Ella Risbridger

"As elegant and energising as a flute of fine
cham

Also by

LAURA WOOD

A Sky Painted Gold
Under a Dancing Star

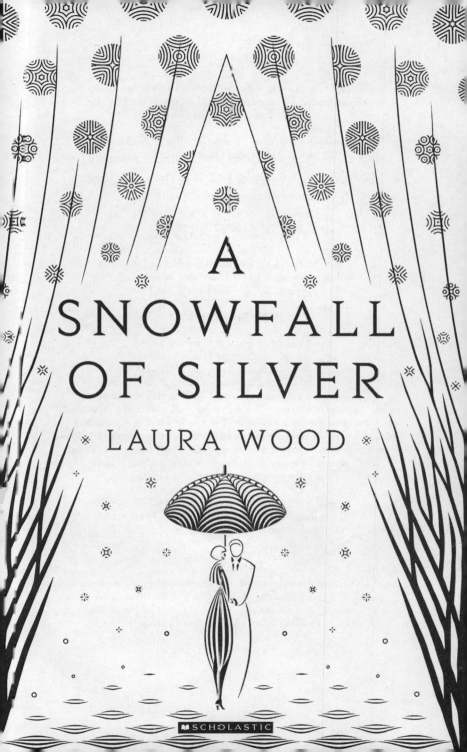

A
SNOWFALL
OF SILVER

✳ LAURA WOOD ✳

■SCHOLASTIC

Published in the UK by Scholastic Children's Books, 2020
Euston House, 24 Eversholt Street, London, NW1 1DB, UK
A division of Scholastic Limited.

London – New York – Toronto – Sydney – Auckland
Mexico City – New Delhi – Hong Kong

SCHOLASTIC and associated logos are trademarks and/or
registered trademarks of Scholastic Inc.

Text © Laura Wood, 2020
Cover illustration by Yehrin Tong

The right of Laura Wood to be identified as the
author of this work has been asserted by her under the
Copyright, Designs and Patents Act 1988.

ISBN 978 1407 19241 3

A CIP catalogue record for this book
is available from the British Library.

Printed by CPI Group (UK) Ltd, Croydon, CR0 4YY
Papers used by Scholastic Children's Books are made
from wood grown in sustainable forests.

1 3 5 7 9 10 8 6 4 2

www.scholastic.co.uk

For my dad, who is very, very proud of me.

"The truth is rarely pure and never simple."

- Oscar Wilde, *The Importance of Being Earnest*

Part One

London
November, 1931

CHAPTER ONE

It is possible that the pantaloons were a mistake.

I realize this now, as I take in the interested glances from some of my fellow rail passengers and head down the swaying corridor towards the compartment marked on my ticket. When I got dressed earlier this evening (by candlelight, so as not to wake Midge and Pa, and – I will admit – for the sense of *atmosphere*), the costume had seemed like such an appropriate choice for a young girl, running away from home to seek glory and fame in the bustling metropolis.

It consists of a scruffy waistcoat over an oversized shirt that once belonged to Pa, a flat cap pulled low over my eyes with all of my hair tucked up underneath it, a pair of long, badly darned socks, and, of course, the pantaloons. (Strictly speaking, they're a pair of ladies' Victorian athletic bloomers that I picked up at the village jumble, but with some very minor alterations they do an admirable job at passing for ragamuffin apparel.) I was particularly satisfied with the dirty fingernails and the artful smudge on my right cheek – it's the little touches that make all the difference.

Looking in the mirror at home in the dingy candlelight I had been pleased with my efforts, and yet now I feel less confident. My intention had been to lurk in the shadows, blending effortlessly into my surroundings, but instead I seem out of place on the night train, soon to be making its way from Penzance to London. The other passengers are wearing very ordinary travelling clothes, their faces pale moons in the lamplight – not a smudged cheek to be seen.

I finally reach my compartment, and slide open the door. With a sigh of relief, I find that I have it to myself.

I make myself comfortable, slumping down into one of the seats and pulling the cap a little lower over my forehead, shadowing my eyes and giving me a feeling of being very discreet – an important feeling for any fugitive.

The train begins to move faster now, the percussive sounds of the wheels against the rails building rhythmically as it gathers speed, and I glance out of the window as Penzance melts away. The world rushes alongside me, draped in an inky darkness that turns the familiar face of the Cornish landscape into a stranger. I shiver, delighted. Here I am, on an intrepid adventure into the unknown. It seems almost impossible to believe, but the gentle swaying of the train is real, the faded green seats are real, the miles slipping quietly away like a silk ribbon running through my fingers are really, deliciously real. Oh, at last, this is living!

I reach for the worn old duffle bag (another of Pa's possessions that I have made off with; it's a good thing he's such an even-tempered sort of man, with all this felonious activity taking place) and open it, extracting a slightly squashed jam sandwich, wrapped in waxy brown paper. I made it before I left home, creeping into the pantry to raid Midge's stores.

Midge is my mother. Her name is Mary, but everyone calls her Midge. I think she got the name because she's very tiny – "a dot", Pa calls her sometimes when he sweeps her up into a big bear hug. Anyway, Midge is an absolutely incredible cook, and her ginger jam sandwiched between two thick slices of home-made bread and butter is a feast that any worldly traveller might be proud of.

After polishing off the sandwich in several hungry bites, and some more staring into the impenetrable abyss beyond the windowpane, it's not long until my eyes begin to feel heavy. I suppose there's only so much staring into the impenetrable abyss that one person can handle. The adrenaline created by my dramatic flight into the night is rapidly leaving my system, and, despite my best efforts to stay awake, my head begins to nod.

It must be after midnight by now, and the train is not due to arrive in to London until seven o'clock in the morning. I settle back into my third class seat, resting my head against the lumpy cushion. I didn't have the money for a sleeping compartment, and anyway, it feels a lot more authentic to travel this way, as if I am a true vagabond. If I wasn't so law-abiding I'd have tried to stow away, but this is the next best thing. I wrap my arms around my bag, clutching it to my chest, and give in to the gentle rocking of the train and my own exhaustion. I let my eyes fall closed, just for a moment.

When I open them again, I realize that some time has passed. It is still dark outside, the lights in the carriages have been dimmed, and we must have stopped at another station – I know this because there is now a boy sitting across from me.

At first, he doesn't notice that I've woken up, because his nose is buried in a book. The light in here isn't very good so he's holding the pages close to his face, like I do sometimes. (Any avid reader who's had to share a room with a younger sibling probably does the same.) What I can make out is a mop of curly red-gold hair above the book, and a pair of long legs stretched out in front of him in dark tweedy trousers.

He shifts slightly, and I see his face. It's a nice face, not exactly handsome but friendly-looking. His nose is crooked, as if it's been broken before and healed a little off-centre, and against his skin, pale in the lamplight, freckles are scattered in light, golden constellations. I think he must be around twenty, twenty-one maybe, not that much older than me.

He looks up then, catches my eye, and flashes a wide smile that shows off two deep dimples, one in each cheek. It's a very good smile.

"Hello!" he says. "You're awake!"

I nod and realize my cap has fallen off. I grab it and tuck my long hair back inside. "Are we nearly in London?" I ask. My voice is croaky.

The boy shakes his head. "About four more hours," he says. "Hope I didn't give you a shock. I did say hello, but you were out to the world when I came in."

"No," I reply quickly, to cover the fact that my half-awake brain is still trying to catch up with where we are and how long I've been asleep. I look at him with interest. "Where did you get on?"

"At Taunton."

"We've been through Taunton already?" I rub my eyes. "I'm missing the whole thing!"

"Not much to miss at the moment." He gestures to the window. Outside I can only see the odd blur – dense, black shapes against a dark sky that skitter away from us before I can make any sense of them.

"I suppose," I agree reluctantly. "Although I can't help but feel it's a bit of a letdown to sleep through one's first proper adventure. It seems to demonstrate a lack of character somehow."

The boy laughs. The laugh is good, like his smile, and it makes me want to hear it again.

I find myself grinning back at him. "I'm Freya Trevelyan," I say.

"Christopher McKay. But please, call me Kit." The boy leans forward and holds out his hand. We shake, solemnly.

"Tell me about your adventure so far, then," Kit says, leaning back again, and arranging his long limbs more comfortably. He looks too tall to be folded into these slightly cramped quarters, and I can tell he's trying not to crowd me.

"Well," I pause for a second, allowing the silence to stretch and some tension to build, "I'm a runaway, of course." The words fall starkly in the space between us with, I think, just the right amount of drama.

"Of course," Kit agrees, as though it's only natural, and I can't help but feel a little deflated at that. I mean, for heaven's sake, this is some high-stakes intrigue. I've just revealed that *I am on the run*. Who knows what dark forces are at play? At the very least he could have gasped.

I try again. "I am fleeing my home. Striking out ... alone."

Kit's eyes gleam in appreciation. "I thought as much. Had an idea that was the case as soon as I saw you. The cap, the Victorian urchin costume – that gave me my first inkling."

"Oh, thank you!" I exclaim. "I made it when I played Oliver Twist in a local production." I hesitate for a second, deciding I might as well tell the truth. "Though, even calling it a 'local production' is a bit grand. It was just something I put on with some volunteers from the village, and they certainly didn't take it seriously enough. I had begun to worry," I continue, glancing down at my outfit, "that the pantaloons were a step too far."

He shakes his head firmly. "Definitely not. You have

to commit to these things, otherwise what's the point in doing them at all?"

"My thoughts exactly!" We share a conspirator's look, and just like that, it feels as though we've known each other for ever. It's a nice feeling, as if I am sitting with a friend or a member of the family, someone familiar and worn in like a particularly cosy jumper.

"So, you're running away to London?" Kit asks. "Hopefully not to actually live as Oliver Twist?"

"No," I reply, a little regretfully – joining a gang of pickpockets really *would* be an adventure. "I'm going to stay with my sister, Lou. One of my sisters, I should say. I have three of them, and four brothers."

Kit doesn't say any of the mundane things that people like to say about us being a big family. To be fair, eight children *could* be considered rather over egging the pudding. Pa sometimes says that there might have been more of us if it hadn't been for the war keeping him and Midge apart for a time, and that we should be thankful for small mercies. It's a sad sort of joke, but quite a good one given the state of chaos that exists in our little farmhouse.

My oldest sister, Alice, is married now, with a little girl of her own, and the next oldest, Lou, is living in London; but that still leaves six of us at home. At just turned eighteen, I have been promoted to head of the siblings. After me comes Tom, who is thirteen, then the triplets, Joe, Max and Davy, who are five, and Anthea-the-baby who is two now but may well be Anthea-the-baby for her whole life.

"That's all right, then," Kit says. "At least you'll have someone to show you around."

"It will only be for a very little while," I add quickly, lest he thinks my adventure diminished. "Until I get my first part. I'm going to be an actress, you see."

Again, Kit nods in easy acceptance. "On the stage?"

"Yes," I say, leaning forward, feeling the pulse of excitement that comes with those words. *On the stage.*

"I really do understand. How funny that we'd end up travelling together. I want to be a playwright, myself."

"*Do you?*" I ask, eyeing him with interest.

"Yes. Always have done. I did my own running away to London a couple of years ago."

"And?" I ask, breathless. "What is it like?"

He shrugs one shoulder and gives a wry half-smile. "Hard, heartbreaking ... wonderful. I haven't had any of my plays staged or anything like that. I've been working stagehand jobs, trying to learn what I can, and working on my own script in my spare time. It's..." He breaks off, as though trying to put it into words is too difficult. "Well, there's nothing like it really."

I sigh. Hard, heartbreaking, wonderful. And all out there just waiting for me. "What were you doing in Taunton?"

"My aunt lives there, I was visiting. I'm just about to go on tour with the company I've been working for, so it's the last chance for a while." He flushes slightly. "It's my first opportunity at stage managing, actually. The man who was going to be doing the job got shingles and had to pull out on quite short notice, so ... they promoted me."

"On tour," I breathe. "How thrilling."

Kit picks up the book on the seat beside him, and with a flick of his wrist, sends it cartwheeling through the air. I catch it between my palms and turn it gingerly so that I can read the title.

"The Importance of Being Earnest!" I exclaim. The play is a favourite of mine. I open the dog-eared paperback and notice that there are a lot of pencil marks and scrawls in the margins and whole parts underlined. "Is this the production that you're going on tour with?"

"That's right." Kit sits back. "With the Queen Anne Theatre's touring company. The theatre is a lovely old place, tucked round the corner by the National Gallery."

I wriggle in my seat. "I can't wait to see it. I can't wait to see *all* of them – the theatres, I mean. I've only been to London once in my life to visit Lou. We went to Drury Lane and saw *The New Moon* with Evelyn Laye, and they set a pirate ship on fire, right there on the stage." The thrill of it comes back to me as I remember the scene. "But that's all I've seen of the theatre. Can you believe it?" I spread my hands, in a gesture that I hope conveys the depth and breadth of my ignorance, and the tragedy of it all. "To have so little to do with the one thing in the world that you know you're destined for? It's been torture."

"Sounds it," says Kit simply. "It's terrible when you

have ambition, but not the opportunity to do what it is that you want the most."

Ambition. Opportunity. Want.

The words thrum deep through me, reverberating like a tuning fork, a pitch that only I can hear.

"If you're around before we leave next week then you should come down to the Queen Anne one afternoon," Kit continues. "I'll give you the guided tour."

"Oh!" I grip the seat either side of me with such force that my knuckles turn white. "Do you mean it? Really?"

Kit's eyes crinkle. They are an interesting pale blue, Kit's eyes. Almost grey, like the sea on a cold day, and fringed with thick sandy lashes. "It would be a pleasure."

CHAPTER TWO

The rest of the journey passes in a blur. Kit and I talk and talk, and at some point I drift off to sleep again, waking with a stiff neck to a pale smudgy dawn, and Kit laughing and promising not to take it personally.

"Sorry," I yawn. "It's tiring work, being on the run."

By the time the train pulls in to Paddington I am trembling with excitement. I have been sitting on my hands for the last ten minutes because the mixture of nerves and anticipation is sending shockwaves through my body; it feels like my limbs might somehow get away from me. I can't stop my left foot from tap-tap-tapping impatiently, as though at any moment I may break into a dance routine like Adele Astaire.

We slow down, down, down, until we're moving *painfully* slowly, and the whistle blows, announcing our arrival like a trumpet call. I try to wait, but the train is still creeping forward as I finally give in and leap up from my seat.

"Come on!" I say to Kit. I grab my bag and shuffle into the corridor, squeezing along past other passengers who are gathering their belongings and emerging sleepily from various compartments. I don't know how they can all be so casual about it. Don't they know we're arriving? Into *London*?

"'Scuse me, 'scuse me," I mumble, ducking and weaving around elbows and raincoats and carpet bags and hearing the same apologies from Kit, following along in my wake.

I reach the doors as the train finally comes to a juddering halt and I'm out and down on the platform before the carriages have finished swaying drunkenly into place.

The roof of the station is enormous, arching up above me like a cathedral, with weak morning sunlight streaming through, and for a fraction of a second I gawp up at it, dazzled. Then, in the next moment, there are people everywhere. A wave of people. A *sea* of people. And they're rushing past me, full of purpose, conveying an intimidating sense of certainty that they know exactly what they are doing, not only now, but for ever and with the rest of their lives.

I am swept forward, along with the crowd, heading unerringly up the platform like salmon streaming upriver. I grip my bag tightly and glance wildly around. "Kit!" I call out.

"There you are!" a voice says at my elbow, and I look up to find the already familiar face of my new friend smiling down at me. I notice he is smiling from quite a long way up, now that he has unfolded himself from the train carriage. He must be several inches over six feet tall – a beanpole, Midge would call him, though he's a fairly sturdy and reassuring one with broad shoulders and strong arms. That must be what comes from dragging all that scenery about.

My spirits lift at the sight of him and I feel foolish for my panic. I'm meant to be on the run, getting by with nothing but my own wits. A very poor job I'm making of *that*, I think – already relying on someone else when my feet have barely touched London soil.

"Let's get out of here," I say firmly, and Kit nods. He touches my elbow very lightly, so lightly that I hardly realize he's guiding me in the right direction and we're through the crowd and past the waiting room and out on the street before I know it.

"We did it," I puff, breathless and giddy, drinking in gulps of the cold morning air. It might be early but London doesn't seem a bit sleepy. There are still so many people around. In fact, there are so many new sights and sounds and even smells assaulting my senses instantly and with such ferocity that for a moment it's hard to untangle the car horns and the shouting and the bright woollen scarves and the tall red buses and the buildings that seem to loom into the heavens. They hit me all at once like an abstract painting, and I think I understand modern art now, which is a rather pleasing development.

"It's wonderful," I breathe, looking around me, and

brushing back the stray lock of hair that has come loose from my hat.

Kit looks around, surprised, at what is, presumably, a rather ordinary bit of London street. But then he's not from a tiny Cornish fishing village with an entire population that is smaller than the number of people currently waiting outside the station.

"If you like this, then you really do have a lot to look forward to," he says diplomatically. "Now, on to more practical concerns. Do you know where you're going? And how to get there?"

"Of course," I say. "I've been plotting this for weeks." I pull a slip of paper from my pocket. "I've written down Lou's address, and I have the correct change for a taxi fare. I found out how much it would be from Mrs Bastion. She's quite a glamorous lady from the village, you see, and she prides herself on travelling up to London once a year and drinking a cup of tea at Fortnum and Mason's. She loves to show off how knowledgeable she is about the *metropolis*, as she calls it, so once I got my hands on a map and worked out the mileage it seemed like I would be able to calculate the cost of the journey fairly precisely."

Kit holds out his hand. "May I?" I place the slip of paper in it. His eyebrows raise and he lets out a low whistle. "That's a nice part of town," he says.

"It's not my sister's house," I say. "Lou lives there and looks after it because her friend Caitlin – who actually owns it – lives in Paris." I lower my voice. "Caitlin and her brother used to be very well off, but then their father died and … I'm not really sure what happened exactly, but they had to sell their big house in Penlyn – they came to the village for the summer, that's how we met them – and they had some great old heap in London that went too, but they kept this place. It all worked out very nicely for Lou." I try to keep the sting of bitterness out of my voice, but I'm not sure I succeed. Lou made leaving Penlyn behind for a dazzling life in London look very easy.

I glance up at Kit a little shamefacedly. "I don't *really* begrudge her happiness," I explain. "I'm happy that she's happy, but sometimes the jealousy, that she's working as a writer, doing what she wants to do, and that she's doing it *here* … it just swamps me." I have never said that aloud to another person before and I feel a bit nervous that Kit will think I am despicable.

"That's understandable," Kit says instead. "But I'm sure it will come in extremely useful when you're playing in a Shakespearean tragedy."

I perk up at that, an aspect of my contemptible emotions that I had not previously considered.

"I suppose this is goodbye, then," he continues. "Are you certain you have enough money for the cab?"

"Absolutely certain. It's the money that my Aunt Irene gave me for my birthday last year. She's a Victorian horror who dresses like a vampire bat and loves to disapprove of everything. It's perfect that she's funding this particular adventure."

Kit laughs, that warm, sun-bright laugh, and lifts up his hand to hail a taxi.

"All right," he says, as I clamber into the back of the car. "I hope the rest of your adventure runs smoothly. And maybe I'll see you at the theatre one afternoon? The Queen Anne, don't forget."

"You may depend upon it," I say gravely.

As the taxi pulls away from the station Kit stands

with his hands in his pockets, watching me go. I snatch my hat from my head and wave it wildly through the back window.

I see him raise his hand in return just before we turn a corner, then, with a sigh of contentment I sit back in the seat and turn my face to the window beside me. I don't want to miss a single thing.

CHAPTER THREE

By the time the cab winds through the crisscross of
traffic-clogged streets and approaches Lou's road, I
am so dizzy with all the sights, I begin to worry about
swooning away. We're in Mayfair now, and the streets
open up a little. The imposing buildings give off a
quiet sheen of old money, as though nothing bad could
happen here. It's quieter. We skirt around the edge of
Berkeley Square, and the elegant old trees there show
off their autumn finery, all dressed up in rippling
amber. I think about all the things those trees have

seen, the way the city must always be changing around them.

The cab driver must be a mind-reader, because he suddenly nods at a large, sandy-coloured building ahead that looks faintly Georgian.

"They're pulling more of them down," he says. "Won't be happy until all the old buildings are gone and they've built more roads, more flats, more offices. Can't keep up with it. It's like the past doesn't matter at all."

I don't know what to say to that. It's hard to think about the past when I'm so excited to be in the present. Fortunately, the driver doesn't seem to want a response.

He turns sharply down a small side street. Here, the frantic energy of the city drops away even further. There are more trees lining the street, their leaves a bonfire flame of red and gold as the sun filters through them. The sound of traffic is muted enough that you can hear the birds singing, and the car glides to a stop in front of an elegant mews house with a gleaming black front door. I recognize it from my last visit and feel a surge of triumph that I have arrived at my destination, navigating the city alone and unscathed.

I pay the driver, pleased to note that the fare is exactly what I expected, and slide from the taxi, slinging the duffle bag over my shoulder.

I stand for a moment, looking up at the house. The sun is shining brighter now, but the air is still chilly. It's going to be one of those golden autumn days, like Keats wrote about.

"*Season of mists and mellow fruitfulness,*" I say, my voice sending his words ringing through the still air. "*Close bosom-friend of the maturing sun; Conspiring with him how to load and bless.*" I'm really warming up now, and I lift my voice further. "*With fruit the vines that round the thatch-eves run; To bend with apples the moss'd cottage-trees—*"

"Freya?" A head pokes out of one of the windows on the second floor, and I see a mop of tousled, conker-brown hair and a pair of squinting grey eyes. "Is that you?"

"Yes," I say, spreading my hands at my side. "It is I."

I'm too far away to actually hear her sigh, but I see the movement of it through her body.

"Of course it's you," Lou says. "Who else would be standing in the middle of the road reciting Shelley?"

"You know perfectly well it's Keats," I hiss, but her head has already disappeared back inside and a moment later the smart black door opens.

"Come in, then," my sister says, and she doesn't sound surprised to see me, only resigned and a little amused. That's sisters for you, though, all over.

I try to retain a sense of dignity as I sweep past her and into the hallway, but this is difficult to do when you have a duffle bag slung over one shoulder, a cap sliding off your head and a rather voluminous pair of pantaloons to deal with.

"I see you've come in costume," Lou says drily, lifting the bag from my shoulder and dropping it on the black-and-white tiled floor, next to an umbrella stand that, alongside a single umbrella, also holds a number of rolled-up magazines and newspapers, a silver-handled cane with a black silk top hat balanced on top of it, and an upside down, empty champagne bottle.

I take a moment to look at my sister. She looks different from how I always picture her, as though she's grown into herself somehow. Even in the few months since I last saw her she seems to have changed.

Her curly brown hair is cut into a short bob and she's wearing the most wonderful wide black trousers and a slouchy bottle-green jumper that doesn't look anything like one of Midge's lumpen home-made disasters. She looks prettier, I realize, and older too, elegant, grown up. Suddenly, I feel like I'm looking at a stranger and a curious panic squeezes at my heart.

Then she smiles her familiar, scrunched-up smile, and I notice the freckles across her nose which certainly belong to my sister and not an elegant London socialite.

She pulls me into a hug and I lean into her with relief.

"What's that delicious smell?" I ask, my nose buried in her shoulder.

"Bluebells," she answers. "My perfume. Now come inside and tell me what's going on."

I think how nice it must be to live in London and smell of bluebells.

She ushers me through the hallway and into a sitting room. There are stacks of books everywhere, and a little upright piano with a jam jar full of sweet violet pansies on top of it. The walls are papered in something pale gold and expensive-looking and covered in framed charcoal sketches of Cornwall.

Sprawled on a worn green silk sofa is the artist himself: Robert Cardew, Caitlin's brother and Lou's ... well, I never know quite what to call him actually. He and Lou are not married, but we all know that they live together – even if everyone pretends they don't. He's reading the newspaper and drinking coffee and looking very much at home here. He doesn't immediately look up as we enter the room.

"Look who I found outside pretending to be a Romantic poet," Lou says.

Robert lowers the paper and his eyes widen.

"Freya?" he says. A smile spreads across his face. My goodness, it's so easy to see why Lou fell head over heels for him. Even after two years, his handsomeness still hits me like a little electric shock. He's all cheekbones and jawline and mossy green eyes and careless dark hair. He places the coffee cup down on the table beside him, next to a plate of toast smeared with marmalade, then gets to his feet and plants a brief kiss on my cheek. The gorgeous smell of him makes my knees a bit weak.

I glance at Lou and her laughing eyes tell me she's well aware of how devastating he can be.

"What are you doing here?" Robert asks me.

"I've run away, of course," I say, twitching a slice of toast from Robert's plate and flopping down into a nearby armchair.

Lou groans. "Of course you have."

"Run away?" Robert's brows draw together in concern. "Why?" He seems to look at me properly for the first time. "And what on earth are you wearing?"

"It's her running-away costume," Lou says.

"Good, isn't it?" I ask, around a mouthful of toast. "Gosh, this is excellent marmalade. Almost as good as Midge's."

"Robert made it." Lou's mouth curls into a smile. "Midge sent him the recipe."

"*Did* she?" I ask, surprised and not a little impressed. Midge doesn't share her recipes with just anyone.

Robert nods, distracted. "I don't understand, Freya. Why have you run away? Is something wrong at home?"

"I should imagine," Lou says, resting her chin on

her hand, "that Freya has run away to seek fame and fortune."

I'd forgotten Lou's annoying habit of knowing just what one is thinking. It comes of being a writer, I suppose. She's so watchful and she always says I'm an open book. As a young woman trying to cultivate a certain air of mystery, that's pretty galling to hear.

"Well, yes, I have actually," I say, a little sulkily. "How did you know?"

"Because you look exactly like a runaway, come to the big city in search of fame and fortune, of course."

"Oh," I say, torn between annoyance at how transparent I am, and satisfaction that my performance was so convincing. I suppose I only have myself to blame.

"I'm sorry," Robert says, looking from me to Lou and back again. "I'm sure I'm being very slow, but … why run away, Freya? Why not arrange a visit? We could have met you at the train station."

"Oh, Robert!" Lou chides disapprovingly, at the same time as I exclaim, "Of all the silly questions! What sort of an adventure would that be?"

Robert gives a surprised bark of laughter and holds

up his hands in surrender. "Ah," he says. "I see I've betrayed a horrible lack of imagination." His eyes meet Lou's and they look at each other for a second in a warm, lit-up way that makes my skin prickle. I lower my own gaze to stare doggedly down at my toast.

"Right." Robert clears his throat. "I'll go and make you some tea, shall I? Then we can have the whole story."

"That would be lovely." I eye him slyly. "How nice to have you around, Robert. And so early in the morning too." Though he tries to look unmoved, a faint pink flush spreads across the top of Robert's cheeks and he leaves without another word.

"That was unnecessary," Lou reprimands me.

I shrug, petulant, already falling back into the role of little sister. "The two of you shouldn't be living in sin, then."

Lou snorts. "*Living in sin*. You sound like Aunt Irene. Anyway," she continues primly, "Robert doesn't live here. He has a flat of his own."

"If you say so."

"I do say so." Lou looks at me from under her brows.

"And you're the one who's not supposed to be here. I hope you at least told Midge and Pa where you were going."

"Of course I didn't!" I exclaim. "What kind of a runaway tells her *parents* where she's going?"

For the first time Lou looks startled. "Freya! They'll be so worried! You should have left a note."

I wave an airy hand. "Oh, I did *that*. I left a note telling them that I was running away to be an actress and that everything was fine and they have nothing to worry about. I just didn't tell them where I was going."

Lou rubs her forehead. "We'll have to telephone," she says at last, looking at her watch. "I'll phone through to the Kimbrells now and see if they can send Johnny up to the farm."

She disappears into the hall to make the phone call. The nearest telephone at home is in the village pub so they'll have to send someone to go and get Midge or Pa, and it will be a while before I have to speak to them. I feel a vague sense of annoyance at Lou's attitude. First, refusing to be surprised by my daring flight from the family homestead, and then kicking up a fuss over my methods. She can't have it both ways!

I toss my cap on the table and shake out my long hair, combing my fingers through it to try and untangle some of the knots. I wonder idly if I should cut my hair short like Lou's. It seems the sort of thing a modern adventuress would do.

"You look so much like Alice." Lou is back, leaning against the door frame and watching me. There's a little pang of sadness in her voice. She misses our older sister. Alice and Lou were practically twins growing up. Joined at the hip.

"Only not as beautiful," I say. "You should see her these days, she glows so much she's practically on fire. Her and Jack and little Rosy – they're the perfect family."

"It hasn't been that long since I saw her," Lou says. "Only a month or so…"

"Three," I mutter. "But who's counting?" I know my words strike a nerve; I can see the flare of guilt in her eyes. "Sorry."

Lou shakes her head. "No, no, you're right. It's been too long." She gives me a slightly watery smile. "I've missed you all."

"Well, aren't you lucky I took matters into my own hands, then?" I say cheerfully, just as the door opens and Robert appears with the tea tray. Thankfully, he's also brought a plate of biscuits. I am absolutely starving, and the toast has barely touched the sides. I reach for one with eager hands.

"Is that plum cake?" I ask, trying not to spray shortbread crumbs everywhere.

"I forgot you were such a bottomless pit." Lou cuts a chunk and hands me a plate. "I'm not sure we've got the supplies necessary to cope with you."

I glare at her. "I don't know how you put up with her," I say to Robert.

"I have a reputation as a charitable man," he smirks, and Lou chokes on her tea.

"If you were really a charitable man, you'd marry her," I shoot back.

This time Robert is ready for me and there's no telling flush on his cheeks. "Alas," he says languidly. "She won't have me."

This time it's my turn to be surprised. "You mean

you've asked her?"

He sighs, flashing Lou a particularly wicked smile before he answers. "Twice."

"Lou!" I squeal. "Is this true?"

Lou groans, burying her face in her hands for a moment before darting a poisonous glance at Robert, who is thoroughly enjoying himself. "We *will* get married," she says. "One day. Just not yet."

"It's a very strange way of doing things, if you ask me," I murmur doubtfully.

"Thank you, Freya." Robert leans forward to offer me another biscuit. I take two. "I've told her I'm not asking again. Next time *she* has to ask me. There's only so much a man's pride can stand."

"Your pride seems perfectly fine to me," Lou grumbles. "I'm not sure I've ever met anyone so pleased with themselves."

"Abused like this in my own home..."

"Aha!" I point at him accusingly. "I knew you lived here."

"My *sister's* own home," he corrects himself smoothly.

"Ignore her," Lou says firmly. "She's only trying to

stir up trouble to distract from the fact that we should be giving her an earful for worrying Midge and Pa. Really, Freya, I can't understand this at all."

"Can't you?" I leap to my feet. "Ha! That's rich, coming from you. You ran off to London to follow your dreams!"

"I understand *that* part. But Midge and Pa were so supportive of me. Why go about it like this?"

"Because I'm an *artist*, Louise!" I say passionately. "I don't need my parents making it easy for me." I regret that I have already leaped to my feet, because I think this might have been a better moment for it. Instead I toss my head defiantly. "My passion and dedication to the craft must overcome every obstacle. Don't you understand what a catastrophe it would have been to encounter no obstacles at all? I have to *struggle*."

Lou shakes her head. "You're being ridiculous."

"You don't understand me at all." I fold my arms. "None of you ever have." I mean for the words to sound hard and angry, but instead they come out with a little quiver.

Lou looks like she might be about to say something

else then, but she's interrupted by the shrill ring of the telephone from the hallway.

"You'd better get that," she says. "It's for you."

CHAPTER FOUR

"So you got there safe and sound." Midge's placid voice comes down the line. She doesn't seem to be displaying any of the anxiety that Lou was worried about.

Unfortunately, she's not the only person intent on taking part in the conversation.

"And what a miracle that is!" a shrill voice chimes in, in the background. "Running away without a word and leaving your poor mother to worry herself half to death! It's the outside of enough, and I've told your parents they should wash their hands of you..."

"What is Aunt Irene doing there?" I hiss.

"Your aunt has been quite … concerned about you," Midge says, and for the first time in our conversation her tone sounds a little strained. I know that my aunt's "concern" is really an excuse to wade in and make her displeasure known.

"Oh, no, she was there when you found my note?" I ask. "I am sorry about that, Midge. What a thing to do to you."

"It's all right, heart," Midge replies softly. "I was worried you'd go hungry, that was all." I almost laugh then, because it's so typical of my unflappable mother to be worried about me missing dinner, and I feel my heart ache a little.

"Oh, Midge," I say suddenly, gripping the phone tightly in my hands. "I *am* sorry. It was an awful thing to do. It just seemed like the absolute *only* way to get a bit of living done."

"Well, you selfish little so-and-so, why, if you were my daughter I'd—" Aunt Irene's piercing voice is back again.

"Reeny, that's enough!" Midge cuts her off, her voice

sharpening. "Freya is with her sister now and there's no harm done, so we'll let the matter drop."

I can hear Aunt Irene continue to grumble in the background. I think I catch the words "eyes" and "ravens" and can only assume that her anger is taking a biblical turn.

"Thank you, Midge," I say, subdued.

"Now, you'd better put me on to your sister so that we can discuss arrangements."

"But I can stay, can't I?" I ask quickly.

"I think that will depend on your sister," Midge points out. There is the faintest hint of a laugh in her voice. "She's the one who's going to have to feed you."

Lou comes through to the hall to talk to Midge and I return to the sitting room, where Robert asks me hundreds of questions about home. Robert absolutely loves hearing about our family. I've never met anybody so interested in how Gerald – the family motor – is running, or how Tom's latest schemes to build his own sail-boat are panning out (not terribly well, actually; there have been some significant buoyancy issues, which is not ideal in a boat), or what rude words the triplets

41

delight in shouting at the vicar. Robert listens to these mundane bits of information like they're fairy stories, his eyes gleaming with laughter.

"I can't believe you actually want to know all of this," I say.

He shrugs. "It's nice having a big family like yours. I wish I did... It's just me and Caitlin now."

"And she's still in Paris?" Caitlin is just as gorgeous as Robert, and she's married to a jazz musician who's getting to be quite well-known. It's all painfully glamorous.

"Yes, though she and Lucky are talking about moving to America. It's difficult there after the crash, people are really struggling, but we have friends over there who think his band could do very well." He suddenly looks unexpectedly forlorn. "I'm not sure what they'll do."

It's strange to think of Robert being lonely. He always seems so self-contained and untouched by things.

"Well, you're a part of our big family now," I say lightly, and the expression on his face is hard to read.

That's when Lou walks back into the room.

"So?" I say quickly. "Can I stay?"

"Of course you can stay."

I throw myself at her, hugging her and jumping up and down at the same time. Lou makes noises of protest.

"You do know that if you'd just asked like a normal person you could have come any time you liked," she grumbles.

"Yes, but now it's part of my story," I explain. "Now, my career begins with a daring act, taking my future into my own two hands, leaving behind provincial life in a tiny village in the middle of nowhere, making a wild dash through darkest night towards the unknown..." I pause, considering. "Calling up my sister and coming for a visit doesn't quite have the same ring to it."

"Well, Midge and I agreed you could stay for two weeks," Lou says easily. "I really do understand wanting to see a bit more of the world. The first time Caitlin brought me to London it felt like something I'd been looking for my whole life."

"Two weeks!" I exclaim in dismay, cutting off this particular trip down memory lane. "But you don't understand! I've run away from home! I'm never going back!"

Lou blinks at me. "What are you talking about?"

I take a deep breath. "I'm going to make it happen," I say. "Do what I've always longed to do. Become an actress on the stage."

There is a silence. "Freya," Lou says, with a gentleness that immediately puts my back up. "You don't just *become* an actress. It takes hard work; you can't simply run away from home without a plan. Of course, if you want to move to London to pursue things at some point in the future, then I can help you. We can look at getting you some sort of work – secretarial college, perhaps..."

"Speaking of work, I'd better go," Robert interjects.

"Coward," Lou murmurs as he kisses her quickly on the cheek and makes his escape, lifting a hand in a friendly half-wave to me as he goes.

"But I'm good!" I say fiercely, ignoring all of this and returning to the matter at hand. "You know I am."

"Of course you're talented, Freya," Lou says, still in that gentle voice. "But you can't just turn up in London and declare yourself an actress. You need to be more practical. You haven't got the first idea how any of it works." She's talking to me as if I was one of the triplets and I feel my temper rising.

Although I have read Sun Tzu's *The Art of War* several times, and I know perfectly well that a hasty temper is a dangerous fault, it is one that I cannot seem to conquer altogether. And right now I feel a hot and righteous anger bubbling through me.

"That just goes to show what you know," I hear myself say. "As it happens, I already have an audition lined up for tomorrow!"

I have the satisfaction of seeing Lou look stunned.

"Yes!" I say firmly. This will teach her to talk to me like I'm a child. "At the – the Queen Anne Theatre! They're doing a touring production of *The Importance of Being Earnest*."

"And you have an audition?" She is frowning in disbelief.

"Certainly," I say calmly.

"Oh." She is obviously nonplussed by this. "Well, that's... I didn't realize..."

"I know you didn't." I use my iciest tones. "Because you still think I'm a child. But you've been gone for two years now, Lou. Things have changed. *I've* changed."

There's a pause.

"You're right," she says at last, and I see a dawning respect in her eyes. "I'm sorry. You're still my little sister, it's hard to ... but that's wonderful news. Why don't I show you up to your room, and then you can tell me all about it?"

"That would be nice," I manage, but the electric pulse of anger has gone, leaving me hollow, and I feel an absolute worm listening to her apologize when I know I've told her a pack of lies.

How else could I get her to listen, though? I could hear it in her voice – the big sister voice. There was no way she was going to take me seriously even if I started talking about hard work and acting classes. Still, Lou is no fool and unless I start to come up with some actual auditions she'll soon see through the lie. I think of Kit, and what he said about my being able to visit him at the Queen Anne Theatre. Maybe, just maybe, something will come of that, I think desperately. Maybe I can *make* something happen.

As Lou leads me up the white, winding staircase my heart thumps unhappily and one question rattles around and around inside my brain.

What have I done?

CHAPTER FIVE

After a good night's sleep I am feeling much better. I am something of an optimist by nature, and I don't tend to stay disheartened for long, I much prefer to think the best. I'm sure that everything will work out.

After all, ever since I was five years old, I've known that I wanted to move to London and become an actress. It's a part of me, this vision of the future; it's bone-deep, ingrained. It feels as if all of my life has been building towards this moment, and now that it's here, nothing is going to stop me. It's as inevitable as winter following on the heels of autumn. Of course I'll make a success of it. Because I have to.

I have slept late, curled up under the blankets like a particularly satisfied dormouse, and it is almost midday already. The bedroom Lou showed me to yesterday is painted a cheerful yellow, and it is light and bright thanks to a large window that looks out on to the street. I allow myself a moment just to enjoy being here. There's an old oak tree outside the window, and I can almost imagine that I'm living in its branches, among the ember-orange leaves. The bed is wide and piled with fluffy pillows and a slightly faded patchwork quilt that I recognize as being from Lou's room in Cornwall. There's a dressing table and a bookcase that holds worn old copies of children's books – *Peter Pan, Alice in Wonderland, Treasure Island*. It's comfortable here, safe and cosy. There's even a very tiny bathroom just for me – a luxury I have never even dreamed of.

I wash, then dress and stand in front of the mirror to comb the tangles from my hair, still damp from washing it in Lou's peppermint-scented shampoo. Lou was right when she said I look like Alice – though Alice is an absolute knock-out, and I am not exactly. My face is not quite as perfectly symmetrical as hers, my hair is not the same burnished gold, but a paler, more silvery blonde. I'm shorter, rounder, with less of Alice's willowy grace. I have the same dark blue eyes, but not the dimples that Pa says could charm the birds from the trees. Still, I like my face. I like the soft roundness of my cheeks and the heart-shaped point of my chin. I like my mouth, even though it is perhaps a little too big. It has character. It is capable of expressing many things.

I turn one way and then the other, craning my neck to take in every angle of myself, before nodding in satisfaction at today's wardrobe choice. Naturally, the Victorian street urchin costume was out, but last night, when I pulled the few crumpled frocks I had brought with me from Pa's duffle bag, Lou had eyed them doubtfully and asked if they were really the thing for auditioning.

I told her I could audition in a potato sack and still make it work, but in the morning reality set in and I realized they really were too shabby. I crept into her room and helped myself to her wardrobe, borrowing a pale, mint green dress, belted at the waist with a skirt that flares out when I move, cut to several inches above my ankle. The shape and the belt mean it fits reasonably well. It is perhaps a tiny bit long and a bit too tight across my chest and my hips, but I'm used to living in cast-offs. As the third daughter I'm not sure I've ever worn anything made to fit me properly.

I could let the dress out myself, but even I know that's a step too far. I have technically stolen it, after all. (Though, really, it's only borrowing, and this *is* what sisters are for.)

Now, standing in front of the mirror, I stroke the material. It is soft and smells faintly of Lou's bluebell perfume. It makes me feel stylish and grown up, and I stand a little taller in it.

I've been making my own costumes for years now – in fact, I'm the only one of my sisters who is any good with a needle – and I know how important clothes are, how they can change the way you feel, the way you move and act. In this cool green dress I too have become cool and unruffled, a confident young woman about town. I sweep my hair up in to a smooth chignon, pinning it back neat and elegant, and apply some of the lipstick that I swiped from Lou's dressing table. It is red as a ripe apple, the perfect finishing touch.

The girl staring back at me in the mirror glitters with a diamond-hard determination. I look so confident that I even fool myself.

I glide happily downstairs. There is a note on the table in the hallway, propped against a vase full of beautiful roses, smelling heavenly, the colour of plum jam. I recognize Lou's untidy scrawl.

Dear Freya,

Didn't want to wake you. Gone to work - help yourself to whatever you can scare up in the larder. The tea is in the yellow tin from home. There's a key on the table, and a map to help you find your way about. Good luck with the audition - Robert says we will open some champagne later to toast your bright future!

Lx

P.S. I know exactly what you're thinking, and while I do not doubt that you have already raided my wardrobe, no you CAN'T borrow my good coat.

I make my way through the house and down the stairs to the basement kitchen. It is small and the remnants of this morning's breakfast languish by the sink on white china plates stamped with blue flowers. When I make my way back up to the sitting room it is with quite a decent picnic: brown bread and sharp cheese, an apple and a few ginger biscuits. I put a record on the record player and eat on the floor in the sitting room, lying on the rug on my stomach, careful not to crease the dress. I leaf through several magazines that Lou has left lying around. One of them is the one Lou works for, and it contains her own story about a fiery murderess called Lady Amelia, which is – though I wouldn't want to inflate her ego too much by actually telling her so – absolutely thrilling.

I think for a moment about Lou's life and how happy she seems. I try to ignore the familiar pang of envy, the greedy feeling that I want to take a piece of this for myself.

The house is still and quiet. I turn on to my back, staring at the ceiling and listening to the crackle of the jazz record playing. Kit must be at the theatre by now. He told me to come down in the afternoon, and it is technically after noon now.

I get to my feet, brush and straighten my skirts, and head for the mirror over the fireplace where I carefully reapply my lipstick. Leaning forward I plant my lips on my own reflection, leaving it there, like a brand on the glass: a perfect, red kiss.

Sweeping up the key and map off the hallway table, I pause only to shrug on Lou's good coat, a rich belted brown tweed with a faux fox fur collar that tickles my neck, and a daring flash of green silk from the lining. Then I sail out of the door.

I turn out of Lou's quiet road, towards the hum and thrum of the city. The streets are full of busy, bustling people who all seem to be in a rush to get somewhere. I like feeling like one of them. After all, *I* have somewhere to get to as well.

I love seeing the women in their modern, colourful clothes, hearing the roar of the traffic, staring, bewitched, into enormous shop windows full of everything from clothes to toys to suitcases to kitchenware to towering patisserie. It all feels so big, the buildings stretching up endlessly into skies the flat grey of a dreary November day. There are narrow roads, cobbled and twisting, springing off vast streets, wide enough to give a confused feeling of space coupled with the thronging and slightly claustrophobic crowds.

Not wishing to appear to be a tourist, I try to look at the map as little as possible, and as a result get lost several times on the way to the theatre. After one wrong turn I find myself outside Hatchards, its tall windows full of beautiful books, and I press my fingers briefly to the glass before stepping through the front door.

The inside is dark and cool, with crowded shelves everywhere I look. I browse, running my fingers over spines, gently leafing through pages, enjoying the feel of the paper, the quiet of the room. Then I make my way slowly up the staircase, my fingers hovering lightly over the bannister, breathing in the lovely smell that only comes from books – a smell that's something like smoke and the way the earth smells after it rains.

I find the drama section and am thrilled to spot The *Importance of Being Earnest*, bound in pale green, with the title picked out in swirling gold. I practically skip downstairs to buy it, gleefully convinced that it must be a sign. The copy that I have at home is so old and well read that it is almost falling apart. It's a story about two men – Algernon and Jack – who have both created fictional personas that they can use to avoid doing things they don't like. Everything goes well until they fall in love, and the women they're in love with think they're both called Ernest – that's when things get complicated and really, really funny. I've never seen it performed onstage before, and it's another reason I'm excited to find out what's going on in Kit's world. Perhaps I'll be able to sneak a peek at some of the performance if they're rehearsing.

Thankfully, it is not a long walk from the bookshop to the theatre. The theatre itself is tucked down a rather unassuming alley, and I think I must be growing immune to all the spectacle around me because it's only after I look at it for a moment that I realize how lovely it is.

The front is stone, painted a creamy white, complete with pillars that look vaguely classical. On the first floor, the marquee is not lit and the white sign where the name of the play currently being performed would stand is empty. The floor above has three tall Georgian-looking windows, nestled between the pillars, and several ornate stone wreaths. The top floor stretches up into a peak, giving the whole place the feeling of a modern acropolis.

I'm here, my heart sings. *I've arrived. This is it.*

I push eagerly against the gold-rimmed doors, but they're locked. Undeterred, I walk down the side of the building and around to the back where a shabby and unassuming door stands propped open.

The stage door.

I hesitate only for a second, my heart pounding in my chest, and then, lifting my chin and taking a deep breath, I push my way through.

It's a bit of an anticlimax to find myself standing in a dimly lit corridor with doors coming off either side. I'm not exactly sure what I had been expecting – something gilded and imposing, perhaps. Rousing orchestral music at least.

"Can I help you, miss?" a voice comes from my left. I swing around to find myself looking into a sort of booth and at a man who I guess must be at least ninety years old. He is small, and largely hidden by a desk that reaches up to his chest. His face has the look of a wizened apple that has collapsed in on itself, his eyes are like two dark currants and a wisp of white hair sits on top of a mostly bald pate. He smiles at me politely, and his smile is full of large, very white teeth, the effect of which is slightly startling.

I hesitate. "I'm looking for Kit. He told me I could call around."

"Mr Kit, is it?" The old man's toothy smile grows wider. "Always seems to know the prettiest girls, that one."

He turns away and from the wall beside him he lifts something that looks like an old-fashioned telephone receiver and speaks into it.

"Kit to the stage door, please. Kit to the stage door."

Faintly, in the distance, and behind the closed doors I hear the words ringing back with a light crackle.

"He'll be up in no time, miss," the man says.

He is right; it is scarcely three or four minutes later when Kit's already familiar face appears. He looks at me for a second in confusion, and then his face clears.

"Freya," he exclaims. "I almost didn't recognize you without the pantaloons." The dimples flash. "Joe, this is the girl I met on the train – the one I said was going to come and have a look round. Freya, this is Joe, a living legend. He's been the porter here at the Queen Anne for over sixty years."

"It's nice to meet you," I say politely.

"So you're the little actress." Joe casts a look of appraisal over me. "Yes, I see."

I'm not sure what he sees exactly, but I smile hesitantly. "Being a porter at a theatre like this must be very exciting."

Joe laughs, a wheezing sound, like the slow compressing of an accordion. "Exciting's one word for it, miss."

Kit groans. "Don't get him started, Freya; trust me, he's got enough stories to keep you here for a week."

"Oh, but I *do* want to hear those stories."

The accordion laugh again. "Don't you worry, miss. I'm not going anywhere any time soon. Maybe young Kit here will bring you for a cup of tea in the porter's office some time."

"I will." Kit takes the parcel with my book and hands it through the window to Joe. "Look after this, will you, Joe?" Then, with a flourish, he holds out his arm to me. "Shall we go? I must say I didn't expect you so soon – you *are* keen."

I place my hand on Kit's arm and we walk down the corridor. As soon as we are out of earshot of Joe, I tug at his arm, pulling him to a halt.

"What's wrong?" he asks, frowning.

"Oh, Kit," I say in a low voice. I find I am actually wringing my hands together, a phenomenon I wasn't sure actually happened in real life. "I've got myself into the most awful muddle!"

CHAPTER SIX

"Let me see if I understand," Kit says. "You told your sister that you have an audition here today. And if you don't get the part you think they're going to send you home?"

"That's about the size of it," I say miserably, pulling my knees up to my chest. We're in a little room off the corridor, no more than a cupboard, full of racks of costumes. I am sitting with my back against the wall, surrounded on one side by a cloud of blue taffeta, and on the other a military uniform.

Kit is sitting on the opposite side of the room, seemingly unbothered by the long feathered gown that he has to keep brushing away from his cheek. "I understand that your sister got you all riled up – sisters have a way of doing that." His mouth lifts here in a way that lets me know he himself is familiar with the despotic ways of sisters. Then, like a cloud flitting across a clear sky, the frown appears again, puckering between his grey eyes. "But what was your plan in coming to London? I mean, please don't rip up at me for asking – but how *did* you think you would get into acting?"

"Oh, the usual way," I say. "Thousands of auditions until I got my lucky break, and I was hoping to be able to take some classes – after all, the only training I've had has been very amateur. I'm not such a fool as Lou seems to think me and I knew I could make it happen eventually. Only then Lou said I could stay for two weeks – and that isn't nearly enough time to get things done!" I take a deep breath. "It was obvious she wasn't going to listen to the truth. I needed her to think I had something lined up, a good reason to stay. Before I knew it the lie was coming out of my mouth, and then Lou was so surprised. It was suddenly like she was taking me seriously and..." I trail off miserably.

Kit nods. "I want to help, Freya, but I don't think I can. I'm not involved in auditions or any of that. And all the parts for the tour have been cast for a while now."

I slump dejectedly, then force a smile. "Of course. I'm sorry for laying all my woes on you like this – it's my own fault that I'm in this mess."

There's a brief silence. "I could maybe get you in to see Mr Cantwell," Kit says finally, lifting a hand to rub the back of his neck. "He might be able to make some introductions for you. Though I must warn you, he's not the most ... *approachable* man."

"Mr Cantwell," I say, and then the words slowly sink in. "Not *Rhys Cantwell?*"

"Yes. He's directing the production."

I stare at Kit for a moment. My lungs feel squeezed of air. Rhys Cantwell is an absolutely legendary theatre director and has been for longer than I've been alive. He's won every award going, worked with all the stars. His name peppers many of the newspaper and magazine cuttings in my scrapbooks. In my wildest dreams I have imagined him calling me his muse as we stage magnificent productions together. Although, now that I think about it, I haven't heard much about him recently. I suppose I thought he had retired.

"Rhys Cantwell is here?" I manage. "*The* Rhys Cantwell?"

Kit laughs. "In the flesh."

"And you'd introduce me to him?"

"That I can do. The rest would be up to you."

I feel suddenly as though the clouds have parted and great beams of sunlight are washing over me. Once again I am pulled back from the brink of despair. Destiny, surely, has led me here; to my big break. I get to my feet. "What are we waiting for?"

Kit takes me through to the back of the theatre, pointing things out to me as we sail past. "That's the men's dressing room down there, women's is the other side. There's the costume department, this is where the scenery is stored and there's a larger workshop down there on the right. It's all in a bit of a state at the moment, because we're getting everything ready for the tour." I scramble to keep up with his long strides.

Kit seems different here, I think. His quiet air of self-possession and confidence is mingled with something else, an excitement that seems to simmer just under the surface. There is a brisk energy to his movements.

Finally, we emerge in the wings of the stage. Stage right, to be exact. The adrenaline that has been racing through me begins to hammer even harder in my veins. I feel like I might be sick. Or faint. Or fly. Everything here feels so big. I look up and see, above the stage, the rigging system – it seems unbelievably high, a mess of ropes, waiting to lower in scenery. Kit walks out on to the stage, and I hesitate for a moment, before following him.

Time slows down.

I'm onstage. A proper London stage. Stretching out in front of me are hundreds of empty red velvet seats. The theatre is tiered like a beautiful wedding cake, all cream and swirling, ornate gold. It is somehow both bigger and smaller than I imagined it would be and exactly how a theatre *should* look.

I am so overwhelmed that it takes me a moment to realize that the lights on the stage have dimmed, and that Kit is talking to someone, out where the audience should be.

"…If you could spare just a few moments, sir," I hear Kit say. Squinting, my eyes finally settle on the man sitting several rows back, a sheaf of papers in his hands and a pair of spectacles balanced on his nose.

Rhys Cantwell.

He is a stern-looking man with steel grey hair that stands disordered around a craggy face. He looks like he's been carved out of stone, ice blue eyes above a beaky, Roman-looking nose. He is wearing gold-rimmed spectacles, which are too small for him, perched on the end of his nose, and attached to a delicate gold chain. They are completely at odds with the rest of his intimidating face and he manages to wear them with an air of disdain.

"Mr Cantwell," I manage to murmur. "Sir!" And then, without thinking about it, I drop into an incredibly low and supplicatory curtsey, one hand gracefully extended, like a prima ballerina making her final bow onstage in a sea of flowers.

I hear Kit gurgle beside me, the sound of a laugh,

quickly stifled, and I freeze there near the ground, wondering what on earth has possessed me. With as much dignity as I can manage, I rise slowly back to my feet.

"Kit!" Mr Cantwell snaps. "Who on earth is this? And why is she acting like she's just been presented to Queen bloody Victoria?"

"This is a friend of mine, sir. She's here because she wants to be an actress."

"Don't they all?" His voice is as cold as those eyes. "What has this got to do with me?"

I decide it's time to take my fate into my own hands. There's no sense standing here like a particularly slow-witted goldfish.

"I'm sorry to bother you, Mr Cantwell. It's not Kit's fault, I absolutely begged him to introduce me. I'm such a tremendous fan of your work. Of course I've never actually seen any of it," I add candidly. "We don't get to see much of anything in Cornwall, but I've read every single review of your plays, every single article about you. I loved what you said about – about *bringing a measure of honesty to the work,* of finding the personal connection to the material – I stuck that in my scrapbook. I have a photograph of you in there as well, though my brother Tom drew a moustache on you in blue ink. He said he thought it made you look more distinguished, and in a strange way, you know, I think he was right."

There's a silence after this, one that is so thick I can almost feel it brushing against my neck alongside the faux fur.

"Who *are* you?" Mr Cantwell asks finally.

"My name is Freya Trevelyan, Mr Cantwell," I say. "And I want to be an actress. It's not even just that I want to act exactly, more a sense that I have to do it as much as I have to keep on breathing. And I've spent my whole life so far, buried away in Cornwall, and now I'm finally here and – oh, *please*, let me at least show you what I can do. I'll never, *ever* bother you again."

"Won't you let her, sir?" Kit asks, his voice firm and serious.

I flash him a look of intense gratitude and clasp my trembling hands together. Mr Cantwell glares at me for another moment.

"Fine," he says shortly. "You may have three minutes.

Go on."

"Three minutes?" I repeat blankly. "What would you like to see?"

"Something worth seeing. I suppose," is all he says.

I don't hesitate. I walk across the stage, unbutton my coat and fling it at Kit who catches it with deft hands. My fingers trembling, I smooth my hair, and twitch the skirts on my dress. I turn so that my back is to Mr Cantwell, and close my eyes for the briefest second, offering up a prayer to Saint Genesius, the patron saint of actors.

Then I turn and step full into the light.

I don't know why, but the scene I decide to perform is Act One, Scene Five of *Hamlet*, where he meets the ghost, and I play both parts, using the space on the stage. As soon as I start I feel the real world melt away as always, lost in the words and the feelings that they stir in me. I think about nothing except the pain, the loss, the sense of betrayal that pours into me as water filling a vase. That's how it feels sometimes; as though saying the lines are an act of obliteration, as though I am emptied of myself and someone else has taken over.

When I finally finish, I stand. dazed, hardly able to

recollect any of the things I have just said and done but faintly aware that I must have said and done them. My ears ring.

I look down, and Mr Cantwell is leaning forward, his elbows on the back of the chair in front of him. His expression is completely inscrutable.

"A very unusual scene choice," he says at last. "Why *did* you choose it?"

"I-I don't know."

"Strange not to do a monologue."

I feel heat rising in my cheeks. "I didn't think," I manage weakly. "At home I often play all the parts. I suppose it was a little…"

"Bizarre," says Mr Cantwell.

"Oh."

There is a pause. "It was … interesting," he says at last, delivering this most lukewarm praise grudgingly. "You are obviously untrained, but it's possible you have an instinct. There's a certain … watchable quality."

"A watchable quality," I repeat, excitement rising in me. The words sound so beautiful ringing in my ears.

Rhys Cantwell thinks I have a watchable quality.

Again, he gives me a long, cold look, and then he returns his attention to the sheaf of papers, shifting the pages in his hands.

"Take her to see Miss Meriden," he says, without lifting his eyes. "She may be able to help. And while you're there, tell her I want to know when my thrice-blasted spectacles will be fixed so that she can have these monstrosities back."

It seems these words are directed at Kit because he reappears from the side of the stage where – to be completely honest – I had forgotten all about him. He is still carrying Lou's good coat over one arm and he quickly shepherds me off the stage and back into the cool, waiting darkness of the wings.

"Oh," I gasp, the word coming out almost a sob. "Oh, oh, oh. Did that actually happen?"

"D'you mean, did you just perform in front of Rhys Cantwell and live to tell the tale?" Kit lifts a brow. "Yes, you did."

"Was it... Was I..." I trail off uncertainly.

"You were good," Kit says. "It was certainly

something, seeing you switch between characters like that." He grins at my worried face. "Honestly, it was good. He would have told you if it wasn't. You can count on that."

"He said it was bizarre."

Kit chuckles. "It was a bit, but it caught his attention. Trust me, he liked you. Why else would he tell me to take you to Miss Meriden?"

"Who is Miss Meriden?" I ask.

"She's his assistant." Kit is guiding me back through the warren of the back of the theatre. We come to a stop in front of one of the doors, and Kit knocks lightly.

"Come in," a voice calls.

CHAPTER SEVEN

My first impression of Miss Meriden is one of particular neatness. Her face, her features, her clothes are all as neat as the room we are standing in.

The room is a very tiny and beautifully organized office with a desk, a couple of chairs, and several tall filing cabinets. She is, I would guess, in her middle fifties, with dark hair pulled back into a severe knot and a grey tweed skirt and jacket worn over a silk blouse the colour of milky coffee. She looks up, and seeing Kit, her eyebrows rise.

"Well, Christopher," she says to him, "what troubles have you brought to my door today?"

"No troubles," Kit replies. "We got the issue with the set pieces resolved as you suggested. He wasn't totally happy, but then, when is he?"

"He likes things the way he likes them." Miss Meriden's voice is firm. "And ours is not to question why." Her keen brown eyes turn on me. "And who do we have here?"

"This is Freya Trevelyan."

I hold out my hand and Miss Meriden shakes it. Even her handshake is brisk and efficient.

"Mr Cantwell has just seen her audition piece."

Again, Miss Meriden gives me a slightly searching look. "Liked you, did he?"

"I'm not sure, actually," I admit. "He said I was bizarre."

"He must have liked you," she says, "if he sent you to me. Now, have a seat." She gestures to the chair in front of her desk. "And, Kit, I'm sure you have better things to be doing with your time. You may leave Miss Trevelyan safely with me."

"I'll drop your coat at the front desk with your parcel," Kit says, then he gives my arm a reassuring squeeze and leaves, while Miss Meriden takes a seat behind the desk and I drop into the chair across from her.

"So, Freya… You don't object to my calling you Freya?"

"Yes, I mean, no." I take a second to control myself. "I don't object – Freya is fine. I'm sorry, I'm just a bit overwhelmed. I can't really believe… I mean, I've been a fan of Mr Cantwell's for a long time."

"I hope you told him so." Miss Meriden sits back in her seat. "He may be an old curmudgeon but he's absolutely not immune to flattery. Of course, he doesn't get as much as he used to these days."

"I did think, when Kit mentioned him, that I hadn't read about him for a while," I say. "But the magazines I get back home in Penlyn are always at least two weeks out of date, and have to go through our neighbour Mrs Bastion first, because she's absolutely mad for all the Hollywood gossip."

"Hmmm." Miss Meriden makes a noise in the back of her throat. "Best not to mention Hollywood around Mr Cantwell."

I wonder briefly why, but Miss Meriden continues. "He has been off the radar for a while; this touring production is a little below his touch." She sniffs here, as though it's a little below hers as well. "But needs must, I suppose. And he managed to get Eileen to come on board, which makes it quite a different matter."

"Eileen?" I ask.

"Eileen Turner. She's playing Lady Bracknell."

My mouth drops open of its own accord. "Eileen Turner." The words come out in a croak. "But she's retired!"

"Not for Mr Cantwell, she's not." The pride in Miss Meriden's face is unmistakable. And rightly so. Rhys Cantwell may be a big name in directing, but Eileen Turner is a grand dame of the theatre, a true, bona fide star. Even in Penlyn her name is golden.

"I can't believe it." I grip the sides of my chair. "Is she here, in the theatre? *Now*?" I feel dizzy.

Miss Meriden shakes her head. "No, but she will be coming in later for another wardrobe fitting."

"Eileen Turner," I say again, "will be here in this

theatre, where I am sitting. It's madness. How can I ever leave a place where things like this happen?"

"Do I take it you are not planning on staying in London?" Miss Meriden asks.

"I'm not sure."

It all comes out then. Growing up in Cornwall with a dream that felt so right and yet so different to everything I knew. How I ran away and came to London. How I can't explain to my family that it is vital I stay.

"When my sister Lou came to London it was different," I say. "She took charge of it all – got herself a job in an office so that she could write in her spare time. Everyone just accepted it and then she started writing stories too, and now she works at the magazine, writing for them and doing editorial work. But I didn't come to London with a sensible job waiting for me. Perhaps that was a mistake, but I'm here and I feel like now I need to at least *try*. What if I go home and then I don't ever make it back again?"

"So why not do what your sister did in the next two weeks?" Miss Meriden asks. "Why not get a job and take some acting classes alongside?"

"I don't have an awful lot of accomplishments that may be helpful in acquiring a job," I admit, making a clean breast of it. "I'm absolutely hopeless at typing which might throw a spanner in the works – Lou can type about a thousand words a minute. I don't know shorthand. I'm useless at anything involving numbers. I could learn, I suppose, over time ... but I don't want to waste my life learning things I don't care a bit about. And I want to move to London *now*."

"Do you have any other skills?" Miss Meriden says.

I shake my head. "I help out on the farm. I read, and I make costumes. That's it."

"Costumes?" Miss Meriden tilts her head like a sparrow.

"I love sewing," I say. "And I'm handy with a needle, which is lucky because no one else in the family is, except Pa. Anyway I've always made the costumes for myself and any kind of amateur production I've been able to be part of, and I love it. I can imagine what the character will wear and how I'll feel when I'm wearing it, how it will look onstage, against the scenery."

Miss Meriden places her elbows on the desk in front

of her and steeples her fingers, regarding me with a steady, searching sort of gaze that makes me want to wriggle in my seat. "Perhaps there *is* something I can do to help. Our wardrobe mistress Nora Felton needs an assistant – someone to help with the costumes, but also to act as a dresser, for the quick changes and so on during the performance. Is that something that might interest you?"

I press my hand to my chest. "A job – here?"

"Well, not *here*," Miss Meriden says. "On the tour. It's six weeks, almost right up until Christmas, and it starts next week. I know it's not acting work, but if Mr Cantwell has seen something in you that he likes, he may be able to offer you some advice, a little polish. I couldn't make any promises, mind."

"I'd get to go on the tour?" I ask, her words sinking in. "To help with the costumes? I'd work with Mr Cantwell and Eileen Turner? In *real* theatres?"

It's possible a hint of amusement flashes briefly in that cool stare, but it's so quick I could be wrong. "You don't need me to sell you on it at all, do you?" she asks drily.

"Of course not!" I jump to my feet. "I think I should pinch myself. This must be a dream."

Miss Meriden holds up a hand. "You'll have to meet Nora, of course; she'll have the final say. And she'll expect you to put in the work."

"No one will ever have worked harder on anything." My voice trembles with fervency. "I swear it to you, on my life. I'll swear it to Nora Felton too."

"That won't be necessary, and frankly, I think Nora would find it alarming. Let's go along now and meet her." Miss Meriden gets to her feet and dusts off her skirt. Then, she adds, with the faintest edge of a smile in her voice, "Who knows? Perhaps she'll have some Herculean labour she can lay before you."

CHAPTER EIGHT

The first thing that strikes me about Nora Felton is how young she is. She must be around thirty, fat and pretty with a round face and a fashionably shingled dark bob, a blunt fridge cut across her forehead. She is wearing a sort of black silk kimono, elaborately embroidered and dripping with pink fringe, and a pair of oversized jet earrings.

The room in which she's working is down the corridor from Miss Meriden's office and, though it is not much bigger, she has managed to squeeze a workbench with a sewing machine along one wall. Above it dozens of sketches are taped, which I assume must be the costumes for the production.

Despite the chill of the day, the window is open, and Nora is perched up on the high window sill, leaning out of it and smoking a cigarette.

"Sorry, I know it's freezing in here, but I don't like to smoke with it shut," she says, stubbing out the cigarette and tossing the butt out of the window before leaping nimbly down. "Otherwise I feel like I'm turning into a smoked kipper myself. These rooms really are wretched little cells, don't you think?"

The question is directed at me, I realize. Startled, I mumble something about how beautiful the theatre is.

"Of course," Nora nods, "but still, we're all squeezed in on top of each other, like sardines in a tin." She wrinkles her nose. "And I think that's enough fish metaphors for one conversation."

"This is Freya Trevelyan, Nora," Miss Meriden says. "I thought she might be a good fit for your assistant. Why don't I leave you two to talk for a while?"

She does so without a backwards glance, her curt

movements indicating she's got much more important things to do than worry about me. I'm beginning to feel a bit like a parcel passed from person to person. Ever since I arrived at the theatre it has felt as though I am being swept along, into a chain of events that are unfolding so rapidly they make my head spin.

Nora has turned away and busied herself making us drinks. Given her sheen of glamour and the cigarettes I am more than half-expecting her to pull out a cocktail shaker, but instead she begins fumbling with a battered electric kettle, copper and standing on three slightly wonky legs. The tin of tea she pulls down is battered too, though it is stamped from Fortnum and Mason.

"I'm sure I've got some biscuits in here somewhere," she murmurs, pushing a bolt of bright pink fabric aside.

My stomach growls and I grimace. "Sorry," I say. "I'm an absolute gannet, always hungry."

Nora smiles, and I see that her eyes are a warm brown and ringed in smudgy kohl. "Me too, and if I don't eat I get increasingly furious. Quite a handy reputation to have, though; the cast often drop in with sweets for fear they'll get put in something puce and covered in ruffles."

I laugh, and as with Kit I feel an instant ease, as though I've known Nora for ages.

"So." She hands me a chipped blue teacup full of steaming tea, and gestures towards a seat, half-buried under bits of costume. "Tell me about yourself."

Again, I tell the story. It's starting to feel more and more like a part that I'm playing. My words are becoming lines in a script. Naive young girl from the country, come to seek fame and fortune in the big city. It's not even original.

When I finish, Nora doesn't ask me about my plans for the future; she asks me about Penlyn and my family, my siblings and the plays I used to put on for them. She asks me about the first costume I made, and how I researched Queen Elizabeth's ruff. She unearths a tin of shortbread biscuits from beneath a half-fashioned corset and we talk and talk.

Eventually, we both fall silent.

"So," I say nervously. "Do you think I might be all right for the job?"

"I should think so." Nora stretches out like a cat. "But I have to warn you that it's hard work, and the pay is an actual pittance, though you'll get room and board on the tour. There will be lots of alterations and repairs, and most importantly, I need a dresser. There are several quick changes between scenes and some of the ladies' dresses are particularly fiddly."

"I can work hard," I say. "And I don't mind about the money. Just to be able to go on the tour and see how it all works up close ... it's a dream."

"We'll see if you still think that when you meet the rest of the cast." Nora stands. "Now, you grab that bag and we'll get going." She gestures to one side of the room, where a worn carpet bag sits.

I pick up the bag. "We're starting now?"

"No time like the present."

And just like that, I am hired. I follow Nora out of her small studio and down the corridor.

"I'll never learn my way around this place," I mutter.

"You will," Nora reassures me, "but you hardly need to – we're going to be leaving soon and then it's a dozen new theatres, all with their own peculiar layouts to learn."

She pushes open a door and we're in a room with two

long rails of costumes on either side. In the middle of the room is a block in front of a mirror, and a chair and a small table sit off to one side.

"Welcome to the wardrobe department," Nora says briskly. "Today we're doing final fittings for Viola and Russ. Viola is playing Gwendolyn, he's Algernon. Her costumes are here." She gestures to one rail. "His are there." She gestures to the other. "On each hanger you'll find a label with the scene and various notes on – they should be fairly self-explanatory. All right?"

"All right," I nod, trying to present a very capable picture.

There's a knock at the door, and a pleasant, slightly husky voice calls, "Nora, are you in here?"

"Come in, Viola," Nora calls back, and the door opens to reveal a very beautiful young woman. She is petite, with glossy ink-black hair cut short with a natural curl, and enormous dark eyes in a delicately pointed face. She moves with an easy grace, and her skin under the hard lights of the dressing room is a light, golden brown. Those beautiful eyes instantly catch on me, and I'm subjected to a long, assessing stare. It feels strangely territorial, like the way Mrs Fowler's tabby eyes up any stray cat that might wander into her garden. Languorously, she drops her bag to the ground and shrugs off her coat.

"Who are you?" she asks.

"I'm Freya Trevelyan." I give her a tentative smile. "Nora's new assistant."

"I hope she's not all fingers and thumbs like that last girl, Nora. I felt like a human pin cushion." These words, addressed directly to Nora, effectively cut me out of the conversation altogether. I glance nervously at Nora, and she rolls her eyes in sympathy. Viola is too busy looking at herself in the mirror to notice.

"What do you think of this dress?" She fusses with the purple crepe she's wearing, smoothing an imaginary wrinkle.

"The colour is nice," Nora says, but she lifts a critical eyebrow. "You should have it half an inch shorter. And I'm afraid it will crush dreadfully."

Viola pouts, then smiles winningly at Nora, the expressions skipping across her face like clouds across the sky. "You're always right, Nora. You'll hem it for me, won't you, darling? You'll make such quick work of it, I know."

"I've got more important things to do." Nora turns towards the clothing rail. "You can ask Freya. Now, step up on the block, and let's get you in to this."

Viola treats me to a charming smile, warm and entreating, very different to the cool appraisal she favoured me with at first. "Will you, Freya?" she asks. "I'm supposed to be wearing this out for dinner tonight with Marco – he's a producer friend of mine, and I want it to be perfect. He claims to be mad about me, but I still need to look just right."

"Of course," I say. "If you wouldn't mind stepping up, I'll just pin it now."

We achieve this quickly enough, and all the time Viola is standing on the block, she keeps up a stream of entertaining chatter that makes Nora and I laugh. She slips out of the purple dress, and I sit in the chair and sew, trying to keep my stitches as tiny as possible, while Nora helps her into various different costumes. Occasionally, Nora will call out a measurement and I'll make a note.

"Do you think the hat needs something?" she says, standing back and looking at it on top of Viola's pretty head. The hat is broad-rimmed, cream, trimmed with silk, and it looks charming; I'm convinced Viola could single-handedly bring this very Victorian creation back into style.

"A feather would be nice," I say tentatively. "Ostrich, along the brim there."

"And then curling down a little," Nora nods. "Make a note."

When they are finished, I hand the purple dress back to Viola, and she checks it quickly, then exclaims in delight. "Well, look at that, Nora. These stitches are so tiny it looks practically fairy made."

She slips back into her dress, just as there is another tap on the door.

"That'll be Russ," Nora says, glancing up at the clock on the wall.

The door opens, and, honestly, it's a good job I'm sitting down because the man standing framed in the doorway is without a doubt the most handsome man I have ever seen. His skin is tanned as if he spends a lot of time outdoors, his teeth a flash of white in an easy smile. Dark hair falls carelessly across his forehead, and there's just a hint of stubble on his face. His jaw is distinctly square. I'm not sure I've ever seen a jaw with actual corners before.

I think I must make some kind of sound of astonishment, because Nora and Viola both turn to look at me.

"Russ!" says Viola, turning back to him. Her voice is vaguely exasperated. "Making an entrance, as usual, I see. Why on earth are you wearing that?"

It's a testament to the beauty of the man's face that I genuinely hadn't noticed his costume until Viola pointed it out. He is wearing an old-fashioned Hussar uniform, deep navy with gold braid and frogging, a scarlet collar, and even a small cape draped over one shoulder. On anyone else such a get-up might look ridiculous, but it looks magnificent on him, as though a soldier has stepped out of the past and into this little room. A room which feels airless, suddenly.

Russ saunters through the door and as he does so he glances at me curiously, a long, lingering look from eyes so dark that they appear almost black, framed with outrageously thick lashes.

"Don't you like it?" he asks, and he has a proper actor's voice, smooth and velvety. "Nora lent it to me for an audition. I thought it would be a lark to wear it back, but I suppose I must look a bit of a fool." His gaze rests on me.

"I don't think you look a fool," I manage, my mouth dry.

He chuckles. This time it's Viola's turn to roll her eyes. I wonder if this means you do eventually become immune to his handsomeness. At the moment it is too much like looking directly at the sun for my brain to function properly.

"Right," Nora says briskly. "That's you done for today, Viola."

"Lovely." Viola smooths her dress, scoops up her bag and grabs her coat. "Wish me luck, won't you?"

"Good luck," Nora and I chorus, as Viola sweeps out of the room, waving lightly to Russ as she goes.

"Where's she off to?" Russ asks, looking after her. "Dinner with another producer?" He snorts. "Ambitious little thing. She'd do better to make sure she's at rehearsal on time. Didn't even turn up on Tuesday, and the understudy had to go on. And then breezing in the next day like nothing had happened, not a word of apology..." He halts, as though realizing he sounds petulant and gives an embarrassed smile. "It's just frustrating when there's so little time before the tour starts. We shouldn't be wasting it."

"Well, she is very good," Nora points out. "Mr Cantwell likes her."

"Oh, yes, she's *good*," Russ agrees. "She wouldn't get away with behaviour like that if she wasn't. And I'll admit her looks are a draw. She brings in the crowds, all right."

"She is beautiful," I say, feeling a strange urge to defend Viola.

"Mother was Indian or some such." Russ shrugs. "Not that she advertises it, obviously."

I don't know what to say to that.

"Marco, is it, this time?" he asks then. Without waiting for a reply, he nods knowingly. "I heard he was sniffing around, promising her a part. Not that it'll come to anything … he's not the first to make her an offer, if you know what I mean."

I have no idea what he means, actually, but I school my face into what I hope is a worldly expression.

"Come on, then," Nora breaks in. "Now that you've made your grand entrance, you can take off that costume."

"Why, Nora, I had no idea you were so forward," Russ murmurs, "But if you insist…"

I blush, hating myself for it, but Nora smirks. "I've no taste for snot-nosed school boys, Russ."

"Twenty-four, Nora," he objects mildly. "Hardly a school boy. Rather, shall we say … in the prime of my life."

"I'll stop calling you a school boy when you stop acting like one," Nora says. "You and Viola winding each other up all day long, it's enough to drive a woman mad."

Ah, I think. So that's it. Russ and Viola are warring lovers or some such. It makes sense; they presumably fight mostly over who is the prettiest. It must be why he's so put out to hear about her being wined and dined by producers.

Russ just laughs at Nora, and then turns to me. The sudden, full beam of his attention is overwhelming. "Now, are you going to introduce me to this young lady?" he asks. "New assistant, is it? What happened to the old one?"

"You know perfectly well what happened to the old one," Nora says tartly. "And I don't want a repeat of that performance, thank you."

"Darling, you wound me," he says. He gives me a conspiratorial wink. "I shall do the honours myself, then. Russell Whitmore." He extends a hand, catching my fingers in his own. His hand is large and warm, pressed around mine.

"Freya Trevelyan," I say.

"Charmed." Russ executes a small bow over my hand, and I have to say that, with his dark hair falling over his brow and the gold buttons of his Hussar's uniform gleaming, it's all I can do not to swoon. "Now," he murmurs wickedly, "which one of you is going to help me with all these buttons?"

CHAPTER NINE

Taking part in Russ's fitting is certainly a test of my professional resolve. For one thing, where I come from, handsome young men are not in the habit of disrobing in front of me. I concentrate very hard on appearing unfazed by the whole thing, and eventually it stops seeming quite so strange, particularly as Nora and Russ are so matter-of-fact. Still, it would be a lie to say I didn't notice the muscles visible under his white vest – which might be what Russ had in mind.

"For god's sake, stop flexing like a bloody circus

strongman!" Nora snaps. "How am I supposed to get these measurements right if you're too busy putting on a show? Freya, pass me the linen shirt there."

The brisk command jars me from my observation of Russ's biceps, and I grab the shirt in question, hurriedly turning it over to Nora's waiting hands.

"What do you think?" Russ asks, after slipping it over his head. His eye catches mine in the mirror, holding it for a moment longer than is necessary.

"I don't know," I say, trying to keep my tone cool. "Perhaps it needs letting out a little?"

"I told you it was going to be too tight," Nora sighs. There's a knock at the door. It's Kit.

"Hello!" I greet him with enthusiasm. I can't wait to tell him everything that's happened since he left me.

"Oh, it's you," Russ says dismissively.

"Yes, it's me," Kit replies easily. "Came to see how the newest recruit was getting on. I see you've put her straight to work, Nora, but I need to steal her away. Miss Meriden needs her to fill out some paperwork."

Nora nods. "Yes, yes, take her. She's done more than enough. There's only Eileen left today anyway."

"Oh, but—" I start to protest.

Nora laughs at my crestfallen expression. "Don't worry, you'll meet her another time. You're going to be seeing plenty of this lot."

"A pleasure I am particularly looking forward to," Russ says. His voice is warm honey, and the look he gives me is mischievous, designed, I think, to rile Nora. I wonder what happened to the old assistant.

"Thank you for today," I say to Nora, ignoring Russ. She waves me away, already absorbed in fitting a jacket. I quickly tidy away the sewing kit I've been using and follow Kit out.

"Kit!" His name bursts from me, once we're away from the others and walking down the corridor. "Can you believe it? I'm coming on tour with the company, and it's all down to you." I give a little skip. "I can never, *never* thank you enough."

Kit shakes his head. "All I did was make the introduction. You're the one who won over Mr Cantwell, *and* Miss Meriden, *and* Nora. No small feat for half a day's work."

"I can't believe I'm going to meet Eileen Turner," I

murmur. "I've had a photograph of her as Titania in *A Midsummer Night's Dream* up on my wall for years."

In the picture, Eileen Turner must only be about Nora's age, with long, pale hair tumbling almost down to her knees and threaded through with flowers. I used to hold whole conversations with this picture, about my dreams, and the theatre, and the adventures I would have – but the Eileen Turner on my wall, she was *my* Eileen Turner. Now, though it still seems absurd to contemplate, I am going to meet the real star herself.

"It's quite the coup that Mr Cantwell managed to get her out of retirement," Kit says, breaking into my daydreams. "She's extraordinary onstage."

"I suppose if anyone could do it, he could." I lower my voice. "Miss Meriden says Mr Cantwell hasn't worked much lately."

Kit rubs the back of his neck. "Yes, he went over to America for a while, to give it a shot in Hollywood, but I don't think things went as well as he'd hoped. He doesn't talk about it."

I wonder what it must be like to be so stunningly

successful and then to fail at something when all eyes are on you. Not nice, I expect.

"I met Viola and Russ," I say, changing the subject.

"Oh, yes, those two," he says absently.

He glances at me and his face suddenly becomes more serious.

"Freya," he says a little awkwardly. "About Russ… I think I should… I mean, I think *someone* should – well, warn you…"

"That he's a tremendous womanizer and I should be careful?" I finish for him.

Kit laughs, looking relieved. "Yes."

"You don't need to worry about that," I say reassuringly. "Of course he's wildly good-looking, but I have no intention of falling for his well-oiled charms. I don't have any intention of falling in love at all."

"You don't?" Kit asks, coming to a stop in the hallway.

"Of course not. My focus is on my career. One must dedicate one's whole self to the craft!"

He looks as though he's thinking this over. "I see," he says finally. "But don't you think – as an actress, I mean – that experiencing all sorts of emotions can only enrich your performances?"

I stare at him, struck by this observation. Penlyn is hardly a seething hotbed of romantic opportunities, but I never went about with the local boys like Alice and Lou did when they were my age. To be honest, if anyone ever invited me to the pictures it certainly wasn't hand holding that I was interested in, it was whatever was happening up there on the screen. I prefer to go to the pictures alone. That way, there are no distractions.

But now, I wonder. *Would* a love affair improve my acting? I think of Viola. She must have had plenty of love affairs; why, she'd implied that Marco the producer she was out with right now was head over ears in love with her. How could you act falling in love if you never had?

I think about all the great parts I've been reading my whole life. Juliet, Hedda Gabler, Cleopatra! I've never experienced anything even close to that kind of passion. The whole love-at-first-sight thing is a mystery to me. How would I know if I was doing a good job at portraying it? I think about how I felt when I first saw Russ, the way he knocked the breath right out of me

– I'm not sure it was precisely Shakespearean, but it was certainly dramatic.

"You may have a point," I say slowly. "I suppose that Russ—"

"Oh, no," Kit cuts in quickly, "I think you were quite right about Russ. I only meant you shouldn't dismiss every possibility out of hand."

"Perhaps," I say thoughtfully. "It's certainly something to consider." I give myself a quick mental shake. "Whatever happens, I have a job. With a real theatre company. And an awful lot can happen in a few weeks, don't you think?"

The smile Kit gives me is slow, like a gas lamp being turned up. "Given what you've achieved in less than two days," he says, "I think the next six weeks are going to be quite the adventure."

Part Two

Oxford
November, 1931

CHAPTER TEN

The following week I find myself squeezed into a van, seated between Nora and a large hat box, as we wind our way towards the first stop on the tour: Oxford.

Nora and I are travelling there together, along with the costumes. I met her at the theatre at the crack of dawn, and we carefully packed up the wardrobe department. Now I watch her, seated behind the wheel of the van, wearing oversized sunglasses despite the clouds and a loose silk dress covered in an abstract design. She nips in and out of the crowds of traffic with great confidence and several exotic expletives that I have never heard before, though I note them down for future use.

I'm not completely clear on how the rest of the cast and crew are travelling from place to place. Like everything about the tour, the transportation seems to be in a state of meticulously organized chaos. The woman with her hand on the reins – so to speak, there are as far as I know no *actual* horses involved – is Miss Meriden, and she is ruthlessly efficient, and can wield a clipboard like it's a scary-looking medieval weapon. So, while I know we're scattered about in various vehicles, I have no doubt we will all end up where we need to be. I do know that Kit is in one of the bigger trucks that is transporting the scenery, and that Mr Cantwell is driving Eileen Turner in his beautiful blue Rolls Royce.

We make quite the peculiar convoy as we leave the city, but as we wind our way further out on to the open roads we drift apart. Mr Cantwell's car glides sedately away, while Russ whips past in a zippy little red car that roars like a territorial lion tribe. Nora and I bring up the rear, rattling along at a leisurely pace.

I tap my fingers, drumming them against my knees

like rain on glass. Though it pains me to admit it, now that we are actually on our way, I am deeply nervous, terrified that somehow I will ruin such a spectacular opportunity. I am also excited. Or perhaps excited is not the right word... Giddy. Euphoric? Jubilant? It is a feeling too big to be contained inside a word.

Last night, Lou said she was relieved I was leaving (with Midge and Pa's blessing) because I was rapidly becoming unbearable with all my theatre talk. Robert scolded her for raining on my parade, which I enjoyed very much, though his eyes did glaze over when I described for him again – in great detail – the differences between Gwendolyn's gown in Act One and Act Three.

I have spent only two more days at the Queen Anne Theatre, and they were increasingly frantic, full of the hustle and bustle of fittings and alterations, and endless lists and packing up. It has been exhilarating work, done mostly in the company of Nora. The kinship I sensed between us when we first met was no fluke – I like her very much. She is funny and spiky, with dazzlingly good taste and an unnervingly fine eye for detail.

The only thing that has been missing from my new

job is Eileen Turner. Despite my best efforts, Nora refused to ask her back in for one more fitting.

"Drag Eileen Turner in for an imaginary fitting, just so that you can gawp at her?" Nora shook her head. "No, thank you."

"But it wouldn't *just* be for gawping," I explained. "It would be to triple-check everything, and then, who knows, maybe we get to talking, she warms to my undeniable charm, taking me under her wing, adopting me as her protégé..."

Nora's perfectly arched brow stopped me in my tracks. I'll admit it is possible I've been getting a *little* carried away, but when one is left alone for days to imagine the impending experience of meeting one's idol, there's sure to be the odd flight of fancy.

It could happen.

It feels like *anything* could happen at the moment.

After all, here I am, on my way to a city I have never been to before, part of the cast and crew of a touring production directed by Rhys Cantwell, and starring Eileen Turner. I think I might have to ask Nora to pinch me black and blue.

We have left the city behind now, and we twist and turn through the country roads, rain pattering against the window, the wipers wheezing feebly. It's still so early that the sun has barely made it above the horizon, lost in a blanket of rain clouds.

Nora starts singing a Cole Porter song in a sweet husky voice, and I join in with enthusiasm, so that soon the windows on the van are trembling, and Nora is tapping the steering wheel like an enthusiastic percussionist. The rain stops, and misty sunbeams struggle to pierce through the thick bank of cloud. By the time we reach the outskirts of Oxford, it's turned into one of those hazy autumn days, weak sunshine against a mist-grey sky.

Oxford seems quiet after London, though it is obviously still much bigger and more bustling than I'm used to. We turn through a maze of narrow winding streets that slither snake-like through buildings of honey-coloured stone. These walls seem radiant with knowledge. I can almost imagine there is something scholarly in the air, as if it is thick with whispered philosophy, crackling with poetry about dreaming spires and white rabbits.

"Oscar Wilde wasn't much older than me when he came here," I say to Nora. "Isn't that funny? He walked around these streets as a young man, and now here we all are about to put on his play at the theatre. Do you think he imagined such a thing happening?"

"Oscar Wilde?" Nora says, taking an extremely sharp left turn in a casual manner that has me clinging to my seat. "I'd say he was certain of it."

"Some people are very self-assured, aren't they?" I ponder thoughtfully, propping my chin on my hand as I watch the world sail past my window.

"And aren't you one of them?" Nora looks at me over her sunglasses.

"I suppose I am," I agree finally, surprised by something I've never considered. "I've always known what I wanted to do, and it never occurs to me that I might fail – that's being self-assured, isn't it?"

Nora laughs. "The dreams we have as children feel very certain. I suppose if you hold on to a dream from childhood then it carries that same feeling of certainty."

I'm quiet at that. She's right; being an actress is such a long-held dream, it has become a part of me, like my blonde hair or my dislike of licorice. I feel briefly uneasy for some reason, but then I shake it off. I am working in Rhys Cantwell's production. All I have to do is prove myself to him, and the future will unfurl itself like a fat, beautiful peony. I'm sure of it.

Finally, the car rounds another corner and pulls up in front of an old wrought-iron double gate.

"Hop out and open that," Nora says, and I do as I'm told. I pull the latches from the ground and open both sides of the gate. The van rattles past me, and I turn to take in the building behind me.

I am standing in a small walled courtyard where a couple of cars are already parked. One of them is Russ's shiny red car, and it's no surprise that he beat us here. The crumbling stone walls are covered in tangled vines, already looking skeletal and wintery. The building at the back of the courtyard is tall and thin, with lots of windows, and a slightly lopsided front porch. It looks as though it has seen better days.

Nora jumps down from the van, dusting her hands off, and comes to help me close the gates back up. "Here we are," she says. "It doesn't look like much, but they're fairly decent digs. The woman who owns it used to be an opera singer and she takes us in for a bit of extra cash. She likes theatre types, so she doesn't tend to mind if things get a little rowdy in the evenings, and she makes an excellent fry-up in the morning."

"Are the others here?" I ask.

"Some of them, by the looks of things." Nora starts shepherding me towards the front door. "Of course Rhys and Eileen won't be staying here – they get put up in a hotel." She reaches up and pulls at a bell, which I hear echoing beyond the door.

The staccato clipping of footsteps across the floor follows shortly after, and the door swings open, revealing a large, smiling woman in her sixties, swathed in a long red gown and clutching a mostly empty cocktail glass.

"Nora, darling!" she exclaims, her words ringing through the air with the perfect clarity one might expect from an opera singer.

"Hallo, Del." Nora leans forward to kiss the woman on both cheeks. "Meet my new assistant, Freya. Freya, this is Adelaide."

"Just call me Del." She beams at me, her mouth a

slash of scarlet lipstick. "Now do come in, it's far too cold to be standing out on the doorstep."

The inside of the house is exactly as I had imagined, dark and worn, and a bit of a warren. The walls are covered in framed posters, faded with age, and advertising operatic performances starring Adelaide St James. This, then, will be our home for the next three days.

Del is already off, leading us on a brisk tour, rattling off the information as though she's shared it many times before.

"This through here is the kitchen," Del gestures. "There's gin in the pantry." Then, after pause, "And milk, I think." She carries on down the long hallway. "Here's the sitting room, where folks tend to gather in the evening, post-performance." The room is large, and contains a battered upright piano, several faded floral sofas, a record player, a large ceramic bulldog with a bowler sitting drunkenly on his head, and a bookcase that is full of empty wine bottles.

"Quite a few of your lot have arrived already. That girl, Viola, well, she's quite the attraction, isn't she? That hair and those eyes ... very exotic. I wonder where she got those looks from."

I think Del means the words as a compliment, but there's something about the gleeful, hushed way she talks about Viola that makes me feel uncomfortable, even though I can't quite put my finger on why.

Nora doesn't reply and Del continues to rattle on as she leads us up the stairs. "And there's Russ, of course – he's been here before, asked if he could have his old room, that sweet boy." Her face is pleased and rosy as she drains the last of the drink in her hand. "I've put you in your usual room, Nora," she says. "And you," she glances at me and I am suddenly struck by the unusual amber colour of her eyes, "you're in here with ... Alma! That's it. Nice girl. Bit quiet."

Del taps lightly on the door and without waiting for a response flings it open. Inside are two wrought-iron single beds with a small strip of faded blue rug between them. Sitting on one of the beds with a book in her hands is a girl about the same age as me.

"I'll leave you to get settled in," Del says and leaves with Nora in her wake.

"Hello," I say a little awkwardly. "I'm Freya."

"Alma." The girl gets to her feet. She is tall and slender, with pansy blue eyes that study me carefully, and slightly mousy blonde hair. She is dressed simply, in a soft blue dress. Her face is rather long and serious, but sweet – like a painting of a saint. She looks as though she should be surrounded by woodland creatures, resting her hand on the head of a slumbering fawn. "It's nice to meet you." Her voice is low and musical, and it matches her face.

"Same here." I step into the room and hold out my hand, which she shakes. "I'm the new wardrobe assistant."

"I'm the understudy," Alma replies.

Of course. Alma is understudying the roles of Cecily and Gwendolyn on the assumption that both actresses are unlikely to be off at the same time – more of the budget cuts Miss Meriden shakes her head over. Like Eileen, I haven't run into Alma at the theatre yet. "So you're an actress," I say with interest, taking a seat on the bed across from hers.

"Trying to be," Alma shrugs, attempting to affect a

nonchalance that doesn't quite come off. "This is my first tour, though."

"Mine too!" I exclaim. "Although really it's my first anything – I've barely even been away from home before, and it was absolute blind luck that I ended up here, I can tell you."

Alma sits back down on the bed and pulls her knees up to her chest, toying with her long braid of blonde hair. "I expect you were hoping to be rooming with someone who could show you the ropes?"

"I'd much rather have a friend I could muddle through it with," I say.

This draws a hesitant smile; she gives me another of those careful looks, as though she's taking my measure. Her face relaxes, and the smile grows. "Me too."

"Besides, Nora will show us the ropes," I say.

"Don't you find her dreadfully intimidating?" Alma asks.

"Not a bit," I tell her. "I know she looks so glamorous, but she's been really kind to me."

"That's a relief." Alma slumps back against her

pillows. "Because everyone I've met so far has been intimidating as anything. Apart from Kit, of course."

"No, Kit's not scary," I agree. "Do you know each other well?" I don't know why but I feel a strange sort of possessive feeling. Kit is *my* friend.

"Only from rehearsals," Alma says, a slight flush rising in her cheeks. "He's very kind."

"Mmm," I murmur noncommittally. "And what about the other actors?"

"They seem nice." She sounds a lot less certain now. "I don't know them very well." She hesitates, then says confidingly, "Russ and Viola don't seem that fond of each other."

"I think they are probably having a big love affair," I say. "Squabbling lovers, you know, like something Shakespearean. They pretend to hate each other, but deep down it's all trembling passion and swooning and—"

Nora sticks her head around the door. "Freya, you'd better come and grab your bag from the van," she says. "Then we'll all head over to the theatre – dress rehearsal in an hour. Get your skates on." She flashes a grin at

117

Alma. "You too – it's all hands on deck. Things are about to get very busy."

Nora sweeps from the room, leaving us scrambling in her wake. Alma looks both thrilled and nervous and I am sure those exact emotions are reflected on my own face.

"This is it, I suppose," I say, giving her an encouraging smile. "Now it all really starts!"

CHAPTER ELEVEN

I miss most of the rehearsal. As soon as we reach the theatre, a large brick building set on the corner of a busy road with a higgledy-piggledy backstage area and a decent-sized auditorium, Nora has me unpacking and pressing and steaming and organizing an endless parade of costumes. Each costume has many parts to it, and they must all be treated as carefully as if they were delicate invalids, and we their weary yet devoted nurses.

Nora is a perfectionist with an eye for detail. "There's a loose thread there." She gestures at the claret-coloured gown in my hands, and swoops down, a pair of gleaming silver scissors already in hand to snip the offending thread, barely visible up this close, let alone in the audience.

I admire her attention to the small things. I find it soothing to do this methodical, practical work. There's a richness to it as well, one that comes from seeing and experiencing the level of detail that goes into a performance – the things the audience may not notice individually, but that become part of their larger impression of the play. Like the embroidery on the bodice of this claret dress. It had been my idea to add it, in gold thread that catches the lights and adds to the sense of opulence onstage.

"You've got a good eye for this." Nora's voice breaks into my thoughts, and she gestures to the embroidery that I have been considering. "That's neat work, and you were right about it finishing off the gown."

I feel a glow of pride at that.

When we're finally done (for the time being, anyway), and Nora tells me to take a break, I slip into the back of the auditorium to get a glimpse at what's happening onstage. It is there, sitting up high, lost in the shadows, that I get my first glimpse of Eileen Turner.

It is only her and Rhys Cantwell on the stage and they are deep in conversation, their voices an indistinguishable murmur, as they discuss some finer point of her performance. Mr Cantwell suddenly throws his head back and laughs, a sharp bark of laughter and the first I have heard from him. Is she funny? Somehow I never imagined that.

I drink in the sight of her. She's smaller than I imagined, but then I suppose it's difficult to imagine your hero being anything but larger than life. Yet here she is, slight and delicate-looking. I search her face for a glimpse of the young woman in the photograph that is still hanging on my wall in Cornwall. She's in her seventies now, and her face is beautiful, elfin, with high cheekbones. Instead of the endless waves falling to her knees, her hair is silvery white and cropped short. She'll be wearing wigs during her performance.

She steps away from Mr Cantwell and moves towards the centre of the empty stage. She pulls her shoulders back, and suddenly she's not small at all – she's a force, a hypnotizing, whirling force of nature. She becomes – in front of my eyes, and despite the lack of make-up or costume – Lady Bracknell, a difficult, haughty, overbearing woman who is used to getting her own way.

"Well, I must say, Algernon, that I think it is high time that Mr Bunbury made up his mind whether he was going to live or to die. This shilly-shallying with the question is absurd."

Her voice rings through the air, and it's a wonderful voice. Deep for a woman, and warm, she lingers on "t"s, and compresses some of the words, giving them a rhythm, a particular music that is unique to her. It's a voice that, once heard, you would recognize anywhere.

She finishes her bit of dialogue and then, as easily as one would slip off a coat, she sheds Lady Bracknell and moves forward, Eileen Turner once more, to talk to Mr Cantwell.

I sit, stunned, as the rest of the cast appear. Kit, his red-gold hair shining under the lights, steps onstage and begins calling to others in the wings. Directions about the scenery, I presume. Mr Cantwell gathers them all together and begins speaking to them. I watch Viola; she is rapt, nodding earnestly, all her attention pinned to his face. Russ sits on the edge of the stage, leaning back on one hand, the very picture of relaxed nonchalance. Dan and Daphne, who are playing the two other lead roles, stand slightly to one side like naughty school children – I see Dan whisper in Daphne's ear, and she stifles a laugh, swatting at him with her hand.

I wish I could hear what they were saying. I wish I was up there with them. I want it, with a ferocity that makes my heart pound. Here I am – so close and yet, still, so far away.

"There you are!" Nora exclaims behind me. "Come on, we've got work to do, break's over." She must see something of my feelings in my face, because her expression softens. "And Lindsey the make-up girl has just turned up with a tin of biscuits. Let's go and put the kettle on."

I scramble to my feet. Biscuits may be the only thing to help ease this particular pain. I follow her out of the auditorium, casting one last, longing look over my shoulder at the stage, at the actors and their director lost in their play.

**

By the time the performance rolls around that evening, I feel as though an entire kaleidoscope of butterflies has taken up residence in my stomach. The build-up to the curtain rising is excruciating – and I'm not even going onstage. I feel like a jack-in-the-box, wound further and further, waiting to explode. I'm not the only one; the tension is a palpable thing. You can practically see the cloud of nervous energy wrapped around each person.

"Is it always like this?" I ask Nora through teeth that seem determined to chatter.

"Yes," she says, with a grim smile. "Though the first night is by far the worst."

It's a relief, then, a blissful exhalation, when the curtain finally goes up, and – like a well-oiled-machine – we all fall into the roles we have practised over and over.

Standing in the wings I watch the scenes unfold between the frantic burst of the costume changes.

There is something deeply pleasurable about watching the cast win over the audience, who seem increasingly eager to be pleased as the night goes on.

The laughter begins almost straight away, but it

builds and builds. There are so many clever lines, so many good jokes, and each one is given space to breathe and to shine.

The audience and I watch, delighted, as Algernon and Jack meet up, as Algernon reveals he has an imaginary friend called Bunbury who he uses to get out of things he doesn't want to do, as Jack explains that he uses the name Ernest when in town so that he can get away with bad behaviour. We hang on every word as Jack reveals he is in love with Algernon's cousin Gwendolyn – daughter of Lady Bracknell – and as Algernon falls for Jack's ward, Cecily. We laugh and laugh at the increasingly complicated tangle as both women believe their beloved to be named Ernest.

Of course it's Eileen who steals every scene she appears in. When she first walks onstage there's a spontaneous burst of applause that halts the production for several minutes. Seeing her work up close is incredible, watching the play of expressions on her face – the twitch of an eyebrow, the flicker of a smile at her mouth – is like a lesson in itself. It's all I can do not to start taking notes. I've still not spoken to her as Nora is in charge of all her costume requirements; she seems to me as unapproachable, as unknowable as God. For the first time, I understand what it means to be *magnetic;* you simply can't take your eyes off her.

By the time Russ and Dan – the actor playing Jack – are arguing over a plate of muffins, the audience are approaching something like hysteria, and I'm finding it hard to smother my own giggles, spluttering as quietly as possible in my darkened corner. Across the stage from me, in the prompt corner, I see Alma clutching the script in trembling fingers and doing the same. Our eyes meet, and I see my own excitement reflecting in the dark, gleaming pools of her eyes.

"How you can sit there, calmly eating muffins when we are in this horrible trouble, I can't make out," Dan snaps. "You seem to me to be perfectly heartless."

"Well, I can't eat muffins in an agitated manner," Russ counters swiftly, a charming sight in his linen suit. "The butter would probably get on my cuffs. One should always eat muffins quite calmly. It is the only way to eat them." He fiddles for a moment with his shirt cuffs, the cuffs that I altered for him with my very own hands, which are now the source of such joy for the laughing crowd.

Russ is a good actor, I think. It makes me like him more, actually, seeing that he's perhaps done something to earn his arrogance, though there's a touch of that slickness that hangs about him onstage.

The whole scene is choreographed perfectly, and I see things in it I have never noticed before. The big-brother, little-brother dynamic, the bickering which hides the fact that both characters are miserable, but unable to seek any kind of solace from one another in sincerity – it has to be through these childish games.

It is a wonderful production and this, I see now, is down to Rhys Cantwell.

All through the last few days he has been invested in every single aspect of the performance – the way a prop is handled, the timing of a line, the fall of a gown. And tonight it all makes sense. The entire staging is beautiful. It's like when you hear a beautiful piece of music – all the different parts coming together in harmony to create something truly special.

Viola appears to make her entrance and I smooth

her skirts and adjust a lock of hair. Earlier, her face was pinched and her eyes looked even more enormous than usual, but when she steps on the stage it's as though she's a flower being revived by the spotlights.

I expected that Viola would be good – but instead, she is a revelation.

She has something of Eileen Taylor's magnetism about her, I think, though not as well developed yet. She's a much better actor than Russ or Dan or Daphne, for all their solid air of professionalism – seeing them onstage together makes it apparent. It's hard to look away from Viola. With the smallest pause or change of expression she reduces the audience to gales of laughter, and she's perfectly cast as Gwendolyn, effortlessly dispensing witty one-liners. She plays the part flawlessly, every gesture absolutely right.

I feel as though I might burst with a mixture of envy and admiration. I wonder why I haven't heard of her before – I follow the theatre world as closely as possible, and Viola is the sort of talent who should be starring in a big London show. There should be girls in Cornwall with her picture on their walls.

When the performance ends and the cast go onstage to take their bows I stand to the side in the shadows with Nora and clap until my hands hurt. The roar of the crowd tells me that they enjoyed it as much as I did. The applause lasts an age and the cast do three curtain calls.

The hustle and bustle after the show is euphoric, riotous, and full of shrieks of laughter, and bouquets of roses and half-dressed cast members swigging from bottles of champagne. There are people *everywhere*. Only Nora remains focused.

"Fetch that hat before it's crushed!" she exclaims, as we dart between bodies that seem to be moving in all directions. "And Viola is missing a shoe, last seen in Act One."

I snatch up the hat in question, and go off in search of the missing shoe.

I find a crowd gathered in Russ's dressing room. He is wrapped in a blue and silver robe, his dark hair damp with sweat, a half-moon white grin on his face. There are people patting him on the arm, telling him what a great job he did. He spots me and winks. I laugh, elated with it all, giddy on adrenaline, still clutching the feathered hat to my chest.

Mr Cantwell appears, looking very dashing in his evening wear, and he too claps Russ on the arm.

"Very good work, my boy," he says, and I think despite his calm he looks pleased. "Very good work by all of you."

I see Miss Meriden behind his shoulder, typically unmoved by all of the heightened emotions on display. Dan, Viola and Daphne join the crowd and a cheer goes up.

Mr Cantwell clears his throat. "You all worked extremely hard, and delivered an impressive opening night performance." There's another whoop of approval. "But there's still work to do," he goes on, his brows lowering impressively, "and I expect each performance to be better than the last." He casts a lingering look around the room. "So make sure you rest well tonight. I will see you back here tomorrow to do it all over again."

As congratulatory speeches go it is not exactly effusive. There's a muted ripple of applause, and then he sweeps from the room, followed by Miss Meriden.

"Rest be damned!" Russ exclaims, when they are safely out of earshot. "I'm gasping for a drink!"

This time, the cheer is much louder.

I spot the missing shoe and snatch it up, then gather the remaining pieces of costume and go to find Nora. As I hurry down the corridor I run almost head first into Kit.

His red hair is tousled, sticking out at peculiar angles, and his eyes are shining. "Freya!" he exclaims. He swings me around in a little jig. "How about that for a first night?"

"It was *wonderful*," I reply, beaming up at him. My heart clatters in my chest, and I feel warm, almost feverish, with a crashing mixture of excitement and relief that everything went well.

"Don't let Nora keep you, will you?" Kit says, releasing me and heading off down the corridor. "Make sure the two of you get back to Del's for the party."

"A party?" I frown. "I thought it was just a drink…" But Kit is already gone.

CHAPTER TWELVE

By the time Nora and I walk through the door at Del's I see that Kit was not exaggerating. This is a party, all right. In fact, it's an absolute squeeze.

"Who are they all?" I ask Nora as we push through the front hallway. People are propped along the wall, deep in conversations, laughing, smoking, and drinking from a variety of strange receptacles. There's a general air of dishevelment, as though everyone has rushed over from the theatre as soon as possible.

I realize that I haven't even looked in a mirror for

hours, and run one hand quickly over my hair, jabbing at the loose pins there, and another down the front of my slightly crumpled frock.

"Nora!" An attractive woman with dark hair cut boyishly short catches Nora by the arm.

"Darling," Nora's voice is a purr, "I didn't know you were in Oxford."

"I heard you were going to be in town." The woman's voice matches Nora's, and smiling, Nora pulls her slowly into her arms and kisses her very soundly, full on the lips.

Blimey. My eyes widen, and I leave Nora to it, pushing my way through towards the sitting room, keeping my eyes peeled for Alma or the flash of Kit's hair.

I follow the compelling jangle of jazz music coming from the record player, weaving my way past a group gathered at the foot of the stairs who – for some reason – are all wearing animal masks. A badger lifts his mask as I pass, in order to give me a leery wink, and a hand brushes – not quite accidentally – across my hip.

I shove and squeeze my way into the sitting room,

where I can see neither Alma nor Kit, but find Russ instead, holding court, telling a story that has the group around him laughing. There's more than one pretty girl there, and he looks extremely pleased with himself, flashing his perfect white smile. I wonder if, like the Cheshire Cat, the rest of him could fade away and the self-satisfied grin would remain. I chuckle at the thought. At that moment, he catches my eye.

"Little Freya!" he exclaims, reaching for my hand and drawing me into the circle. "Someone fetch a drink for little Freya, the only girl here who's had the pleasure of undressing me. So far, anyway," he adds in a low voice and the giggles that greet this remark leave me raising my eyes to heaven.

Someone presses a chipped teacup full of water into my hand. I take a swig and almost spit the whole thing out. Not water. Gin. Neat gin.

Russ looks upon me with the sort of fond amusement one may reserve for a young sibling and I straighten my spine, instantly riled. I certainly don't want him thinking of me in that light. I sip carefully at my drink and try not to grimace.

He must notice, because he drops an easy arm around my shoulder. "Don't be cross, darling," he murmurs, close to my ear, his breath warm against my cheek. Then he pulls away, his dark eyes dancing. "Although you do look adorable when you pout."

I shrug his arm away and feed my cup of gin to the sad-looking potted fern beside me. "I'm not cross," I say. "And I'm perfectly happy to be adored." I hesitate. "Although, to be honest, I wasn't pouting so much as making a face over the gin, and I find it hard to believe *that* was especially attractive. I think you must be a little drunk."

He stares at me for a moment, and then, suddenly he laughs, a real laugh, long and loud, and – after a very brief pause – his crowd of sycophants join in.

That's when I spot Alma, marooned across the room with a young man, who is wearing a lot of black and standing much too close to her while gesturing earnestly. Her eyes are darting around the room and I get the strong impression she is not enjoying herself.

"I must go," I say, and Russ clutches at his chest.

"You can't leave me. Stay!"

I laugh, and leave him to his fans, though I feel his eyes on my back as I cut through the crowds until I reach Alma.

"Freya!" she exclaims in obvious relief. "I was just telling … um…"

"Nathaniel," the young man supplies, frowning.

"Yes, Nathaniel, of course," Alma says. "I was just telling Nathaniel that I was meeting a friend tonight, and here you are. Should we…"

"Go and find Kit as we promised," I agree swiftly, taking her arm. "Come on."

"Nice to meet you, Nathaniel," she calls over her shoulder.

"*Was* it nice?" I ask teasingly.

"Not really," she sighs, and then obviously feels bad about it. "I shouldn't say that. I didn't want to be rude. But I just *couldn't* stand another minute of listening to him talk on and on about Brecht."

"Gosh, there are a lot of terrible men here," I sigh as I dodge another wandering hand. "Are theatre parties always this bad?"

"Don't ask me," Alma replies glumly. "I'm new to

this too, remember?"

"Not enjoying yourselves?" a voice asks from behind me, and I see my own relief mirrored in Alma's face.

I turn to find the reassuringly rangy form of Kit standing next to Dan, who, unlike the rest of us, is immaculately turned out, his fair hair neatly oiled, his shirt crisp, his shoes shined – you would never guess that a couple of hours ago he'd been sweating under the stage lights.

"It's the men!" I say. "Either it's Russ and his fan club, or it's leery men, or it's men who want to bore you to death with the sound of their own opinions."

Kit looks amused, and Dan sniggers.

"It is rather slim pickings," Dan drawls, his eyes running around the room, "but, then, not everyone's arrived yet. Del's crowd usually attracts a devastating man or two to keep things interesting."

I look around the crowded room. "Where is Del going to put them?" I ask.

"Oh, I'm sure we can find somewhere." Dan raises his eyebrows suggestively, and we laugh.

"Here," Kit says, holding out a glass to me. "We got

our hands on some champagne."

I take the glass saucer, cool to my touch, and Dan hands one to Alma as well. "Thank you," I say, taking a sip and enjoying the sharp sting of the bubbles. "Much nicer than the gin."

Kit grimaces. "You haven't been forced to drink that muck, have you? I heard Del brews it herself in the bathtub – it's absolutely lethal."

"I fed mine to the plant."

"Poor plant."

"Congratulations on tonight," Alma says to Dan. "You were wonderful."

"I was rather, wasn't I?" Dan smirks, pleased with himself, then the smirk drops away and he gives a much more genuine, slightly lopsided smile. "As a matter of fact, it was a hell of a lot of fun." His smile widens. "And speaking of fun, here she is."

Daphne appears at his side, the bubbly red-headed girl who plays Cecily, Russ's love interest. She and I have not had much chance to talk, but she seems to me like the glass of champagne in my hand, sparkling hard and fizzing with energy.

"You were ravishing, darling." Dan loops an arm around her waist, and she lifts her own glass.

"I'll drink to that," she whoops happily. "Particularly when everyone else seems to be."

We chat more about the performance, and I feel a thrill at the easy way in which I am taking part in a conversation with the performers. *I was there,* I think. I helped make it happen too, in a small way.

It feels almost as though I am watching myself, hovering above the scene and looking down on my body as words come out of my mouth. I'm so painfully, crushingly aware that what is happening right now in this moment is a dream come true. Or, I suppose it could be the champagne – never having really drunk much before, I can't be certain.

I catch Kit's eye and he's looking right at me, through me almost, and suddenly I know that he knows just what I'm thinking. It's a moment of startling telepathy, the kind that I suppose is only possible between kindred spirits and good friends. I beam up at him, wrapped up in the thick delight of it all.

Talk turns to the other guests and Dan and Daphne

entertain me with scandalous tales of cast, crew, theatre workers and hangers-on. They keep breaking into impressions. The room fills with more people and in the crush I find myself leaning back against Kit, laughing so hard that my own legs won't hold me. I feel his own body rumbling with laughter, a deep vibration against my back.

Somehow, we end up being swept towards the piano. Never one to shy away from the spotlight, I ask if it is in tune, and tap out a tremulous scale.

"Oh, yes, a song!" Daphne exclaims joyfully. "Just what we need!"

I sit down at the stool and crack my knuckles, my fingers hovering over the keys. I am not a particularly brilliant pianist, but Midge always says that what I lack in talent I more than make up for with enthusiasm. I bring my fingers crashing down on the keys and launch into "I'm Sailing on a Sunbeam" by Des Tooley, shouting out my goodbyes to all my cares and sorrows.

The rest of them join in enthusiastically. Alma, I notice, has a particularly beautiful voice, and she and

Dan begin harmonizing like a pair of songbirds.

Others join in. Someone produces a trumpet, from where I do not know, and starts playing along.

Daphne hops up on the stool beside me, an open bottle of champagne in her hands as she conducts the crowd, all joining in the chorus. We sing the song through three times, getting louder and rowdier and more pleased with ourselves on each pass at the chorus.

As I bring the song finally to a clattering halt, Daphne exclaims, teeters suddenly on the stool, rights herself briefly and then, in a fog of expletives, crashes to the ground.

"Daphne! Daphne!" I exclaim, crouching down, reaching out to touch her arm. "Are you all right?"

She looks up at me. "Well, that's torn it," she says, and then her eyes flutter closed.

CHAPTER THIRTEEN

Dear Midge and Pa,

So, here I am in Oxford at the start of the
tour. The place we're staying in is very nice, and
I'm told the lady who owns it makes a good
breakfast, for which I'm very grateful as these
theatre types don't seem terribly worried about
scheduling meals at proper times. Still, you
mustn't imagine I am fading away. For one thing

Lou sent me off like a child to boarding school
with a full tuckbox. I shall have to start having
midnight feasts with my new friend Alma - she
and I are sharing a room. I'm having so much
fun already, I love it all. Our first performance
last night was a triumph and everyone very
pleased.

Will write again soon, love to you and all the
babies,

Freya xx

Dear Lou,

Drank gin that was brewed in a bathtub.
Danced until the early hours. Almost out of
shortbread.

Don't miss you one bit,

Freya xx

***

The next morning, I wake early. Alma is still asleep in her bed, her long hair tumbled across the white pillowcase. There is barely any light filtering through the gap in the curtains, and I snuggle under the blankets with my torch, careful not to wake my roommate as I write a couple of quick postcards.

There's a restless kind of buzzing in my limbs and I dress as quietly as possible, bundling up in a thick and misshapen jumper, the product of Midge's misguided belief that she can knit. The jumper is a soft russet colour, and when I press it to my nose I almost believe that I can smell the sea.

Slipping out of the room I tiptoe down the hallway, the floorboards creaking monstrously as I try to be wraith-like and silent. It's no matter, though – I can hear snoring coming from one of the rooms off the hallway. The party went on extremely late – it was still going strong when I stumbled into bed around two-thirty. I'm much more used to early nights and early mornings, and it's going to take me a while to adjust. I should think it will be ages before anyone else is up.

Downstairs, I pop my head into the kitchen. It's

freezing, and no one is there, but the mess from the party litters every surface. I head into the pantry in search of sustenance and find half a slightly sad-looking loaf of bread and a jar of honey, as well as fat, yellow butter in a butter dish shaped like a white cow. I pour water into a tin kettle and set it on the stove. I'm not sure there's a finer feast on earth than tea with bread and honey. I eat hungrily, mulling over the details of the night before.

As soon as we helped Daphne up from the floor it became clear that she had badly hurt her ankle. Del hurried off to call the doctor, and several of the others spirited Daphne off to her room to lie down. In that moment I looked at Alma and saw that her eyes were wide. I knew just what she was thinking, and I knew that she didn't like herself for it one bit, but there it was: if Daphne couldn't perform, then Alma would. I suppose in this business you need a degree of self-interest. I remember what Russ said about Viola being an "ambitious little thing".

My own sense of ambition is complicated. On the one hand I've known I wanted to act pretty much since I could talk, and I'm extremely determined to get there – if that's not ambition then I don't know what it is. On the other hand, I never thought much about *how* to get there.

Certainly I never imagined dining with producers like Viola does. I suppose I just thought one did a good job and was rewarded for it. But Viola, despite being undeniably talented, is not starring in a big theatre, and she's chasing all the opportunities she can. There is clearly more to it than I imagined.

I lean back against the stove, my hands cradling my mug, the warmth seeping into my cold fingers. When I've finished I make a half-hearted attempt at tidying up a little. Then I decide I can't stand it any more and I need to go out. I feel claustrophobic in this stuffy room, as though I've been too much inside, as though I need to feel the sting of cold, sharp air on my face. I have a sudden, searing longing to see the sea. I've never been so far from it before and for some reason it leaves me unsettled.

I am in the hallway, wrapping a scarf from the teetering coat rack around my neck, when I hear footsteps on the stairs. Looking up, I find Kit, yawning.

"Hello!" he says in a low voice. "I wasn't expecting

anyone else to be awake."

"I couldn't sleep. I wanted to explore."

"Would you like some company? You can say if not; I know it's hard to get time to yourself on tour."

I beam at him. "No, I'd like you to come. But it's cold out there."

"This isn't cold! Wait until we get up north. You're not going to know what's hit you." He grabs a coat and we go about the business of wrapping up, buttoning jackets, and tying shoelaces, side by side.

"Right, then," says Kit, as we step outside into the chill morning. "Where are we going?"

"I woke up missing the sea," I say. "So I thought I might try and find the river."

"That sounds perfect."

We walk through the quiet streets in silence. I think it must be around seven o'clock. The sky is a gentle gold, still lightly pink around the edges, the sun struggling and sleepy. When we reach the river a low mist hangs over the bank, giving the place a strange feeling – almost as if we have stepped out of time. I feel like some ancient traveller, walking along the well-worn riverbank. I think about all the feet that have walked this path, about all the lives and the stories and the triumphs and the failures. Great artists and not-so-great artists. Many of them walked here over the years. Even Oscar Wilde was here. And now so am I.

Willows weep over the water, and trees line the banks. Some of them are still clinging to their finery, jewel-like flashes of ruby and amber, others are elegantly spare, skeletal against the early morning light.

"Is it helping?" Kit asks, breaking the quiet. "With missing the sea?"

"Not exactly," I say finally. "It's different, I suppose. I miss the size of the sea, the way it stretches out into the horizon, the way it's always changing... It makes me feel small. And that feels like a healthy dose of perspective. Walking here isn't like that." I laugh. "I think I'm starting to get ideas of grandeur instead."

"Perspective is overrated," Kit says. "Places like this, with all of their history – it makes me feel close to the people who came before me. The ones who did what I'm trying to do."

"That's just what I was thinking!" I exclaim. "I was

thinking about Oscar Wilde and how he must have walked along those streets and here by the river. I know it's the same in London, but somehow it's easier to imagine here..."

"London is always changing." Kit nods in agreement. "Growing, spreading, eating itself up and becoming something else. It's harder to imagine people from the past there sometimes. You catch glimpses, but for the most part I think it belongs to the present."

"Yes, that's it," I say. "That's what I was trying to work out in my head. The way London feels like the most modern place on earth, where it's all happening right *now* – but it's where it's *always* all been happening for whoever was there at the time." I'm not explaining myself very well, but I know Kit understands. It's like when you tie two tin cans together with a piece of string; our thoughts whisper straight down the line between us.

We walk a bit further, the grassy path twisting and turning alongside the water.

"So, do you think Alma will be taking over from Daphne?" I ask after a moment.

"I should think so. At the very least it's a bad sprain.

Daphne will have to go home."

"Poor Daphne," I murmur.

"She'll be all right," Kit says. "She's good – and hopefully she'll get a nice write-up in last night's reviews, although I think most of the critics are coming tonight." He pauses. "I wonder if Rhys will want to appoint a new understudy."

There it is. The sharp thud of my heart in my chest acknowledging how close I've been to wondering this too.

"If he did," I say carefully, "he'd probably choose someone with lots of experience."

"Maybe," says Kit. "Or maybe he'd choose someone close to home."

And then, without another word he takes my hand in his for a moment and squeezes it lightly. With that, it's as though he's saying all the things he doesn't want to say out loud. *This is exciting for you, this could be good, this could be a big break. I don't want to get your hopes up, but I'm pleased for you.*

I squeeze back, just for a second, just to let him know I understand, and then he drops my hand. We carry on walking, and Kit turns the conversation to home, asking me about my family. He laughs at my stories. Kit tells me about his sisters.

"Three of them," he grimaces. "And I'm the baby. You can imagine."

I can. "Are you close?" I ask.

"Yes and no. They're older – just a few years but it makes a difference growing up, doesn't it? I was always off with my mates from school. I love my sisters, of course," he adds quickly, as though I might not take that as a given.

"I understand." I look out over the river and rub my nose. "My sisters – Alice and Lou – they're older than me, and it was always the two of them. I always felt like the odd one, the one that didn't quite fit. It was like they had everything they needed in each other so I was by myself a lot." I wrap my arms around my stomach. "It's one of the reasons I got into acting. I got to try on different parts, I got to mess around with who I was, *and*," I grin up at him, "I could force them all to pay attention to me while I did it. A captive audience."

For once Kit doesn't smile back. Instead he looks

a little sad, and I realize that he is sad for me. That makes me feel uncomfortable, as if I've peeled too much away, as if my words have shown him something too vulnerable. I rub my arms and clear my throat.

"You know," Kit says after a moment, "we're almost at Binsey. We can go and see the treacle well."

"The treacle well?" I frown, remembering. "Like the story the dormouse tells in *Alice's Adventures in Wonderland?*"

"Yes. Apparently Lewis Carroll based it on the treacle well at Binsey."

"You can't really think we'll find a well full of treacle."

"We'll never know if we don't look," says Kit. "This feels like just the sort of morning when we might."

"That's true," I agree. "All magical mists and trips through time."

We reach the outskirts of the village and Kit leads the way towards the church. The path winds between the old gravestones, which erupt from the grass like teeth forming a jagged grin. The ground is carpeted in fallen brown leaves that crunch as we walk.

"There it is," Kit gestures, and I'm surprised. I had

expected a round structure above the ground. Instead, the stone well is a long rectangle cut into the earth, lined with white marble above light brick walls. It looks like one of the graves.

"St Margaret's Well," I read the inscription on the stone at the top.

"Patron saint of treacle, of course."

I clamber down so that the stone walls of the well rise around me. In front of me, and beneath the stone bearing the saintly inscription, is a triangular gap, and under *that* is a small round hole. I peer into the damp darkness there. "No treacle, as far as I can see," I sigh.

"Oh, well." Kit reaches into his pockets. "We'll have to make do with chocolate instead." He breaks the bar in half and holds a piece out to me.

"Even better." I climb back up and take it from him, perching on the edge of the well. He sits beside me, and the sleeve of his coat brushes against mine. I have a sudden, strange urge to rest my head on his shoulder. It must be because I'm so tired. Instead, I lift my eyes to the sky. It's brightened up now, the sun having summoned the energy to burn away the morning mist. It's going to be a nice day.

"Tell me about your writing," I say. "When we met, on the train, you said you wanted to be a writer."

Kit nods. "I do. I've been working on something for a while. I think it's almost done." He frowns. "Although it's hard to know."

"Have you shown it to anyone?"

"No. I keep thinking there will be a moment when I put a final piece of punctuation in place and then I can, you know, *lay down my pen,* finally satisfied … but that never seems to come. I think I could probably fool about with it for ever."

"I don't think you can wait for something to be perfect before you do something with it." I chew thoughtfully on my chocolate. "It's like a performance. You need the rehearsals to refine it."

"When did you get to be so wise?" Kit asks, laughter rippling through his voice.

"Must be the magic properties of the treacle well."

He smiles. "Must be." A clock strikes in the distance, and I jump to my feet. "It's eight o'clock! Nora wanted me today for Alma's fitting."

"Don't worry," Kit says, standing and stretching. "She'll still be sound asleep."

But I am already hurrying back down the path. "Come on!" I call over my shoulder. "We've got work to do!"

CHAPTER FOURTEEN

When we arrive back at Del's house the place is no longer in slumber. In fact, it is wide awake and buzzing with activity. The delicious smell of sizzling bacon fills the air and there's a great deal of clattering coming from the kitchen. This must be Del's famous fry-up. My stomach growls happily. Man cannot live by bread and honey alone, and Kit's chocolate has done little to dull the edge of my appetite.

"Where have you two been?" Viola appears in the hallway. I don't remember seeing her at all last night, but I suppose she must have been at the party. Her face is a little pale, but other than that she looks no worse for wear. In fact, she looks charming, in a very stylish sapphire blue dress, her dark hair artfully mussed.

"Out for a walk," Kit says.

"We saw the treacle well." My voice is muffled as I unwind the scarf from my neck. "Sadly, treacle free."

"You have mud on your coat," Viola says and for a second I think she's talking to me but then I realize her attention is focused on Kit. Somehow, from her, the words sound seductive. She puts out a delicate hand and brushes the lapels of his coat.

If I wasn't so utterly stunned, I'd be impressed. Making mud sound suggestive is, after all, an impressive feat; I doubt even Greta Garbo could have done more with the subject matter.

Kit moves away slightly and shrugs his coat off. "That's what coats are for," he says easily.

Viola laughs softly and steps closer to him, their arms almost touching. Next to Kit she looks even smaller and daintier than usual. "You didn't come and find me last night," she says in a low voice, though not low enough to keep me from hearing.

I take a quick step back. "I'd better go and see if Nora's up," I say, and I hurry down the corridor, only now realizing with dismay that I am also moving further away from the kitchen and the delicious food smells.

I stick my head in the sitting room. The only person in there is Russ, sprawled out on one of the sofas, wearing a pair of dark glasses despite the gloominess of the room. I wrinkle my nose. The curtains are pulled closed and the air smells musty. There are empty bottles everywhere.

"Ah, Freya, my love," he says, pulling the glasses down his nose and looking at me over the top. His eyes are slightly red, and he hasn't shaved.

"You look thoroughly seedy," I tell him.

"Too much gin," Russ agrees wearily, his head lolling back against the cushions. "Come in here and keep me company for a moment. The others are all running around in a flap over Daphne."

I step cautiously into the room. "Shouldn't *I* be running around in a flap over Daphne?"

"What in the world are you going to do about her? Got a secret medical degree I don't know about?"

"I need to find Nora—"

"Nora has still not appeared after last night's festivities. And incidentally neither has that delicious brunette she was with, what's her name – Sandra or Sarah or Sally or something."

"Gosh," I manage, dropping into the seat across from him. I suppose I'm really seeing the world now.

Russ chuckles indulgently. "What a lovely, naive thing you are, Freya," he says.

"It's difficult not to be naive when nothing has ever happened to you," I say briskly. "And I may not have read *The Well of Loneliness,* but I have heard about it – we do get the papers, you know, even in darkest Cornwall. I think Nora's business is Nora's business, just like anyone else's and I'm happy that she's ... having a nice time."

Russ grins at this slightly confused speech. "But I like your naivety, Freya. I find it deeply charming."

"Don't get too attached to it," I say. "I don't imagine it will last long while I'm hanging about with you lot. I'm sure Nora's not the only one who spent the night with someone else." I treat him to a very level gaze.

He chuckles, lifting his hands in a gesture of surrender. "A gentleman never tells." His eyes twinkle. "And, darling, if you'd ever like to learn a little cynicism, you know just where to turn."

I eye him thoughtfully. I know that Russ is not a sincere person – he would flirt with a potted plant if it wore a skirt. But when he's not trying so hard to be devastating, when he's making fun of himself or really laughing, there's something very appealing about him. I remember what Kit said to me about being open to all sorts of different experiences. And Russ is *very* good-looking. In fact, if I look at him hard enough, I can make my heart beat a little faster – surely a sign of infatuation. Perhaps we could have the kind of passionate affair people have onstage.

"You're making me feel nervous," he says, looking at me uneasily. "May I ask why you are examining me like a prize-winning pig at the country fair?"

"When have you ever been to a country fair?" I ask.

He waves a hand airily. "One doesn't have to go to a

country fair to know precisely what a country fair is."

"Nonsense," I murmur, but my mind is already on other things, particularly that little scene just now in the hallway. "Listen, there's something I want to ask you. Are Kit and Viola ... you know..."

"At it again, are they?" Russ sighs. "She does seem to dig her claws in. Mind you, I thought she had moved on to pastures new and a producer with deep pockets. Were they off together last night? I noticed she did one of her disappearing acts."

"I thought there was something between *you* and Viola."

He makes a horrified, spluttering sound. "My god, *no*," he says vehemently. "I mean, she's nice to look at, but a complete harpy. And," he adds, with surprising self-awareness, "we couldn't both be the centre of attention all the time."

"I thought it was one of those passionate, sparky, enemies to lovers-type things."

Russ shakes his head. "Not *everything* is a play, darling. Sometimes people just don't get on."

I laugh at that, though my mind is still reeling at the

idea of Viola and Kit as a couple. I don't like the idea of it one bit, though I'm not exactly sure why.

Perhaps it's that, yet again, I'm being left out. It seems that there are plenty of romantic entanglements already taking shape on this tour. My gaze flickers once more to Russ.

He yawns. "Yet again, I feel like a prize pig," he says. "What exactly does that look mean?"

"I was assessing you for romantic potential," I say, deciding not to be coy about it.

Russ looks delighted. "Oh, *were* you now?" he says, his voice a self-satisfied purr. "Do let me know what you discover."

I am about to put him in his place when we are interrupted by the appearance of Nora, wrapped in a silk dressing gown covered in a swirling red and gold paisley pattern. Her hair is sticking out in all directions, but her red lipstick is perfectly applied.

"What on earth possessed Daphne to jump off a wardrobe?" she asks with a groan, sinking down beside Russ.

"It was a piano stool," I say. "Is she badly hurt?"

"Off her feet for at least four weeks, according to the gossipy youths in the kitchen," Nora grimaces. "No more tour for her."

"How awful," I say. I feel a pang of real sympathy, followed on shamefully swift wings by other, less altruistic, feelings. "What's going to happen to her part?" I ask, trying to keep my tone neutral.

I'm obviously fooling no one. Nora arches an eyebrow and Russ snorts.

"Alma will take over the part, I suppose," Nora says, and she stretches her arms over her head, the sleeves of her dressing gown falling back to reveal dimpled elbows and what looks to be a telephone number written on her forearm in kohl eyeliner.

"And ... the understudy?" Despite my best intentions my voice squeaks on the question.

Nora gives me a tolerant smile. "You'd better ask Miss Meriden. She was arriving as I came downstairs."

I leap to my feet, an action clearly too energetic for Nora and Russ who both groan loudly. Honestly, these theatrical types – always *so* dramatic.

"We'll need to go over to the theatre for Alma's fitting

in about half an hour, Freya," Nora murmurs. "Make sure you're ready." She leans back, her eyes closing.

"I will," I say, hurrying off.

I find Miss Meriden in the dining room, sitting at the long table and talking earnestly with Alma.

"Hello," I say cautiously. "I hope I'm not interrupting…"

"No, no," Miss Meriden replies. "We were about to look for you."

Del bustles in behind me with two plates in her hands.

"There you are!" Del says to me. "Did you want some breakfast?"

"I would love some," I say, reaching out for the plate she offers which contains fried eggs, bacon and toast as well as two plump brown sausages. "Thank you," I manage, already chewing on a piece of buttered toast.

Del laughs. "At least sit down. You'll give yourself indigestion." I follow her down the table where she places the other breakfast plate in front of Alma. "There you go, darling, get that in you."

I perch in the seat beside Alma, putting my own plate

in front of me and getting stuck right in.

"I don't think I'll be able to eat a thing," Alma says weakly, and then, in a burst she adds, "They're going to put me on tonight!" The look on her face is one of mingled awe, excitement, and despair.

"But that's wonderful!" I exclaim, taking her hand in my own slightly buttery fingers and squeezing hard. I try to ignore the inevitable stab of jealousy and focus only on Alma. "It's awful for Daphne, but such a lucky break for you. You'll be wonderful. Mr Cantwell wouldn't have hired you if he didn't believe that."

"Exactly what I said," Miss Meriden agrees in her cool, impassive way.

"I feel sick." Alma, who is looking a bit pale, sways in her chair.

"Don't say that," I chide, making inroads into the sausages. "You'll feel much better if you eat. Midge always says one doesn't go into battle on an empty stomach."

"Midge?" Alma asks.

"My mother. She's always right." I grin at Alma. "Now eat."

Like an encouraging mother hen, I cluck until Alma

165

has eaten some toast and drunk some of the steaming coffee Del places before her. After a while she looks less green. Miss Meriden nods approvingly.

"There," I say, having cleaned my own plate and polished off one of Alma's sausages. "Everything feels better after breakfast. It's a law of nature. Besides, this is what you wanted, isn't it? To be on the stage."

"Oh, it's a dream come true. It's not that I don't appreciate the opportunity." Alma plucks at the tablecloth. "I just didn't think it would happen, at least not so soon. I'm not sure I'm ready..."

"Of course you are," I break in. "Why, you know the whole thing backwards by now."

"You're right," Alma nods. But she still looks as though she's about to face the gallows. I decide she probably needs teasing out of her mood.

"Oh, Alma, you look *exactly* like you're about to be martyred at the stake. You should use it in a performance one day, perhaps Joan of Arc."

The martyred look dissolves into laughter, and she bats at my arm. "All right," Alma says, "I'm being ungrateful." She turns to Miss Meriden. "Thank you,

Miss Meriden, I'll go and get ready."

"I'll wait and walk over to the theatre with you," says Miss Meriden.

Alma pushes away from the table and makes her way out of the dining room, throwing a tremulous smile over her shoulder at us.

"You did very well with her," Miss Meriden says, picking up her own cup of tea and looking at me over the top of it. She sounds a little bit surprised.

I shrug. "I'm used to siblings. Dramatics don't faze me. She'll remember how much she wanted the opportunity once we're at the theatre."

"And you?" Miss Meriden asks. "Do *you* want the opportunity?"

Our eyes meet for a moment.

Ambition. Opportunity. Want.

The words dance around inside me.

"You know I do," I say at last.

There's a pause and then Miss Meriden nods. "It's possible Mr Cantwell will ask you to step in as understudy. He seemed to like your audition. You will still have to keep on top of all your other responsibilities, of course."

"Of – of *course*," I manage.

"It's a lot of work. Mr Cantwell will want you word perfect and it's unlikely you'll perform."

"That doesn't matter. If I could read lines with Mr Cantwell, I wouldn't ask for anything more."

I say it so fervently I almost believe it, but I know that it's not true. I know that my greedy, gluttonous heart is already hoping for more. I know that my insatiable, out-of-control imagination is already picturing the lights, the applause, the accolades.

I think Miss Meriden knows it too, because the look she gives me is slightly pitying.

"Well, then," she says, "I think we'd *all* better get to work. Time to find out if Alma can live up to expectations."

CHAPTER FIFTEEN

It turns out that Alma *is* good. Better than good. Better than Daphne was, even.

That night she gives a performance more than worthy of a Rhys Cantwell production. It's strange watching her from my position in the wings. In real life she's so quiet and self-contained, a little bit serious, but onstage she becomes a different person altogether – it's like someone has lit a candle inside her.

I had thought that she would try and copy Daphne's performance and mannerisms, but she doesn't – she goes further in showing Cecily's mix of innocence and wit. The scenes between her and Viola are especially good; they spark off each other and it lifts the whole play. She's *funny*, and I realize I've only seen her be serious. It's a bit of a shock. By the end of the play, I can't imagine anyone else playing the part.

When everyone piles back to Del's house that evening Alma is lifted on people's shoulders. She's toasted with champagne, and the earnest young man from the night before – still dressed all in black – throws his glass to the floor, smashing it into a million pieces, so that it may never be raised again to a lesser mortal.

Alma absorbs this quietly, graciously, but with a pucker of confusion between her brows.

"All I can think about is what I did wrong," she whispers to me.

"You were wonderful," I whisper back. "Let them tell you so."

Instead of the expected pang of envy, all I feel is pride in my friend. I think about how much she was shaking before she went on, and the moment I saw her take her courage in her hands, straighten up and walk onstage, about how truly good she was. I realize – almost with surprise – that being happy for her, being impressed by her, doesn't take anything away from my own attempts. Though it does make me want to be better, to push myself harder.

The party is the same as the night before, just as full of people and gossip and gin, only now people call me by name.

"Freya! Freya!" Dan calls, looping a casual arm around my waist. "You must hear the story Lindsey was telling me about when she was working with Dirk Hadley – it will shock you to your core!"

Lindsey, the friendly make-up girl with a cloud of dark hair, laughs. "It didn't shock you," she grins at Dan.

"Not a lot *does,* my sweet. But I do get a vicarious thrill watching Freya blush."

It is a delicious feeling, being a part of this team. I hadn't realized until we came to Oxford how alone I had always been. I never thought of myself as lonely – I was part of a big, noisy family, and I had my books, my costumes, my plays. Thanks to them, I spoke with kings and villains and saints, I travelled to Italy, to France, to America. It had all felt so real to me, and yet now that I am here, in the land of the living, this whirlpool of creativity and energy and laughter, I am starting to understand how insular it was. I was buried inside my own imagination, and however rich that imagination was, it didn't, *couldn't*, compare to the reality of going out into the world.

"I've got it." Russ's voice suddenly cuts through the noise. He is waving a newspaper. "Friend of mine slipped me a copy of tomorrow's *Times*. And our review is in!"

Dan whips it from his hands and begins to rapidly scan the page.

All sound ceases then and people press eagerly towards Dan, surrounding him as he finds the review and begins to read aloud.

"A charming and witty production that keeps the audience laughing, and which teases out the shadow as well as the light," he begins.

The review is glowing, praising everything from the staging to the individual performances. It's hailed as a "triumphant return" by both Mr Cantwell and Eileen

Turner, dwelling at length on Eileen's "sublime, definitive" performance. It mentions Russ and Dan – and pays special tribute to the muffin scene that I had so enjoyed.

"Stepping in from her role as understudy, Miss Alma Blair is a fresh new talent and one to watch," Dan reads, and I gasp, gripping Alma's arm. She turns to me, dazed, as people reach out to pat her on the shoulder. I imagine briefly what it must feel like to have your first review, to step in as an understudy and to wow people like that.

"Anything else?" Viola asks. Her voice is calm, but there is a nervous energy to her.

"Yes, yes," Dan says, scanning the piece of paper. "Here you are, darling: Miss Viola Edwards is a star, drawing every eye with her grace and exotic beauty."

"My *exotic beauty?*" Something flickers across Viola's face. "I see."

"It says you're a star," Dan laughs, tapping the paper with the back of his hand. "Right here in black and white."

Viola's mouth twists. "An *exotic* one, no less." She turns away slightly. The others push forward, urging Dan to read the piece again, and I think that only I see the flash of hurt and anger in her eyes.

Exotic. It's the same word Del used to describe Viola, And I realize, suddenly, that it's not the compliment I thought it was. It's a way of saying *other, foreign, different*. No one would use the word exotic to describe me or Alma. It puts Viola in a box that has nothing to do with her talent but with something else entirely.

I wonder how many reviews Viola has read where she is described like this, how many times she's heard that word *exotic* to describe a performance she has worked hard at. And for the first time I wonder whether this is the reason why an actor as talented as Viola is touring with a small company rather than stepping out on to a West End stage. Maybe it's all she's been allowed to do. I want to say something to her, though I'm not sure what. I take half a step towards her, but she has pushed her way through the crowd before I reach her side.

Eventually, the excitement over the review calms down and I get swept back in to the party. Alma and I chat and laugh, and when the record player wheezes to life, we dance. Russ appears then, and sweeps me into his arms. My heart clatters appreciatively. He looks down at me with those ink-dark eyes, and a smile tugs at the corner of his mouth.

He smells delicious, and he doesn't say very much. I look at his mouth and wonder what it would be like to kiss him. The thought makes my cheeks warm, and the way Russ looks at me makes me think he knows what's going through my mind. At the end of the song he lets me go with a winning display of reluctance, and another man takes his place.

When I leave the makeshift dance floor to go in search of a glass of water, I run into Kit, leaning one shoulder against the door frame, talking with a pretty girl who assists with the props. He catches my eye and excuses himself.

"There you are," he says. "Alma did a great job, didn't she?"

"She did," I agree. There's an awkward silence between us then. There has never been anything awkward between Kit and I before. I keep thinking of Vola laying her hand on his coat, the way her voice dropped as she spoke to him. It was intimate.

"About earlier…" Kit begins.

"It's none of my business," I say quickly. "I just didn't realize that you and Viola were – well…"

He shakes his head. "We're not. Not any more."

"Like I said, it isn't any of my business," I say. It really isn't. But the thought of the two of them being together still makes me feel strange.

The look Kit gives me then is hard to read. Thanks to the press of the crowd, we're standing close together, almost as close as Russ and I were when we danced.

"It's complicated," he says finally, running his hand through his hair.

"Isn't it always?" I say brightly, because I'm not sure I want to talk about this. "Anyway, I'm going to turn in soon." I lower my voice a bit. "Mr Cantwell has asked to see me tomorrow."

Kit's eyes widen. "That's wonderful!" he says.

"I hope so." I pause, and then add a little sheepishly, "I kept telling Alma not to be nervous, and now – just at the *possibility* of it – my heart is in my mouth."

"That doesn't sound too good, medically speaking." Kit's dimples flash. "I prescribe raiding the larder for cake, followed by a good dance."

"I didn't know you were a doctor," I laugh. "But I do love cake."

"I know."

I feel some of the tension leaving my shoulders. Whatever the link is between Kit and I, the invisible gossamer thread, it's still there, still easy. He's still my friend, whoever his girlfriend might be.

We head to the kitchen in search of sustenance, and find Nora holding court. She's perched on the counter top, a cigarette in her hand as a crowd of men and women gaze up at her in open admiration. Nora wears her confidence, her whole attitude, with the same style as she wears her incredible clothes. Tonight it's tapered black trousers and a crisp white shirt, rolled up at the sleeves and unbuttoned so low that it shows the top of a black silk slip underneath and a generous amount of her cleavage. Around her neck is an elaborate green and gold necklace that on anyone else would look ridiculous, but on Nora – well, it's the perfect finishing touch. She's got something about her, something that makes people look at her the way they do.

"Hello, children," she says upon spotting us. "Kit, Viola was in here looking for you."

"Was she?" Kit says, and I think I catch a flicker of concern in his voice. "I'll go and find her."

"I think you should," Nora agrees. Then she jumps down from the counter and moves to put an arm around my waist, dispersing the crowd with a flick of her wrist. "I'll keep Freya company."

"Let me know how it goes tomorrow," Kit says to me.

I nod, my stomach lurching at the thought of what the next day might bring. "Of course."

"The big meeting with Rhys, is it?" Nora takes a drag on her cigarette as Kit goes off.

"Yes." I swallow. "How badly do you think he'll take it if I cast up my breakfast onstage?"

"Not terribly well," Nora chuckles. "But you won't. You'll see. It will be the start of something wonderful. Which is a shame for me, because I've finally found a decent assistant who doesn't spend all her time mooning over Russell Whitmore," she finishes on a grumble.

"He *is* very handsome," I say fairly.

"And he knows it."

"There is that," I concede, then after a slight pause, "When I first saw him and Viola together I thought they were a couple. But actually, it was Viola and Kit."

Nora snorts. "Russ and Viola, god, what a nightmare that would be. They don't believe there's room for two stars in one show, let alone a relationship, you know."

"That's pretty much what Russ said."

Nora flicks her cigarette into a nearby saucer. "Yes, he can be disarming like that sometimes. Why on earth did you put them together?"

"Well," I say, struggling to articulate it. "They're both so beautiful. They go together more than her and Kit."

"But Kit's so attractive. All the girls go mad for him," Nora says, shrugging.

"Kit?" I exclaim, stunned.

"Haven't you noticed?" Nora says. "It drives Russ wild, which is great entertainment. Kit doesn't even have to try; they all want him. Viola set her sights on him instantly, of course. The two of them were inseparable for a while."

"You're talking about Kit?" I ask. "*My* Kit?"

Amusement creeps into Nora's gaze. "Your Kit?"

"I don't mean it like that!" I put in hastily. "I meant my *friend* Kit, obviously."

She watches me through a cloud of smoke. "*You* don't find Kit attractive?"

"I've never thought about him like that." I flounder. "I mean, he's not handsome like Russ, is he? Not that he's not good-looking. I just..."

"I didn't say he was handsome, I said he was attractive." Nora gestures with her cigarette. "Those are not always the same things. Kit has a ... quality. I mean, it's the height and the strong arms and the dimples ... but it's something else too, his personality, the way he carries himself. He has an ease about him that draws people in."

I realize that what Nora is describing is exactly what I was thinking about her. It's too strange to think of Kit that way. "If you say so," I say, sounding doubtful to my own ears.

"I suppose Russ is rather the obvious choice," Nora muses, as if I haven't spoken. "Dull, perhaps, but one can see the appeal."

"I don't think he's dull."

"No?" Nora's look is enigmatic. "But then you're so young."

I can't help feeling a bit miffed by that, and Nora obviously sees it in my face because she laughs. "I'm sorry, darling, there's nothing worse than being told you're too young to understand something, is there? I didn't mean to be patronizing; you seem like a girl with her head screwed on right, and you work your socks off. You've got an eye for design too," she adds. "Not many do. There might be a future in dressing for you, if you ever wanted to look outside of acting."

I am torn between pride at her hard-won praise, and horror at the idea of giving up acting.

"Oh, no," I say quickly. "It's always been acting for me. It's what I've wanted my whole life."

"Then I'm sure it's what you'll end up doing." Nora's red lips part in a smile. "Perhaps starting tomorrow."

CHAPTER SIXTEEN

It is frighteningly early the next morning, and I am perched on the edge of the stage while Rhys Cantwell sits in the front row, all of his intense energy concentrated on me like a sunbeam through a magnifying glass. It feels as though he might burn me up without a hint of remorse, like a small boy torturing an ant.

"What I need from you, Miss Trevelyan, is a proper audition," he says crisply. "Can you do a scene from the play?"

"Yes, sir," I say quickly. "I know every part off by heart."

"*Every* part will not be necessary," he growls. I wish his face were not so unfriendly – it's very off-putting. He's not even wearing the silly spectacles which took the edge off last time. "We will do the scene where Algernon and Cecily meet in Act Two. *You*," he pauses here, "in case it is not obvious, will play Cecily. I will read in Algernon's lines."

"Of course." I get to my feet and move upstage.

"You may take it from, 'I have never met any really wicked person...'"

So this is it, I think. *I'm really going to read lines for Rhys Cantwell.* I feel sick, dizzy, feverish, shaken. I try to empty my mind, to feel nothing, see nothing, hear nothing – nothing but the words coming to me, like a voice whispering them in my ear. I close my eyes for a moment, and then I begin.

"I have never met any really wicked person before. I feel rather frightened. I am so afraid he will look just like everyone else."

Rhys Cantwell fires Algernon's lines back at me with

speed and precision and I match them without pause. It's exhilarating and strange, more like a game of tennis than any acting I've done before.

It goes all right, I think. I remember the lines, and I fill them with as much wit and meaning as I can, remembering how Alma played the part. When we finish the scene I stand in front of Rhys, my hands clasped. He's not looking at me. He's looking somewhere past me, into the middle distance, his expression thoughtful. He picks up a pen and twirls it in his fingers.

"Please, sit down."

I do so, my legs swinging over the front of the stage. It leaves me feeling vulnerable, a bit like a child, my feet too far off the ground on this big stage, but Mr Cantwell doesn't seem to notice.

"Tell me what you think of the play," he says finally, surprising me.

"Of *this* play?"

"Yes," he snaps, an impatient hand flapping. "Of course this play."

I gulp. *Not exactly dazzling so far, Freya.* "Well, I think it's wonderful," I manage, and then, mortified by the trite words and gathering my scattered wits together as best I can, "It's funny, and it makes people laugh, but it's funny in a way that's not quite warm. It's witty and clever. It's cutting. It can be cruel. It's saying things, about the way people behave, about the way people want to be seen and the way they really are..." I trail off, embarrassed by my miserable little schoolgirl's analysis of a speech.

"Tell me about Cecily," he says.

"She has this romantic fantasy about her cousin Ernest, but I don't think she's as innocent or naive as people think. She holds her own against Gwendolyn, she asks Miss Prism difficult questions. She has to be knowing and – and unknowing at the same time." I'm floundering now. *Did I just say unknowing? Is that even a word?*

Mr Cantwell fires more questions at me. He asks me questions about the different parts, he asks me questions about the individual performers and what I've learned from them so far. He asks me about the costumes and the decisions Nora made and why I think she made them. He asks me about the sets and the props and even the lighting. I like these questions, I like the way they're making me think about the play differently. I feel alight with enthusiasm, as though I'm somehow producing my own electricity. And though Rhys Cantwell never goes so far as to smile, or nod, or actually soften in any perceivable way at all, I begin to feel that I am not doing so badly.

He has me walk up and down the stage and then do exercises that project my voice further and further towards the back of the theatre. Finally, at the sound of a door opening in the auditorium he says, "Ah, Eileen, there you are."

I freeze, actually freeze, my limbs unmoving, my brain empty save for a dull buzzing sound, I am like the proverbial rabbit in the headlamps, just waiting to be squashed, flattened, obliterated.

Eileen Turner is here. In this room. And unless I am much mistaken I am going to have to speak to her. A feat that will prove complicated if I cannot formulate coherent thoughts, let alone translate them into coherent words.

Eileen Turner walks down the aisle of the theatre

towards the stage and Mr Cantwell meets her. She is magnificent, regal in an enormous fur coat. Her eyes are flinty, assessing. I think I'm going to faint.

Eileen Turner, my brain says. EileenTurnerEileen-TurnerEileenTurner.

She and Mr Cantwell confer in low voices, and then she turns to me.

"Miss Turner," I say, and, unthinking, I fall into another one of those awful supplicatory curtseys, like some sort of dying swan.

There is a moment of silence.

"She does that," Mr Cantwell says. "I don't know why."

"Call me Eileen," is what Eileen Turner says in that beautiful voice of hers, her grey eyes resting on me for a long, measuring moment.

"Eileen," I croak, lifting myself from my prone position. *Of course I'll call Eileen Turner, Eileen,* I think. For some reason my teeth are chattering as though it is cold, and I have a desperate urge to laugh, which I am trying very hard to keep from doing lest I look like more of a maniac than I do already.

"I shall just go and dispose of my coat," Eileen says, managing to imbue these words with the kind of imperial coolness with which a queen might announce she was going to dispose of several of her more annoying subjects. "And then I'll be ready for you."

"Wonderful," I say airily. After she's disappeared I turn to Mr Cantwell. "What does she mean, ready for me?" I hiss.

His shaggy eyebrows rise. "She's going to do some scene work with you."

"Oh god," I murmur.

"Yes, well, get used to it. Heaven forfend lightning does strike twice and you do have to be onstage with the woman. You can't spend the whole time gawping at her like she's a bloody zoo animal."

"Go onstage?" I gasp. "You mean – you mean you're going to let me understudy?"

"There's not a lot of choice at this point. And you'll do. You need work, of course, a lot of work. But I think we could make you passable. In a pinch. I'd rather not cancel a performance unless we absolutely had to."

I am too thrilled to care how lukewarm he sounds.

"I'm an *understudy!*" I squeal, and I do a little jig on the stage.

"Hmmmm." Mr Cantwell's mouth turns down in a way that gives him the appearance of an angry turtle. I cease my jig at once, folding my hands and schooling my face into an expression of mild obedience that always seems to go down well with Aunt Irene.

"I mean, thank you, sir, for this opportunity. I won't let you down."

He smiles faintly. "Don't make promises you can't keep, Miss Trevelyan."

"Well, then; I promise to try my best not to let you down and to work very, very hard."

"I suppose," he says, "that will have to do. Now, let's go back to the beginning of the last scene and take it again, shall we? And this time do *try* not to flap your hands around; you're supposed to be drinking tea, not conducting an orchestra."

Part Three

On Tour
December, 1931

CHAPTER SEVENTEEN

4th December, 1931

Dear Lou,

I know I owe you a good long letter because
I haven't written since Birmingham. Well, here
we are in Nottingham. Do you remember when we
used to play Robin Hood? You and Alice were
Robin Hood and Maid Marian and I was the
Sheriff of Nottingham. I always did like playing

the villains best, so much more interesting.

I persuaded Kit to drive me out to Sherwood Forest this morning and a whole bunch of the others came too. Alma, of course, and Viola because she never seems to like Kit and I going off together. Russ and Dan came too, and I must say we made quite the band of Merry Men. The forest was just like I had imagined, and I longed to scramble up the trees and stage a daring ambush, but I couldn't in front of all the sophisticated theatre types. Only think how disappointed Tom would be in me!

The play has been very well received here, and Alma continues to perform so well it makes my teeth hurt. Yesterday, and quite out of the blue, Mr Cantwell actually complimented her. She and I just stared at each other in amazement and then, as soon as he left the room, we whooped around like a pair of banshees.

Both she and Viola are in excellent health, so I continue to see no reason that I will have to fill in - for which I think Mr Cantwell is mightily grateful. My own rehearsals have not gone smoothly - even Dan lost his temper a little when I stepped square on his foot for the third time - and Viola gets truly furious with me. She has a reputation for being flakey, missing rehearsals, but she seems an absolute tyrant to me, wanting everything completely perfect. Not that I mind, I quite agree with her, only it's galling when the thing that isn't perfect - or anywhere near it - is me. Still, Eileen (did I mention that Eileen Turner told me just to call her by her first name?) said she thought I was "improving". That is something, I suppose.

I can't help wondering whether my lack of worldly experience is contributing to my inability to manage a scene. The more I see of the world outside Penlyn the more I realize I haven't the first idea of anything much at all. It's as though life has passed me by and I feel utterly dried-up and ancient. When I said this to Nora she told me that all eighteen-year-olds feel ancient, but I think she was being facetious. Still, you should hear the stories the company tell about the adventures they've had, the places they've travelled, the endless stream of lovers and rivals. It's thrilling and outrageous and I have nothing to contribute. Maddening!!!!

The digs here are absolutely the worst yet. Even worse than the ones in Leicester. I can't tell you how cold it gets at night. The leading cast members like Viola and Russ get their own rooms - but Alma elected to stay with me and I'm so grateful. She and I have been sleeping in one bed with all our clothes piled on top of us, and this morning the water in the sink had frozen over! She had me in hysterics with her impression of the landlord when we raised the point with him. Alma's the most wonderful mimic, I think it's because she really sees people - just the way you do. She's quiet, but she doesn't miss anything. I hope you and Robert are well, and-

I am interrupted in my writing by a knock at the door. "Come in," I call out.

It's Kit. He takes in the sight of me wearing my coat, scarf and gloves while under a blanket and laughs.

"Come on, before you turn into an icicle. We're going to the pub where it's warm."

"Hallelujah," I exclaim, leaping to my feet and abandoning my letter without a second glance. "Lead on, Macduff! Did you know," I say, following Kit out into the hallway and down the stairs, "that *lead on, Macduff* is a misquotation?"

"In fact, I did," Kit grins, raising his voice dramatically above the clatter of our feet. "*Lay on, Macduff, and damn'd be him that first cries, 'Hold, enough!'*"

"And then, we fight," I say, wielding an imaginary sword.

"I'd rather we went and ate fish and chips instead."

"Fish and chips? *Heaven.*"

We chatter happily along the road in the direction of the pub. This week it feels suddenly as though winter has struck in full force, and the wind blusters around us with icy determination, leaving us huddling further into our coats. The sun has set, though its ghost remains behind, warming the sky to a rich navy, rather than the star-strewn black velvet it will soon become.

"How did the writing go today?" I ask.

Kit huffs out a breath that forms a white cloud in front of him. In Kit speak that means, *not well*. He still hasn't offered to let me read his work, and I have to admit it's driving me mad.

It's a Monday, our one night off from performing. We all needed a break. The work has been gruelling, the accommodation miserable, the conditions tough, and I've been enjoying every moment of it.

Nottingham is a nice city, bustling and cheerful without feeling overwhelming. I like it here. We round the corner towards the pub, which is nestled at the foot of a hill, the castle on top looming over us with a faint air of menace. I didn't have much experience with pubs before this trip. It's not precisely the thing for young women to visit them usually, but the rules don't seem to apply to theatre troupes, which is just fine with me.

It is a very old pub, cosy and full of hidden corners, that stays open late, and it has been adopted by the cast and crew as a source of food, drink and warmth, thanks to the horrors of our current boarding house. I don't think I had any idea how lucky we were staying first at Del's place, as it's certainly been all downhill from there. Nora seems resigned to our new surroundings. "Just be grateful for the lack of rats," was her prosaic advice.

As we push through the door a wave of warm air hits us like a curled fist, along with the deafening roar of chatter. The pub is full of people, talking, eating, and clutching pint glasses full of frothy amber beer. That now familiar hoppy smell, mixed with sawdust makes me feel happy.

"Freya! Kit!" I hear Alma's voice, and I spot her in the back. She has climbed up on to her seat to wave at us. Several others in the pub swing around to look at her appreciatively. With her long fair hair rippling down her back and her pink cheeks she looks angelic.

Kit and I weave through the crush of people, trying not to jostle arms or step on toes.

"Phew!" I exclaim, when we reach the table where Alma, Dan and Viola are waiting for us. "It's even busier than usual." I begin the process of unwinding my long scarf, and shedding my many layers.

"We don't usually come until later," Alma points out.

Russ appears then, parting the crowd like the Red Sea. In his hands is a tray full of heavy beer glasses, which he plonks on the table, sloshing the drinks over the edges.

"Here we are, friends," he says. "The food's on the way too, courtesy of the delightful landlady."

I find I don't mind Russ's charm so much when I'm the one benefitting from it. "Thanks," I say. "I'm starving." I slide into a seat and take a sip of beer, the foam clinging to my top lip. I wipe it away with the back of my hand.

"You're always starving," Russ says, slipping into the seat beside me and leaning close to my ear. "Why don't you let me take you out for that dinner one night?"

It's not the first time Russ has asked me out, but I've always put him off. I don't want to be just another one of his conquests; it feels too predictable, somehow. Now, though, I'm thinking about the letter I was writing to Lou. Here I am, languishing for some experience, while all the while experience, in the very nice-looking form of Russ, hammers on my door. This is my chance to get swept away in a passionate affair, to make some stories of my own.

"All right," I say. "Why not?"

Russ looks startled and I wonder whether he only continued to ask out of habit. He corrects himself swiftly enough, turning his smile on me. "Wonderful," he murmurs. "I know a charming little place. Tomorrow? After the show?"

"Yes, that sounds good."

"What's tomorrow?" Viola asks. Trust her to notice.

"Freya is finally letting me take her out to dinner." Russ leans back in his chair, looking pleased with himself.

"How nice," Viola says drily, at the same time as Alma's doubtful, "Really?" rings out.

"Don't fall for it, darling." Dan leans across the table towards me, a cigarette clasped between his elegant fingers. "You're the first wardrobe assistant yet to resist his charms. He's only looking to cross you off his bingo card."

"Oh, for god's sake," Russ splutters indignantly.

"Perhaps," I say, "I am looking to cross him off mine."

Dan smiles at that. "In that case, good luck."

"I think I'll grab some water," Kit says abruptly.

"I'll come to the bar with you." Viola jumps up, and the two of them walk off together.

"What is going on with those two these days?" Russ asks, leaning forward so that Dan can light a cigarette for him.

"Well." Dan lights Russ's cigarette with a flourish. "You didn't hear it from me, but *apparently* Viola told Daphne before we left London that she was going to win Kit back over the course of the tour by fair means or foul."

"I still can't really believe they were together," Alma says, her eyes lingering curiously on the two of them.

"Oh, yes, love's young dream for a while," Dan says.

"Until she chucked him over for a producer who could do more for her career," Russ snorts into his glass.

"No!" Alma exclaims.

Russ nods. "David Spelling – he's pretty small fry, actually, but I think he made her a lot of promises. After things didn't work out the way Viola hoped she went back to Kit. I think she expected he'd welcome her with open arms." He pauses. "She was wrong."

"Oh." Alma's mouth softens. "She broke Kit's heart."

It has become clear over the last few weeks that Alma has a soft spot for Kit. After Nora spoke about Kit's appeal I started to notice the way girls look at him. She's right; there's more than one girl in the company who'd be happy to step in to Viola's shoes should she fail in her quest.

I look over at them now, standing at the bar. She's talking animatedly, her eyes smiling up at him. He laughs. They look good together, I admit.

"Did she?" I ask quietly. "Break Kit's heart?"

Dan purses his lips. "Not sure," he admits. "It's hard to tell with Kit. He doesn't give much away."

I feel a sharp pain in my stomach then, at the thought of Kit being hurt.

"And now I hear she's seeing Marco." Dan's eyes narrow thoughtfully. "I wonder why she's still got an eye on Kit?"

"Perhaps she's still in love with him," Alma says.

"Perhaps she likes the challenge." Russ is far less generous.

"Let's change the subject," I say, feeling suddenly

uncomfortable. "It's not good, all this gossip."

"Darling," Dan drawls, "if you're going to work in the theatre, you're going to have to get used to it. It's a small world and it absolutely runs on the stuff."

"Speaking of which," Russ murmurs, glancing surreptitiously around, "did you hear about a particular leading man and his problems with – shall we say – certain recreational substances?"

"No!" Dan leans forward, delighted. "Do tell."

They keep talking about people I don't know, in that funny, coded way. Alma smiles politely.

Kit and Viola return, and behind them comes a barmaid with steaming plates of fish and chips. We fall on the food, snatching at the hot, greasy chips. I lick salt from my fingers and take a swig of my drink as I relax against the battered red leather seat that smells sweetly of tobacco.

"This is so good." Russ pats his stomach. "Nora's going to be taking out all my trousers by the end of the week."

"Do you remember last summer, when I stomped on

my hem and tore that dress onstage?" Viola asks.

"It made that awful loud ripping noise, and you were so into your performance you barely noticed," Kit chuckles. "The audience thought it was part of the scene."

"And then I came off and Nora drew herself up like the Queen of Hearts, about to order my beheading!" Her eyes dance, and she leans back against her chair. "I thought I was going to get such a scolding. But before she could get going I told her I'd stay behind and sew it up myself."

"Which you *never* thought she'd agree to." Kit takes a swig of his beer.

Viola grins at him. "But she called my bluff and stood over me while I tried to mend the wretched thing with stitches like great gap-teeth because I'm so useless. I thought she was going to make me wear it, but the next night of course the dress was perfect, and she'd taken all my hems up. She's not let me wear anything the least bit trailing since."

She laughs, and her laughter is genuine, infectious. We all join in. That's the thing with Viola, she's mercurial. She can be cold and sulky, but she can be so charming too. You never quite know what you're going to get with her.

The conversation around the table turns to other things, including the new *Frankenstein* film that everyone's been talking about. The pub is warm and I'm starting to feel sleepy.

"Film is the future," Viola says, her eyes glowing. "Hollywood, that's where I'm going. That's where we should all be aiming for."

"Don't let Rhys Cantwell hear you say that," Russ says.

Dan makes a murmur of agreement. "Chewed him up and spat him out, the poor old darling."

"I don't think film could beat the theatre, though, could it?" I ask. "Acting in front of a real-life audience…"

"And what would you know about that?" Viola asks dismissively. "When you've never acted in front of an audience before?"

"No, but I've been there when you do," I point out. "It's like there's something electric snapping between you and them."

"That's because *I'm* good," Viola says, not boastful, merely dispensing facts.

"And I suppose I'm not?" I throw the words down like a gauntlet, trying to fake a confidence I don't feel.

"I'm sure that's not—" Alma begins.

"Well, I don't think we're doing her any favours pretending she's a real talent," Viola breaks in, tilting her chin up. "It's ridiculous having someone so inexperienced as an understudy. I can't understand why Mr Cantwell fusses over her." She shoots me a look that is not one of dislike so much as one of perplexity. "If you want my advice you should stick to costumes." She jumps to her feet then and throws some coins on to the table. "I'm going back," she says. "Some of us have a performance tomorrow."

We sit in silence while she leaves. Then Kit says awkwardly, "Don't let her bother you, Freya." He rubs his forehead in a tired gesture. I notice that his fingers are flecked with black ink stains. "Tensions always start running high this far into the tour."

The others murmur in agreement, and gently return

to a discussion of America and the opportunities it might offer.

I stare down into my drink as they chatter. Maybe Viola just said what they are all thinking. That I'll never be any good, no matter how hard I work.

I can hear the blood pumping through me, the dull thump of my heartbeat as I wrestle with a feeling that threatens to overwhelm me.

Then I straighten my spine. Viola is wrong. I'll be onstage one day, and when I am, she'll eat her words. I'll make sure of it.

CHAPTER EIGHTEEN

I spend the following day trying very hard to stay busy and not to think of Viola's words, words that struck at some deeply vulnerable part of me. Fortunately, this evening is my dinner with Russ, which provides an excellent distraction. I feel strange about it – a little nervous, a little excited. I have already decided to throw myself into it, the romance of it all. Russ is practically a paper cut-out of the perfect man, and so – for tonight, at least – I will be the perfect girl on his arm. Perhaps I'll get swept up in the feelings that dominate so many of my favourite stories – the passion, the desire, the soul-searing connection between two people. I can give it a go, at least.

After the performance, my head full of kisses and whirling music, I head to the wardrobe closet to get changed, and I find Nora there waiting for me.

"I hear you have a big evening planned," she says.

"I don't know about that," I reply. "After all, Russ is the one doing the planning."

She laughs. "I know you don't need yet another person warning you off, but..."

I hold up my hand to stop her. "Honestly, I'll be fine. I know who Russ is. I want to take a little risk. I don't have any stories of my own yet, and you all have so many! Whatever his faults, Russ is a story. I like him, when he's not taking himself too seriously."

"Fair enough," Nora says. "But for what it's worth, I like the stories you already have. The ones about your family and your friends. Don't confuse drama with living, Freya. That's all I'm going to say." She grins. "Well, that, and if you are going to go out for dinner with Russ for the story, then you should wear something sensational. Something to make him sit up and take notice."

"I don't own anything sensational." It has actually been a bit of a sore point for me, because when one is determined to live out a fantasy, one imagines doing it in something other than an old frock that doesn't quite fit because two older sisters have worn it first.

"Don't I know it." Nora gives me a pained look. "You must start making your own clothes, Freya, you've got such a good eye, and these old hand-me-downs you wear do nothing for you." While she's talking she's riffling through the clothes rail and then she pulls something from the rack. It is an evening dress the colour of saffron strands, sleeveless with a trailing bow holding one shoulder together, and falling into a long tulle skirt, embroidered with a design of golden petals.

"Oh, *my*," I say.

Nora looks pleased. "I know. It's one of mine."

"Nora, you're so good." I stroke the material with reverent fingers.

"I know that too. Now, get out of that horrible thing."

I slip out of my cheap (but quite pretty, I'll not concede everything to Nora) dress, and stand in my underwear as Nora lowers the frothy golden concoction over my head.

There is the merest sigh of silk as it slips down over my hips, and then Nora begins fussing with the straps and the fall of the dress. It fits beautifully, falling just above my ankles. I peer past Nora into the mirror, admiring my reflection.

"That's enough of that," Nora chides. "You and Russ can't *both* spend the whole night admiring your own reflections in every shiny surface." She returns to the clothes rail, and despite her advice, my eyes drift back to the mirror.

"These," she says firmly, producing a pair of strappy gold sandals. "And these," a small beaded bag and a winter green wrap follow. "Now, sit." She pushes me down into the seat by the small dressing table.

"You're so bossy," I grumble.

"Save all of us clever, resourceful, confident women from that horrible word," she replies. She begins brushing out my hair. "I think you should wear it down, actually."

"It's not fashionable," I say doubtfully. "If you're going full Fairy Godmother you should throw in a haircut too."

"Don't cut it," Nora says. "It suits you this way. Fashion is not something you should follow blindly, Freya. You can make it yourself." She pulls one side away from my face and pins it, and then she starts on my make-up. More brisk orders. "Look down. Look up. Turn this way. For god's sake, Freya, stop talking for five seconds so I can do your lipstick." And so on, and so on.

"Right, then, Cinderella – if that's who you are – I think you're ready."

I jump to my feet, smoothing down my skirt and giving myself another once over in the mirror. I barely recognize myself. Nora has used kohl to make my eyes look enormous, and the gold in the dress makes my hair even lighter than usual, a stream of almost silver. There are butterflies in my stomach, all of a sudden, as though I'm about to go onstage. But then, I suppose this is the perfect costume. If you're going to have an evening of romance it *should* really be in a cloud of golden tulle. I feel like the ballerina in the middle of a jewellery box.

"Thank you, Nora," I say, and she squeezes my arm.

"Just behave," she says. "Don't let the dress go to your head."

I emerge into the corridor and begin making my way through the throngs of performers and crew. Lindsey whistles as I walk past and flashes me a wink, and a girl I don't know stops me to compliment my dress in awed tones. There are some less polite catcalls from the male crew, but I sweep past them, channelling Eileen Turner at her most regal.

I head towards the stage door where I've arranged to meet Russ, and find that my heart is pounding. Surely pounding hearts and sweating palms are all signs of romance. And I suddenly wonder whether he will kiss me. The thought makes me feel tingly. Another good sign.

I step out into the shock of the cold air. Although it's been a while since the performance finished, there are still a few hopeful audience members waiting with their autograph books in hand. Heads swing to look at me for a moment, clearly thrown by my glamorous appearance, before coming to the conclusion that I am simply a well-dressed nobody.

"Freya?" The word comes from my left, and I turn to see Kit. He's holding a cigarette in one hand and leaning against the wall. For some reason, nerves probably, my pulse stutters alarmingly.

"Hello," I say. He is looking at me very oddly. "What are you doing out here?"

He lifts the cigarette. "Just needed some air," he says.

"What's the matter?" I ask, unthinkingly taking a step towards him.

"It's just been a long day," he says. Then, after a pause, and in a low voice: "Viola and I had a disagreement. I think I upset her. I hate that. I don't..." He trails off, and there's something in those winter grey eyes of his that looks like pain.

"I'm sorry."

He shrugs. "You look nice," he says, clearly changing the subject.

I do a little spin. "All Nora, of course."

"I don't think she can take quite all of the credit."

"Just most of it?"

"I don't know." His smile is real again now. "I think most of it is just you."

"There you are!" a voice booms, and the mass fluttering and twittering of the autograph hunters before me tells me that Russ has arrived.

I turn around to face him, and his eyes travel slowly over me. He is devastating in a dinner suit, his dark hair curling over his collar.

"Well, well, well," he says, looking like the proverbial cat. "Just give me a moment, will you, darling?" He turns the full beam of his charm on to the gathering of fans. They look dazzled and I can see why. When Russ makes his mind up to charm you, it is like nothing else.

Kit stands beside me, watching as Russ signs autographs, smiling his enchanting smile. "Have a good time tonight," he says.

"Don't you want to warn me off him?" I ask. "I promise you, everyone else has."

"I don't need to warn you off anyone, Freya," he says lightly. "You should make whatever decisions you want." He grins at me. "And, anyway, you and I both know you're not going to get your heart broken by a man as trivial as Russell Whitmore."

"I'm not?" I say. "That's a shame. Experiencing

heartbreak would probably enrich my performance no end."

Kit laughs and shakes his head. "Be careful what you wish for. Have fun," he says, dodging round the group huddled about Russ and heading back inside.

For a second I look after him, wishing that he and I were going out for dinner instead. Everything is so easy with Kit.

Russ appears at my elbow, leaning down to kiss me lightly on the cheek. "Sorry about that," he murmurs. "Fans." He says it with a grimace, but he can't disguise his obvious enjoyment. "And may I say, you look ravishing?"

"You may," I reply as he touches my elbow, guiding me lightly down the street. "You do too," I add, because of course he does. His hair falls just right over his forehead, his jacket fits him like a glove, emphasizing his broad shoulders, his white teeth flash, perfect like a toothpaste advert. He is like a collection of beautiful parts: difficult to take him all in at once. The effect is overwhelming.

I feel as though a Hollywood icon has stepped out of

the screen and taken me by the arm. And I am enjoying it; of course I am, I'm eighteen and wearing a beautiful dress and there's a handsome man taking me out for dinner and dancing. My heartbeat accelerates at the thought of it all. I feel, I realize, quite like someone else.

The restaurant Russ takes me to is exactly what I had imagined – white tablecloths, heavy silverware, dim lighting. We're seated at a table in the corner, and I get the impression that Russ arranged it that way – and not for the first time. He pulls out my chair for me, his hand brushing against the bare skin at the top of my arm, just for a second.

As he sits down opposite me, and orders drinks from the waiter, I look about with interest at the crowd, mostly older, well-dressed, and already on to their desserts – thanks to the play, we're eating decadently late.

"I like this place," I say.

"I'm glad," he smiles, as the waiter returns and hands me a perfectly chilled saucer of champagne with a twist of lemon and a sugar cube in the bottom. Of course the girl in the golden dress drinks cocktails.

Russ lifts his glass, and winks at me over the top. I take a sip, and it is sweet and delicious, melting the tension from my body.

"So, this is where you take all your girls?" I ask, admiring the monogram embroidered on the perfectly pressed tablecloth.

Russ chokes on his drink, and I look up.

"Sorry," I say. "Is it bad form to mention the other girls?"

"It's ... not typical," Russ admits, a gleam of laughter in his eye.

I think about that. "I won't ask about them, then." I lean my elbows on the table. "I want to be very typical tonight."

"I don't think it's possible for you to be typical, Freya," he says. "You are unique."

"How well you turned that around into a compliment." I look at him admiringly. "That was very smooth, even if being unique is actually true of every girl."

"Thank you," Russ manages, taking another swig of his drink.

I turn my attention to the menu which is large and bound in red leather. "I'm starving."

"Me too." Russ's tone is innocent, but the look he gives me is pure Big Bad Wolf eyeing up Red Riding Hood.

I try for a moment to take him seriously, to simmer in a seductive way, but I can't help bursting into a laugh that rings around the murmuring quiet of the dining room.

Russ's mouth tugs up in a rueful smile. "All right," he says. "None of that. How about if I tell you what's good on the menu?"

"That I *would* like," I say.

It is not long until we have the place mostly to ourselves. A discreet waiter appears at my side to top up my wine glass whenever it is getting low.

Russ is charming and attentive, asking me questions about home, and he seems genuinely interested in the answers.

"Seven siblings?" He grimaces in alarm. "What was *that* like?"

"Complicated," I admit. "And noisy. I was always a bit of an odd one out."

"Me too," he says, taking a sip from his glass. "I think lots of us actors start off as misfits."

I like that. *Us actors*. I like to think of Russ as a misfit, like me.

I ask him about his own childhood but he's evasive, only letting slip that his family don't approve of his acting work. I get the impression they're quite well off. He much prefers to talk about his life in London, the performances he's been in, the people he knows, the parties he goes to.

"You don't need to impress me, you know," I say, chasing a morsel of steak around the plate. "After all, we know each other quite well by now." I smile at him. "Which must put you at quite a disadvantage when it comes to seduction."

"That's a disadvantage?" He puts a hand to his chest. "Christ, Freya, you know how to wound a man. Are you suggesting you would like me more if you didn't know the first thing about me?"

"Well, only that I would be more easily dazzled, you know," I say, a little apologetically. "Like those girls by the stage door. I expect that's why you make such quick work of the wardrobe assistants usually."

A frown briefly mars his perfect brow, and then, reluctantly, he laughs.

"You are direct, Freya," he says. "I'll give you that."

I can see that he has decided to find me amusing, and from then on everything is easy, so easy. The wine we're drinking is good, red and spicy, warm on my tongue, and it leaves me feeling boneless.

Without knowing exactly when it happened I realize Russ is holding my hand across the white linen tablecloth, toying lightly with my fingers. On the one hand it is sending quite interesting little tingles up my arm, and on the other it is preventing me from being able to properly attack the towering dessert that has been placed in front of me – all thick cream and whisper-light meringue.

"Dessert first," I say sternly.

Russ's smile is one of delight.

After we've finished eating, he orders brandies. They come in wide glasses, swirling amber and sending a shot of heat right down to my toes. It all feels impossibly grown up. I sit there, twirling my glass and feeling sophisticated.

"So this is what a romantic evening feels like," I say dreamily.

Russ chuckles. "We're not done yet, you know." This time the look he gives me is much more effective, a warm pulse in my belly.

There's no one else left in the restaurant now. The waiter hangs back, waiting for the gesture to get the bill. The candles have burned down in their silver candlesticks, and the soft music continues to buzz in the background.

While Russ pays for dinner I slip off to the loo where I touch up my red lipstick. The girl looking back at me in the mirror sparkles, young and alive, and exactly as I imagined I could be. I feel a million miles away from Freya Trevelyan.

When we leave the restaurant, Russ gently places my wrap around my shoulders, his hand sliding down my arm. I watch it with a sort of fascination – how practised he is, how utterly polished.

He "knows a little place" where we go to dance.

It's nothing like as classy as the restaurant we've just

been to. A tiny door in an unappealing alley, jazz music, scattered and sultry, rippling through the air in a smoky little bar. We dance close together, and I can feel the heat of his body. It feels intimate, that heat, coming off his skin. I am taut, full of anticipation for ... *something*.

By the time we leave I have no idea what time it is. The sky is pitch black, stars wheeling overhead. The dim light of the street lamps reflect off the road. It must have rained at some point because we skip around oil-slick puddles, hand in hand.

When we reach our digs, Russ doesn't hesitate. He kisses me.

The kiss is very good. Then again one doesn't expect a man like Russ to kiss badly. I lean into him, wrapping my arms around his neck. The kiss deepens. I feel again that sense that I am playing a part as I sigh, his hand cupping my cheek. And that that is all wrong – the point was to feel something so that I could act it later. I try to concentrate on the kissing, the breathing, the hands, but part of me feels like I'm not really there at all, like I'm watching a girl in a golden dress being kissed by a handsome man. Finally, I break away.

Russ stares at me, his breathing hard.

"Thank you for a wonderful evening," I say, taking a step back.

There's a beat. Something like disappointment flashes across his face, but it's quickly replaced by the familiar, charming smile. "You're very welcome." He holds the door open for me. We kiss once more, briefly – it feels almost perfunctory at this point – on the landing, and then I slip through the door into my room.

Alma is asleep, but at the sound of my entrance she stirs.

"Well?" she says, lifting herself up on her elbows. "How was it? Did he sweep you away with talk of your radiant beauty?" She shifts into a perfect imitation of Russ's smirk at the end of this, and I chuckle.

"It was nice," I shrug.

"Not Romeo and Juliet?" Alma's blue eyes are full of sleepy laughter.

"No," I sigh, stepping out of the golden dress. "Not that."

CHAPTER NINETEEN

8th December

Dear Lou,

    Told Russ I didn't think things were going to work out between us romantically - fairly sure I just beat him to it, but he still managed to look crestfallen, which I thought was very nicely done of him. I despair, though, what does a girl have to do around here to be swept off her feet? It was all so perfect on paper, but when he kissed me I just felt rather flat and like I was pretending. Anyway, I worried it would be awkward, but if anything Russ is being nicer and more attentive than ever. Boys are strange.

Freya xx

10th December

Dear Midge,

Thank you, thank you, thank you for the saffron cake and the jam which was waiting at the theatre in Sheffield! I can't believe you thought to send it there. It was such a lovely taste of home, and I could almost imagine I was there with you sitting around the kitchen table. Particularly as I was surrounded by noisy actors fighting over the last slice. (As if I would share the last slice with anyone, the fools!)

Still, you should know that your baking has garnered much praise, and Russ would like me

to convey a proposal of marriage, should you find
yourself at a loose end. I tried to tell him he
could never "win the hand of the fair maiden"
(as he put it) from Pa, but he insists his stage combat
training would come in useful. Kit says to pass on
his special thanks for the ginger biscuits – he was
surprised I had told you they were his favourite,
and even more surprised that you remembered. He
was so pleased, Midge, his cheeks turned all pink
    All my love,
    Freya xx

                                    10th December

Dear Tom,

    No, you absolutely cannot keep your newts in
my wardrobe. My costumes are in there, and I
don't want you in there AT ALL. I don't care if you
have named one of the newts Rhys Cantwell, it is
still an insult to my art.

    Freya

Dear Lou,

The company runs like clockwork these days, moving from town to town. I barely know where I am, but I seem to always know where I'm going. The play continues to draw a big crowd. We were sold out in Leeds last night, and the audience were laughing themselves into the aisles. I can't tell you how tired I am, or how happy. Every night is different, every performance a clean slate. It's exhilarating.

Reasonable digs here, warm enough to leave off the thermals indoors at least! Alma swears she heard a ghost on the stairs last night, but I didn't hear a sound, I was fast asleep. So upsetting to miss a possible spectre, but then I daresay it was just Russ sneaking another girl into his room.

That's not true, actually, he's been on his very best behaviour, and I can't help suspecting he might be trying to win me around. I don't

know what to think about that, having very little
experience in the matter. What was your first kiss
with Robert like? Was it a bit flat?

Freya xx

POST OFFICE TELEGRAPHS

Time handed in: 14.37

Office of origin: Westminster

Words:5

NO IT WAS NOT

ROBERT

From Nottingham we continue north to Sheffield, Leeds and York. We have fallen into a routine now, and while the hours are punishing, the thrill of the performance continues to hold its spell over me. I've never worked so hard, or been so tired, or felt so fulfilled and exhilarated as I do in those weeks. My own rehearsals – squeezed into our busy schedule – have improved, and I feel a general sense of achievement.

The temperature continues to plummet, and by the time we head into the last week of the tour it has started to snow. We are driving towards the Yorkshire coast when this becomes a problem. The increasingly narrow roads we are driving down are banked with snow. The wheels of the van skid a couple of times, and I learn some more colourful swear words from Nora. I thought I had heard them all by now.

"This is getting ridiculous," Nora murmurs as we creep carefully forward in the van. "Thank goodness we left early and there's nothing else on the roads. Have you seen anything that looks like it might be the town yet?"

"I think we're almost there," I say, projecting more confidence than I feel. I frown over the map, trying to trace the exact route we should be taking, with very little idea of where we actually are.

The snow is falling thick and fast now, a flurry of fat flakes that splat audibly against the windscreen. The wipers are going full force but we can barely see a few feet in front of us.

"Look!" I exclaim. "Civilization!" I see a snow-covered sign and realize with relief that we have reached the outskirts of Runleigh, the small town that is to be our next stop. It's such a small town that I'm not entirely sure why it's on the tour. When I asked Nora she said that Mr Cantwell had a special affection for the theatre here, which piqued my interest.

"Oh, thank you, thank you, thank you," Nora mutters under her breath as we crawl along the road, shadowy buildings looming up alongside us.

"Here," I say. "This is the boarding house, I think. Just there on the left."

We pull bumpily off the road. I see that Kit and Mr Cantwell have already arrived. Mr Cantwell's car is still humming, and through the snow-covered window I can see Eileen Turner all wrapped up in her fur coat. We abandon the van and slip and slide across the driveway towards the two men. It begins to dawn on me that neither of them look at all happy. They are having a conversation with a third man that involves much angry gesticulating.

"What's going on?" Nora asks when we finally reach them.

"They haven't got room for us," Kit says. The man they've been talking to takes this opportunity to slink unobtrusively away and back towards the boarding house.

"I don't understand it," Mr Cantwell murmurs darkly. "Meriden has never let us down before but the blasted man says he hasn't got any record of us coming and that he's completely full."

"Miss Meriden will know what to do, won't she?" I say.

"She's not coming," Kit says. "She sent a wire to the boarding house, not that the manager had a clue who it was for at the time. The roads were too bad. Most of the company turned round and headed back to York. Apparently we missed the worst of it by the skin of our teeth."

"Not coming?" Nora says blankly. "Miss Meriden?" And I agree, it seems impossible that that capable woman should be thwarted by anything as mundane as the weather.

"What are we going to do?" I ask, shivering.

We're interrupted by a screeching sound as Russ's car suddenly swings into the road, coming to a precarious stop almost on top of us.

Viola emerges almost instantly. "My god, Russ, you could have killed us all!" she shrieks. Russ steps, laughing from the car, and Alma and Dan emerge from the back seat, pale and shaken.

"Things got a little hairy," Dan murmurs, coming to stand beside me. "Between Russ's driving and Viola's banshee impression, I began to think it possible I'd died and been sent straight to the abode of the damned."

"Well, you were wrong." Alma smiles weakly. She too looks a little green-tinged around the edges. "We all survived, and anyway, you're an angel and you're going straight to heaven."

"Sweet of you, darling, but I'm afraid heaven sounds dreadfully dull."

The situation is swiftly explained to them and then we all stand, undecided what to do next. At last, Kit suggests we go to the theatre.

"We can't just stand around here all day," he says reasonably. "I don't think anyone else is coming. Perhaps the manager there will have some suggestions."

This is met with a chorus of agreement.

"I am *not* getting back in a car with that madman behind the wheel," Viola insists.

"We can leave the cars here and walk," I suggest. "It's just around the corner. I saw it on the map."

We make a funny kind of procession, slipping and sliding along the road, forging our way through the very air around us which has turned white and freezing. My eyes are watering, and my cheeks sting. I barely take in the outside of the theatre once we reach it, I am so relieved simply to be there. When Kit pushes at the door and it swings open underneath his hand I am not the only one to let out a weak cheer.

We tumble into the welcoming warmth of the building like a litter of overeager puppies. Even Mr Cantwell and Eileen seem to have lost their usual dignified air, bedraggled as the rest of us, with pink noses and windswept hair.

"Mr Cantwell!" a voice exclaims in tones of deepest horror. "What on earth are you doing here?"

The voice belongs to a small, anxious-looking man with a bald head, round gold spectacles, and a nervous habit of twisting his hands. "I'm Hubert Pennington, the theatre manager." His eyes lock on to Eileen and widen comically. "Oh dear, oh dear," he says, almost to himself. "I thought for certain that you would have turned back in this weather."

"We missed the worst of it," says Mr Cantwell.

"But – but we can't hold a performance here tonight!" Mr Pennington exclaims, and I realize he looks exactly how I imagine Mole in *The Wind in the Willows*.

"Don't worry about that," says Mr Cantwell wearily. "Most of the cast are trapped in York anyway. We just need a place to stay – the boarding house has no room for us."

I had not thought it possible for the man before me to look more anxious, but at this he turns positively grey. He shakes his head. "There isn't anywhere else," he says sadly. "Nowhere with any room, and of course because of the snow no one is leaving and…"

"We'll have to go somewhere else," Mr Cantwell says.

"I don't see how," Kit points out. "It's going to be hell trying to get out of here in this weather."

The theatre manager nods eagerly. "The main road always gets blocked off just up the hill when it snows like this," he says. "I'm surprised you managed to make it through. I really didn't expect…"

"He's quite right," Dan says. "We shouldn't have come through ourselves, only Russ drives like an absolute demon. I thought we were going to be swallowed up in some sort of avalanche."

"But if we can't stay, and we can't go, what *are* we supposed to do?" I ask.

There's a silence then.

"We could stay here," Kit says finally. "If that was all right with you, Mr Pennington?"

"Here?" Mr Cantwell, the theatre manager and Viola all exclaim in equal tones of horror.

"It couldn't really be worse than most of the places

we've been staying," Kit says. "It's warm and dry, at least. There's a bathroom…" He turns to the manager. "Do you have any camp beds we could set up in the dressing rooms?"

Mr Pennington nods. "I'm sure we could cobble something together," he says uncertainly.

"No worse than where *we've* been staying," Nora says, "but those two are used to finer things." She nods at Mr Cantwell and Eileen, who are looking rather apprehensive at the talk of camp beds.

"Oh!" the little manager squeaks. "But it would be my pleasure, indeed, my honour, to host you both at my home." He looks as though he's about to fall and genuflect at Eileen's feet.

"It would be most kind of you," Eileen says in her beautiful, stately voice. She inclines her head by the merest fraction of an inch. "I can't tell you how much we appreciate it." Mr Pennington turns bright pink.

"I only wish I had room for all of you," he adds weakly.

"Oh, the rest of us will be all right," Nora says briskly, though Viola's pursed lips tell a different story.

"Right," the manager says, relief writ large across his face. "That's a plan, then. I'll have one of the lads dig out some camp beds and see about some other home comforts for you."

"Come on, Russ, let's get the bags," says Kit.

"If we must," says Russ, tugging up his scarf. I catch his eye and he smiles. "You know I live to serve you, darling."

"Do stop fawning over Freya for a minute and see sense," Viola says, at her most icy. "This is a ridiculous idea. Sleeping in a rundown old theatre."

"It'll be fun," says Alma, her eyes shining. "An adventure."

"I think you'll find it all quite snug," Mr Pennington says, eyeing Viola coldly. "The theatre is a very special little place. In fact, why don't I give you a tour?"

He leads us through the foyer and deeper into the theatre, talking all the while.

Alma and I bring up the back of the group. "So?" she asks. "What do you think?"

"I agree with you." I wriggle in excitement. "Camping out in a theatre. *What* an adventure!"

CHAPTER TWENTY

It turns out Mr Pennington is quite right; the theatre is special. I've never seen anything like it before. I had wondered what it was that was bringing us to this small coastal town, but as we begin to look around I find that now I understand Mr Cantwell's affection for it completely.

The Theatre Royale is a tiny, perfect chocolate box of a theatre, built – Mr Pennington informs us – in the 1780s. The boxes that line the wall of the auditorium are painted a pale, mint green, and are embellished with golden scroll work. The seats in the stalls are opulent green velvet, and the walls are painted a blushing peach colour. The ceiling is covered in a painted fresco of a swirling sunrise, and suspended from the centre is an elaborate golden chandelier that shimmers with the promise of mellow morning light.

The stage is slightly smaller than we have worked on before, and surrounded by swagged green curtains. The complete impression is one of delicious folly, as though the whole theatre has been constructed on a whim, like an oversized dolls' house for grown-ups to play in. Even Viola's frown vanishes, and she looks as enchanted by it as I feel.

The backstage area is less interesting, but scrupulously neat and clean. The dressing rooms at the back, being near the boiler, are deliciously warm, and I think we will be quite snug and cosy here.

Several boys appear muffled in thick coats, obviously drafted in by Mr Pennington, dragging camp beds which we set up in the dressing rooms, laden with thick quilts and downy pillows, donated by various generous townspeople. It almost feels like a dormitory. Nora,

Alma, Viola and I will be sleeping in one room, and the boys in the other.

Russ and Kit arrive with the last of our bags, windswept and cheerful, and we scatter to unpack and make things as comfortable as possible. I can hear Dan next door, singing an Al Bowlly tune in his rich baritone.

Hubert Pennington returns with supplies – candles, bread, jam, butter, a whole carefully wrapped fruit cake and a crate of gently clinking bottles that contain – according to the handwritten labels – home-made ginger beer and elderflower wine.

"We are going to have quite the midnight feast later," I say, and Alma squeezes my hand.

Now that the cold has worn off, I'm not sure there could be anything nicer than being snowed in at this little theatre. I was never sent away to school, but this is always how I imagined it might be. There's something about all this, the unexpectedness of it, the feeling of magic, that makes me feel like a young child.

"This is a first," Nora says, sitting on her bed with her back against the wall. "I've done a lot of things, but

I've never slept in a theatre before. This will be a story you can tell one day, Freya."

I hug myself tight. "It does feel like being dropped into the middle of a story, doesn't it?"

"How long do you think we are going to be stuck here in limbo?" Viola asks, plonking herself in front of one of the mirrors and fiddling with her hair.

Nora shrugs. "Your guess is as good as mine. We can't go anywhere until the road clears. We're due to perform here for the next three nights – tonight is obviously cancelled, but who knows what we'll wake up to? It could all be back to normal tomorrow."

I hope not, I think.

The boys drift into our room. "Shall we investigate this wine, then?" says Russ.

I feel a light, familiar touch on my shoulder.

"Do you want to go and explore?" Kit asks.

"I've been waiting for you to turn up," I say. "Let's go."

We slip out of the room, leaving Viola and Russ arguing over the bottles. I think Alma is the only one to notice us leave, but then she's a noticing sort of person.

We leave the dressing rooms behind and step into the heavy silence of the theatre. It's strange, this silence, in a place that would usually be filled with such noise and energy; it leaves us creeping quietly, talking only in hushed tones.

Behind one door we discover what must be the wardrobe department, filled with rails of costumes.

"Kit, *look* at these," I exclaim, the excitement in my voice splintering the quiet, my hand trailing over the dresses. Some of them look a hundred years old. "Nora is going to be in heaven."

There are dresses, tissue light, like something spun by fairy magic, rich velvets in jewel tones, rippling silks in every colour of the rainbow. There are gowns that flash, heavy with glass stones that weigh a ton, and elaborate frock coats made of swirling jacquard or severe black silk, delicately embroidered.

I reach out and stroke a stiff apricot silk gown shot through with gold, that looks like something Marie Antoinette would wear. "Viola would look so beautiful in this," I say, without thinking, imagining how the simple neckline and elegant lines would suit her.

Kit nods. "She would," he says. Then he pushes through the doors to the next room. "Look at this!" I hear him call and I follow the sound of his voice. Stacked neatly on their sides, against the end of the room, are dozens of pieces of scenery, hand-painted and beautiful. There are intricate woodland scenes, fairy groves, deliciously detailed drawing rooms, even desert sands shimmering under an achingly hot sun.

"I think a lot of these are quite old." Kit's voice is low, reverent. He handles the fragile painted flats carefully. "Some of them may even be from when the theatre opened."

"This whole place is magic, isn't it?" I say.

"Absolutely magic," he agrees.

We leave and climb up dozens of narrow steps until we're high above the stage. When he reaches the top Kit turns and holds out his hand, his fingers wrapping around mine as he pulls me up to join him. We sit up there, where the ropes for the rigging live, our legs dangling over the side. I produce a slightly squashed piece of cake that I had taken from Mr Pennington's hamper and wrapped in paper, and we share it between us.

"One day they'll put your plays on here," I say.

He laughs. "You've never even read my play. It might be terrible."

"It won't be," I say, and I'm sure of it. Then, after a pause, and because I've been dying to ask: "*Could* I read your play?"

"If you like." Kit seems totally unruffled.

"You don't mind?" I ask, feeling a little put out by his relaxed attitude. "I thought writers were meant to be all tortured about this sort of thing. I've been wanting to read it for weeks. I thought you might ask me to."

He grins. "I suppose someone has to read it some time. I'd like it if it was you." Then he looks at me, his eyes dancing. "I'm sorry I didn't ask you earlier, I had no idea you wanted to."

"Yes, you did!"

"No, I didn't, honestly. I've been hoping you'd ask."

We sit in companionable silence for a while until somewhere in the distance a clock strikes five. When we return to the dressing room we find only Nora, sprawled across her bed, a magazine in her hands and a half-eaten bar of chocolate at her side. Her feet are bare and I notice her toenails are painted a dark, vampy red.

"My sister Lou writes for that magazine," I say. "She writes the Lady Amelia story."

"Your sister writes Lady Amelia?" Nora says, laying down her magazine. "But Lady Amelia is too thrilling! Wait, don't tell me you're *Lou's* sister?"

I nod. "Yes, I am. I've mentioned her to you before."

"Oh, but I didn't put the pieces together at all!" Nora exclaims. "I've only met her once or twice at parties. She's wonderful. And what a talent."

"I suppose," I say grudgingly, as only a little sister can. Nora is mine and I don't like the idea of Lou knowing her first one bit. I know I'm being childish, but this is the first time in my life I've carved out something away from home and my family, and even though I love them, I want this to be just for me.

"She's a great writer," Kit says admiringly. "To keep a serialization like that going at the pace she does is quite something. I heard she was turning it into a novel."

"Maybe," I say doubtfully. My sister, the novelist. It makes her sound awfully grand.

"Where have the others gone?" Kit asks then. I think he is changing the subject on my behalf.

"They're on a mission to find a hot meal," Nora says. "If they manage to find one, they're going to send someone back for us."

"I hope they do," I say fervently. "I'm famished."

"You shock me," Nora replies. She pushes the chocolate bar over to us. "Have some chocolate."

We break up the chocolate and sit, sharing it and chatting contentedly for a while, before there is a thumping on the door, and Dan appears, muffled up to his eyes in an enormous blue scarf, and looking like some sort of Arctic explorer.

"They've taken pity on us at the pub," he says. "The landlady says she can rustle us up some beans on toast. Wrap up – it's a blizzard out there!"

The four of us battle our way out and along the street to the pub where the others are waiting. We're the only guests.

The pub is warm, and the landlady, Sophie, is extremely welcoming. Sophie is small and round with luxuriant gold hair and green eyes that tilt up a little at the corners like a cat. Nora has been staring at her ever since she arrived, uncharacteristically tongue-tied.

We sit at a long table in front of a merrily crackling fire, and Sophie places steaming plates in front of us, thick toasted brown bread spread with butter and topped with baked beans from a tin. It is, honestly, one of the best meals I've ever eaten.

"I'm only sorry I couldn't sort you anything better," Sophie fusses. "I had no idea anyone would need feeding tonight. You must have been so put out not to have a proper room waiting for you."

"This is wonderful," Alma says, her eyes briefly closing. The rest of us murmur in agreement.

The spell that has been cast over us all seems to hold. Even Viola is happily attacking her food with gusto.

We talk and laugh, and a heavy, drugging warmth creeps through my bones.

Kit and I tell the others about what we found on our exploration through the theatre.

"I can't get over that place," I say, shaking my head. "It's so special. No wonder Mr Cantwell wanted to come."

"I heard he staged his first production here," Dan says, taking a swig of his drink.

"How romantic that he'd want to come back," Alma sighs. "All these years later when he's a big success."

"It's just a shame that no one will get to see it," says Russ.

After eating and drinking our fill, we decide to head back to the theatre. Nora offers to stay behind and help Sophie clear up.

Everyone is in good spirits, and we sing – a little rowdy – as we make our way back down the quiet, snow-softened road.

"Let's raid Mr Pennington's supplies," Alma suggests when we get back to the theatre. "I'm not ready for bed yet."

"We can have our midnight feast!" I exclaim.

"Finally, the boarding school experience I've always longed for," Dan drawls, delighted.

We return to our dressing rooms and gather our quilts and pillows, arranging them in a circle on the empty stage like a nest. Viola lights some of the candles, and Russ opens a bottle of elderflower wine with a pop that makes us cheer.

We stay up late, telling ghost stories that become increasingly bloodthirsty and outlandish, until I'm shaking with a curious mixture of fear and laughter.

I think Viola will be the best at telling ghost stories, but it's actually Alma, her eyes lit with ghoulish glee as she has us all screeching.

There's something so nice about the whole evening, from the beans on toast to the midnight feast. It feels like we are all naughty schoolchildren up past our bedtime. An uncomplicated sense of happiness settles around us.

Eventually, yawning, we make for the dressing rooms. At the door, Kit stops. "Wait here," he says, and ducks into the room. He returns and hands me a sheaf of papers, neatly bundled together. "My play," he says, his grey eyes serious and no hint of his dimples on display. "If you'd really like to read it?"

"Of course I would." I take the bundle and hug it to my chest. "I'm going to start it *right* now."

"It's late," Kit laughs.

"I'm not tired," I say. And, suddenly, I'm not.

"Well ... then I await your verdict. Goodnight, Freya."

"Goodnight, Kit."

CHAPTER TWENTY-ONE

The next morning, I wake to the sound of the others moving around. I have fallen asleep with Kit's play underneath my pillow, and as I stretch and open my eyes, I hear the crackle of the pages near my ear. I stayed up reading it, burrowing under the covers with my torch so as not to disturb the others.

"What time is it?" I manage, blinking owlishly.

"Only just gone nine," Nora groans from her bed. "Why aren't you all still asleep? Young people today are far too up and at 'em for my taste."

Alma plonks herself down on the foot of my bed. She's wearing slacks and a jumper, and her cheeks are flushed with excitement. "I looked outside. It's stopped snowing!"

"Do you think we'll be able to leave?" I try to keep the disappointment from my voice. I don't want to leave this magical place, so cut off from the outside world. I want to sleep another night in my camp bed and drink elderflower wine and wander through this beautiful old theatre.

Alma shakes her head. "There's a drift of snow out there. I don't think we'll be leaving any time soon. Unless we can *dig* ourselves out."

Alma's prediction proves correct. It's perhaps an hour later when the six of us, without Nora (who has declared firmly her intention to stay in bed "where it is warm and does not resemble deepest Siberia"), are trying to push our way out of the stage door.

Russ is wielding the coal scuttle which is the closest thing we could find to a shovel and digging with his shirt sleeves rolled up. "If I just dig a little more here," he pants, "I think I'll have it."

"Come on, put some effort in," Viola says. "Try to get further round towards the middle."

"Sadly, my dear, the laws of physics make that impossible," Russ drawls. "So you can take it up with them." He looks dishevelled this morning, but no less handsome for it. "Obviously, not all of us have your flexibility."

"You're doing a wonderful job," Alma says encouragingly, her eyes shining. "I think you've almost got it."

After a bit more complaining, and huffing, and swearing, the door finally swings forward with an unhappy groan.

"Freedom!" Russ waves the coal scuttle in the air. He tugs on his thick, grey woollen coat, and then holds out his hand to help me through the gap and into the pure white snow. He pulls me towards him, so that I fall briefly against his broad chest.

"Russ!" I laugh, disentangling myself.

"Clumsy me," he smiles, with his wolf smile.

"Come on," Alma says quickly, tucking her gloved hand through my arm, and pulling me away from Russ. "We've got exploring to do."

It is impossible to describe the scene that greets us this

morning. Impossible to capture the dreamlike feeling of emerging into a world transformed so completely.

The previous day our excursions had been spent head down, battling through freezing winds and icy rain. Now, the sky is a celestial blue, arcing above us and punctuated by the odd wisp of white cloud. The sun is pale beaten gold, weaker than on the kind of miraculous blue-sky days you find in summer, but all the sweeter for that. We crunch through the snow, our footprints the first footprints, breaking through the crisp crust like a spoon tapping against burned sugar.

We make our way slowly, arduously, through winding streets and past small, stone cottages. Underneath their blanket of snow, they look like something you might find on a Christmas card.

Eventually, after much puffing and panting, we round a corner on to a steep road sloping down and away from us.

"Look," Kit says, his eyes instantly seeking mine, full of pleasure. "Look, Freya."

I catch my breath.

The sea.

I feel a rush of emotion at the sight of it. The road we're on now angles down towards the harbour, with its long stone wall. Out to the sides the beaches spread, the tide out and the sand covered in an icing sugar dusting of white snow. The sea itself is grey and wild, crashing against the harbour wall with a roar of defiance. I was right, I realize in a flash, to compare Kit's eyes to a winter sea.

But there's no time for that now.

With a cry that I don't intend to make, I stumble down the hill, laughing and sliding through the snow, steadying myself as I go with the black iron handrail, the old-fashioned lamp posts, anything my hands scramble over. It is far from dignified, and more than a little of the journey is achieved flat on my bum, but I don't care. I can hear the others scrambling behind me, making their own whoops of exhilaration.

When I reach the bottom I fly on to the beach, right up to the edge of the water, the sound of it filling my ears, the wind whipping my hair around my face and the sharp taste of salt on my lips.

"Aaaaaooooooooooooooooo!" I shout into the sea,

howling like an animal. The noise is instantly snatched away from me, spiralling out into the waves and the sky. I shout again, louder this time.

Viola appears at my side, her nose pink, her eyes wide with delight.

"Aaaaaaaaoooooooooo!" she howls with me. We grin at each other, for once completely in harmony. On my other side, Alma appears. I find that the three of us are holding hands. Soon all six of us stand in a line, hand in hand, tethered to each other like a string of lobster pots, shouting and laughing as the wind snaps and growls around us.

We break apart, wandering over the sand, picking our way across the rocks.

I bend down over a large rock pool and tug my glove from one hand, touching my fingers to the water, an ice cold kiss, that leaves me tingling.

"What can you see?" Alma asks, coming to stand beside me and leaning over the pool.

"Anemones," I say. "Loads of them. That one," I point to a red sea anemone, clinging to one of the rocks, its tentacles waving gently in the water, "is called a strawberry anemone. For obvious reasons."

"It does look just like a strawberry!" Alma is delighted.

Russ appears, peering over the side. "What's that?" he says. "It's got red eyes!"

He plunges his hand in the pool. "No! Russ!" I exclaim, before he violently withdraws his hand, sending a spray of freezing seawater over me and Alma, a string of curse words falling from his mouth.

"It's called a velvet swimming crab," I say, half in sympathy, half-laughing at the outraged expression on his face. "They're notorious for giving you an angry nip if you bother them."

"A nip?" Russ's eyebrows raise incredulously. "That thing almost had my hand off!"

I take his hand in both of mine, rubbing it gently. "It hasn't even broken the skin." I look up at him.

He smiles lazily. "But it hurts. I think it needs further ministrations."

"What seems to be the problem?" Dan arrives.

"Russ has hurt his hand," Alma says drily. "He appears in need of a nurse."

"I volunteer," Dan smirks.

"No offence, Daniel, but yours is not exactly the tender care I was hoping for." Russ pulls his hand away, a reluctant huff of laughter in his voice.

He and Dan climb further along, daring each other higher and higher up the rocks.

Alma and I watch them for a moment. "Be careful," Alma says finally.

Her tone is so serious that I look at her in surprise.

"Of what?" I ask.

She squints up at the boys. "Of Russ. There's something…" She trails off, and then looks at me again, her gaze earnest. "Just be careful."

I don't know what to say to that, but we're interrupted then by the sound of the boys hollering and beating their chests, showing off how high they've climbed.

I notice Kit and Viola walking by the edge of the sea, their heads turn towards Dan and Russ too, and Viola lifts her hand in a wave. She looks happier than I've seen her down here, by the sea, her eyes sparkling, her hair being ruffled by the playful hand of the breeze.

"Let's skim stones," I say suddenly.

"I haven't the faintest idea how to skim stones," Alma replies. "Not a lot of sea in London."

I laugh and lead her down to the shore. I think I see a flicker of annoyance in Viola's eyes, but Kit greets us easily. I can hear snatches of Dan and Russ squabbling as they climb back down to join us. Soon I'm teaching all of them how to skim stones across the surface of the water.

Kit watches quietly as the others' stones sink with sad splashing sounds. Then he pulls a stone from his pocket and sends it skipping across the water.

"Six bounces!" I exclaim. "You've been holding out on me!"

"All those summer holidays in Devon," he grins, the freckles on his nose scrunching up.

"Pah! Cornwall knocks Devon's socks off every time." I begin to search around for a likely looking stone, determined to best him. Which I do, of course.

"Nine!" Kit lets out a low whistle. "I bow before the master."

I don't know how long we're there in the end, on the beach, laughing like children, exploring, but eventually the others start to peel away.

"I'm freezing," Viola says through chattering teeth. "Do you think we should go and see if Sophie's got the fire going at the pub?"

"Oh, yes, that sounds like bliss," Dan agrees.

"I'd kill for tea and toast." Alma tugs Russ's arm, and he wanders off with her, talking about lunch.

Finally, it's just Kit and I left. I've been waiting for this moment all morning.

CHAPTER TWENTY-TWO

"I read your play," I say baldly. "I loved it."

He stands very still, his lovely tousled hair blowing about his face, and the look that flashes in his eyes then, just for a second, is one that I'll remember until the day I die.

"Thank you." His voice is little more than a low rumble.

"Now let me tell you all my thoughts," I say. "Because I have so many. Starting with how clever I thought that second scene was." Kit laughs, and we walk, heads close together, him pulling me in to his side as we move and talk, shielding me from some of the cold with his long limbs.

I have only told the truth about Kit's play. I did love it. It surprised me. I don't know what I was expecting, but I suppose something quite earnest and worthy. Instead, Kit has written the funniest comedy of errors. I spent most of the night biting down on my knuckles to keep from waking the others with my laughter. It is witty and warm, and clever in its simplicity. There are only five characters – two couples who become increasingly tangled up in misunderstanding, and a narrator, who speaks directly to the audience. Her part is the best, full of wry observations and the occasional stinging critique of the lovers' ineptitude.

"When I read it, I could see it exactly," I say to Kit now. "The narrator, suspended slightly above and to one side... She can step into the set at times. Fix herself a drink..." I sketch the scene with my hands.

Kit looks thoughtful. "That could work."

"It *would* work," I say firmly. "She's amazing. She reminds me a little bit of Nora, but older – cutting, sometimes, but warm with it."

We've been walking back towards the town. I stop suddenly.

"What's that?" I say. At the top of the cliff, the silhouette of a great building is outlined starkly against the sky.

"Shall we go and have a look?" he asks. "Or are you desperate for something to eat?"

I pat my cloth satchel, into which I placed the pages of his script this morning, alongside several emergency jam sandwiches and a bottle of ginger beer. I knew if it were me, I'd want the first person who read my script to talk about it as soon as possible. "I come prepared. Let's explore."

We climb the hill, offering one another the occasional steadying hand. The cliffs above the town are high and steep, and the climb is hard work. Despite the freezing cold I start to feel warm, my cheeks pink with exertion, my breath feathering in little white clouds through the air in front of me. "I'm always scrambling up hilltops at home, but this is a bit of a challenge."

"You probably don't do it in such deep snow," Kit points out, breathing hard.

I stop for a minute and squint out over the view. "I've never seen so much snow before!" From here the view towards the beach and the harbour is even more startling. Thin clouds have begun to roll in, draining the sky of that vibrant blue we saw this morning. Now it is a flat, blue-grey, and with the dazzling white of the snowfall, against the slate grey sea makes for a scene curiously bleached of colour. It should be bleak, but the effect is more wild and mysterious.

"Come on," Kit says. "We're almost there."

The last bit of the climb is so steep that I feel my feet sliding from under me several times. On every occasion Kit's arm is there to catch me, steady, always.

Finally, we crest the hill and I let out an audible gasp. I can tell from Kit's expression that he's as startled as I am.

It is the wreck of an old abbey. The scale of the ruin is hard to believe, towering far, far above us, up and into the sky. We walk – the only two people on the planet, it feels like – through the snow and inside what remains of the building.

The remains are skeletal; it is like standing in the belly of a once-great beast. The roof is completely gone, and turning your eyes skywards produces a dizzying feeling of infinity. There are no windows or doors, only enormous spaces where they would once have been. These stone gaps frame the views – across the cliff top, over the water – with all the drama of a magician revealing their trick.

The silence has a quality that I have never known before. A bone-deep kind of peace. In its dilapidated state you can feel even more keenly the scale, the endless work that went into building the abbey.

I'm surprised to find tears blurring my eyes. I don't know why, only that this place is so beautiful it makes my chest ache. The feeling it gives me is so big, I don't know what to do with it.

I brush the tears away, the wool of my glove rough against my cheek. I wander off, moving in and around the ruin so that I can look at it from different angles, the gilding of snow only adding to the desolate beauty. Each view is different, revealing new secrets about our surroundings.

Finally, Kit comes to stand beside me. "Beautiful," he breathes.

"Yes. *Yes*."

We find a low wall to perch on and eat our picnic. The heat from the climb has certainly worn off now, and my fingers are cold as I unwrap my sandwich. I quickly realize that a picnic in Yorkshire in December was a trifle optimistic.

"Ginger beer is all very well in the summer," I grumble through chattering teeth. "But what I wouldn't give for a nice flask of tea right now."

"We can't sit here like this," Kit says practically. "We'll freeze."

"We'll end up perishing in a tragically beautiful posture, like a pair of doomed lovers," I agree.

"Found weeks later. Our story will be told for centuries," he adds.

"Well, that sounds nice. But it's hard to think about being a tragic romantic heroine when I can't feel my toes." I jump to my feet and stomp them a bit, trying to get the feeling to return. "I know!" I exclaim. "We can rehearse your play."

"My play?"

"Yes, I have it with me in my bag, and I've made

notes. I hoped we'd get a chance to talk all about it. I can show you what I was thinking. Come on," I grin, pulling the pages from my bag. "Just read it with me."

Half-laughing, half-groaning, Kit allows me to drag him to his feet.

I sketch out a rectangle in the middle of the abbey with a stick to represent the stage, then put my hands on Kit's shoulders and position him.

"You stand here, you see. We're in a drawing room, a bit old-fashioned, you know – as if there was money once, but it's gone now. Now go on, you start."

Kit reads the lines of ones of the lovers, and I read back to him, pausing occasionally to adjust the way we're standing.

"What about this line here?" He breaks off. "I'm not sure how to play it best."

"I suppose the question is whether or not he is actually in love with her – or whether he just thinks he is? It will make a difference to the way you play it."

"I think he loves her," Kit says quietly. "He just doesn't know how to tell her."

"I do too," I say. "He's nervous, which is

uncomfortable for him. I think if he delivers the line a little more offhand then it will be funnier. Like he doesn't quite dare say it seriously. Try it again."

And so it goes on. We work through the first scene, making ourselves laugh, arguing over certain lines, sharing our ideas of how you could make it work. We're so involved that we don't notice the voices until they're on top of us.

"Well, hello, you two." The unmistakable voice of Eileen Turner greets us, and I swing around to find her walking towards us on the arm of Rhys Cantwell. They are both wrapped up in thick coats, and Eileen has a round fur hat pulled down low on her head.

Do not curtsey, I tell myself sternly.

"It looks like you're having a good time," Eileen continues. "True that you can make a stage anywhere, it seems."

"How did you two get up here?" Kit asks. Like me he is clearly trying to imagine Eileen Turner scaling the cliff face. Perhaps Mr Cantwell carried her on his back like a daring mountaineer. I stifle a wave of laughter.

"We followed the path." Mr Cantwell gestures across

the clifftop towards the top of the town. "It's not a bad walk, even in this weather. I assume you two climbed up from the beach?"

I wonder if it's our completely bedraggled appearance that has led him to this conclusion.

"And what are you up to, that has you in such high spirits?" he asks. "We could hear you laughing all the way along the cliff path."

"We're acting out Kit's play," I blurt out quickly. "It's completely wonderful, Mr Cantwell. You must read it."

I hear Kit's sharp intake of breath at that, and I know I've crossed a line. I don't dare look at him. The play is too good for him to keep it a secret. It needs to be out here, in the sunlight where people can see it.

"We were just working on the first scene," I say.

"Will you show us?" Eileen asks. It's not really a question; she knows we'll bow and scrape as much as she likes, like courtiers before our queen.

I risk a quick glance at Kit and his expression is slightly stunned. "If – if you'd like," he says uncertainly, his eyes going to Mr Cantwell.

"Yes, show us," the director agrees, taking a seat on

271

the low stone wall where Kit and I shared our picnic. Eileen gives the wall a brief, dubious look but as there is no alternative, she dusts down her thick fur coat and perches gingerly next to him, her back rigidly straight.

I smile reassuringly at Kit, who has gone so pale that his freckles stand out against his skin.

"All right," he says, collecting himself. "Well, in this scene, the man is in love with the woman, but she has no idea. She thinks he loves her friend, and so their wires get crossed while he tries to bare his soul to her. The narrator comes in when the action freezes and unpicks what's really going on."

"She's sort of world-weary," I add. "She's seen it all before and she critiques them as if they're in a play."

I don't suppose that you often know something important is unfolding right in front of you, but that is how it is now. We play out the scene, on our stage set in the ruins, for an audience of two, and it goes over like a dream. Mr Cantwell laughs several times, something I have never seen before up close. The exhilaration of it pours through me, more warming than a tot of brandy.

"Is there more?" Eileen asks, getting to her feet and

walking towards us. I rush over to my bag and pull out the carefully tied pages. Eileen takes them from me, her eyes skimming them, an occasional smile pulling at her mouth.

"This is funny," she says. "What the narrator says here."

"Freya had a terrific idea about staging the narrator's scenes," Kit says then, and I flush.

"Tell me," Eileen says, quietly passing the pages over to Mr Cantwell to read.

I do, and then, I'm not completely sure how it happens, but the four of us are practising the scene.

"No, no, Mr Cantwell," I break in at one point. "Wait a beat longer and *then* turn back – think how funny it will be for the audience. And, Eileen, you must hang back too."

We only stop when it becomes really too cold to carry on. The sun has slipped precariously low in the sky and the four of us make our way back along the much easier path Eileen and Mr Cantwell arrived by. Kit and I walk side by side. I am still thrilled by what has just happened and I feel – in this golden moment – that everything is perfect.

CHAPTER TWENTY-THREE

"It's gone four already," Mr Cantwell says, glancing at his watch. "We'll come back to the theatre with you and speak to the troops." He sighs. "I don't like just kicking my heels here like this, but it doesn't seem we have a choice."

Over the course of the afternoon I have found I am a lot less intimidated by him. I suppose when you see someone mopping their eyes with laughter then they become a bit less daunting.

"Well, I think it's a charming place to be stuck," Eileen muses.

"How is Mr Pennington's house?" I ask.

"Hubert has been a dear," says Eileen placidly.

"Yes, because he has a great thumping crush on you," Mr Cantwell grumbles. "I half-expected the place to be covered in Eileen Turner pictures."

I flush at that, and Kit flashes me a wicked grin.

"You never can stand it when men prefer me," Eileen says calmly. "Not that we have so many to fight over these days." The two of them exchange a sparkling look that makes me absolutely long to sit them down and drag out all their stories.

At the theatre we find Russ and Alma playing cards onstage while Dan lounges, strumming an old guitar beside them.

"There you are!" Alma jumps to her feet. "We were starting to wonder if we should send out a search party for you."

"We found an abbey up on the cliffs," I explain, peeling off my gloves and walking over. "And we ran into Mr Cantwell and Eileen." I don't mention the rehearsal, or Kit's play. It feels too precious, like the whole afternoon is a gift I can't yet bear to share.

"You're looking very lovely, Freya," Russ says, glancing up.

"I don't believe it," I say. "Unless you have a particular taste for red noses and tangled hair."

"But I do," he says lightly. "You look all fresh and healthy, like a girl from the country. I can practically see you now, milking a cow on a picturesque mountainside."

"I *am* a girl from the country," I say. "I've milked plenty of cows, and there wasn't a single picturesque thing about it."

"Hello, Eileen. How are things staying with Hubert?" Dan asks. "Is he wearying you with his attentions?"

Eileen shakes her head at him. "He's a delightful man and he's done us all a huge service," she says. It seems the grand dame has a bit of a soft spot for the little theatre manager. "I'd love to do something nice for him. He's been such a good egg."

"He is certainly as bald as one," Russ mutters, and Dan makes a snorting sound.

"Well, why don't we say thank you in style?" Nora's voice chirps. She has appeared from the wings, with

Viola in tow. "Viola and I have a plan."

"What plan?" Kit asks.

"As we're stuck here again tonight, we thought perhaps we'd have a party," Nora says.

"A party?!" several voices echo in astonishment.

Nora nods. "While you were all lazing around, I bravely undertook another visit to the pub where Sophie and I had a chat over a mulled cider or two … or three. To cut a long story short, she's been slaving away over a hot stove all afternoon to deliver us a rather spectacular indoor picnic."

"We thought we could have a dinner party on the stage," Viola says. She comes forward. "There's plenty of furniture in the props cupboard, and candles and scenery."

"And costumes!" I exclaim. "Can we make it a costume party? You wouldn't believe the stuff in their wardrobe department."

"Excellent," Nora agrees with a nod. "I will dress you all to perfection; I've been dying to get my hands on some of those dresses."

"There's the most beautiful apricot silk dress that

will look wonderful on you, Viola," I say. She glances at me, her expression startled and slightly suspicious.

"Wonderful," Eileen says serenely. "And we can invite Hubert."

"And Sophie's coming," Nora adds. "Quite a supper party."

I think it's a relief for everyone to have something to plan after sitting idle, and Nora sweeps Mr Cantwell and Eileen off to help them choose their costumes.

"And we must choose something for Hubert," Eileen murmurs as they walk away. "I think he'd make a splendid vicar."

"What are you going to do?" I ask, turning to Kit.

"Revise my first scene," he says. "It's not every day you get feedback from Rhys Cantwell and Eileen Turner."

"It was really good, Kit, truly."

"Do you think *they* liked it?"

"Yes, I do. How many times have you seen Mr Cantwell laugh like that?" He flushes at my words. "But don't go getting a big head about it. And try and remember us little people when you've made it, won't you?"

"Of course I will, you'll be my leading lady," Kit says.

I feel something twist in my stomach then, an anxious feeling that I don't understand.

For once, Kit doesn't seem to notice my mood, and he wanders off, his brow furrowed, already far away from here, thinking about the changes he wants to make.

I sit and join Russ and Alma's card game, my mind only half on the cards in my hand. I can't stop thinking about Kit's play. It *is* good – and what a relief! How awful it would be to care about someone so much and to have to tell them their work was bad.

Viola appears at my side. "All right, then," she says rather gracelessly. "Come and show me this dress you were talking about."

I scramble to my feet and lead the way towards the wardrobe department. We walk through the theatre in silence and into the backstage area.

When we reach the right door, I knock.

"Wait a minute," calls Nora. "We're still finding

Hubert the perfect clerical robes."

We sit in the corridor outside, our backs pressed up against the wall.

"I want to ask you something," Viola says, breaking the silence between us. She looks at me and lifts her chin. "Is something going on between you and Kit?"

"Nothing!" I say, relieved at being able to clear this up once and for all. "At least – we are good friends, but romantically, there is nothing going on at all."

Viola raises her eyebrows is apparent disbelief. "Honestly," I rush to explain. "The only person I've had any kind of romantic *anything* with is Russ, and that didn't end up going anywhere."

"I think Russ likes you," she says. The unspoken, *though who knows why,* hangs clearly in the air.

"Russ is just contrary," I say. "He sees me as a challenge, I think." I sigh. "Our evening was nice enough, but it wasn't the stuff of dreams. I was hoping for proper romance, like in books."

Viola looks at me curiously. "What do you mean?"

"Well, all the melodrama. Not being able to tear yourself away from one another, and high passions, and tragic pining and not being able to sleep or eat. No one I've met has so much as made me want to miss lunch. Certainly not Kit… most of the time we eat together."

"Hmmm," Viola sniffs. "I've had my fair share of melodrama, and it's not all fun and games."

"With Kit?" I ask.

"I suppose," she sighs. "When I broke it off with him I know that I hurt him, and I feel badly about that. I thought he understood, but…" She trails off then and gives a little sigh of frustration. "I'm not worried about Kit anyway, not really. He and I will get back together eventually. It's just – these small, provincial tours make me wild. I want to get out."

"Get out?" I feel my eyes widen. It never occurred to me that this tour, with all of its excitement and delight, might be something to break free from.

She shoots me a quick, irritable look. "I thought you, at least, weren't going to be shocked by a woman demonstrating a bit of ambition."

"I'm not," I say hastily. "I suppose I've just had quite a painfully small life so far. It seems to me that this production – well, it's something to be proud of. On tour with Rhys Cantwell and Eileen Turner, of all people! And you're doing great work."

"My work is not the problem," she says. "And, yes, Rhys and Eileen add some clout. But the rest are no good. Provincial audiences are easily pleased, and Rhys could drag a decent performance out of a rock, but Russ is middling at best, no matter what he likes to think of himself. Dan too – he's passable but he'd be out of his depth without the rest of us to carry him."

"What about Alma?" I ask anxiously.

Her eyes narrow. "She's all right," she says slowly. "She's got potential, anyway. But that just brings its own set of problems, doesn't it?"

"Does it?"

"Don't be so naive," Viola says coldly. "You can't be if you want to act. If Alma's talented then she's a threat – she and I will end up competing for the same parts. And her looks are a director's dream, all pale and blonde and blue-eyed and saintly. The crowds will love her even before she opens her mouth. We're all competing against each other, and pretending that we're not is dishonest. I may be a lot of things, but dishonest is not one of them."

"But you don't need to compete with Alma," I point out. "No matter how good she is, she's just starting out, whereas you've got experience. The audiences love you. Just look at the write-ups."

She gives a short laugh. "They don't review my performance. They just go on about my looks, like I'm a plant or a parrot," she says. "It's the same with directors and producers. They want me to be the 'exotic' beauty, but never *too* exotic. Did you know," she says, leaning forward, "I met with a producer once, who had a whole story planned for me that could explain my background. He suggested I could say I was born in Australia, rather than India. Said I was fortunate that I could *pass*."

"Pass for what?" I ask, confused.

"White." The word is blade sharp, slicing through the air. "Of course."

The breath catches in my chest and my lips form a silent, "Oh."

"You really haven't seen much of the world, have you?"

I shake my head. We sit in silence for a moment, and then I say hesitantly, "I'm sorry about – well, I'm sorry about all of it. I didn't know, I mean, I hadn't thought..."

"You wouldn't."

There's another pause then and Viola pulls something from her pocket. A piece of paper, severely crumpled, as if it's been folded and screwed up and smoothed out again many times.

"Do you know what this is?" she asks, but she doesn't wait for an answer, because how on earth would I? "It's a telegram from Marco. That producer I was seeing. He's so sorry but he doesn't think I'm right for the part after all. It's going to someone else. Someone well-known and uninspiring who looks an awful lot like your Alma. He feels awful, but the decision's been made. How unoriginal it all is."

She leans back, briefly closing her eyes. When she opens them again they're full of fire.

"I'll get there, though." Her voice is low. "I'll show them all."

Nora sticks her head round the door then, and Viola jumps up and moves forward. I try to organize my scattered wits. I know that Viola is right – growing up in a small Cornish village means I have a very shuttered view of the world. It is one of the reasons that I wanted so badly to get out. I suppose I just hadn't really thought about what I would find once I did.

I think about what Viola said, and about the question that had been tugging at me ever since I had first seen her perform – with her talent, why hadn't I heard of her? Why was she having to work so hard to charm the producers and get the parts she wanted? Was this the answer?

I follow Viola into the room where Nora is showing her some of the beautiful gowns that hang from the rails.

"It was this gown you meant for Viola, wasn't it, Freya?" Nora drapes the dress over her arm. "You do have a good eye."

"Yes," I manage. "That's it."

Viola strokes the silk with elegant fingers. "I don't know if it's my colour."

"Try it on," Nora urges her.

She does. When the dress settles around her it looks as though it has been made exactly for her, as if some unknown dressmaker in the distant past took her measurements, and the dress has sat on the rail for all this time, waiting for Viola to wear it.

"It's … acceptable." Viola tilts her head in the mirror, but her eyes meet mine there and there's nothing she can do to hide the pleasure in them.

"Perfect," Nora murmurs in satisfaction. "Now, Freya, for you," there's a gleam in her eyes, "I have a few suggestions."

CHAPTER TWENTY-FOUR

Our little dormitory has become a dressing room once more. What had begun as Nora's spontaneous dinner party has turned into a real event Alma, Nora, Viola and I have spent an enjoyable few hours getting ready, while the men "set the scene" as Kit mysteriously put it.

Nora has curled my hair and piled it on top of my head, but I've been so busy helping the others I'm still not in my dress yet.

Viola looks predictably beautiful in her golden gown, her hair swept up; the only make-up she wears is the tiniest bit of rouge on her cheekbones and lips. Alma is dressed in pale blue with flowing sleeves. Nora has rapidly altered a man's evening suit so that it clings to her generous curves. The suit is midnight blue, the jacket close-fitting with tails, embroidered in gold thread, and a matching gold waistcoat. She looks sensational.

"My goodness, Nora," I exclaim when I get my first look at the full outfit. "Just think what they were all missing out on not letting the women wear breeches!"

Nora smiles, pleased with herself. "I imagine I'd have scandalized a few regency ladies given half the chance. Here, help me with this button, I don't think it's attached properly."

After helping Nora with more minor alterations, I sit down with Alma to braid the front of her hair back and away from her face, leaving the rest rippling down her back. When I'm finished I step back to admire her.

"You look absolutely wonderful," I say. "Like Guinevere."

"I *feel* wonderful," she says. "If only we could always dress this way. It makes me feel so regal."

"You won't be saying that when you are trying

to keep your sleeves from trailing in the soup," I point out.

Somewhere down the hall a bell clangs loudly.

"That's it," Nora exclaims. "The signal! The boys are ready."

"Oh!" I exclaim. "And I'm not even dressed yet. You go, and I'll be right behind you."

"All right, all right," Nora laughs, following after Viola and Alma. "But don't be long, you don't want to miss the fun!"

Finally, I am alone in the dressing room, and I press my hand to my stomach, taking a deep breath. Kit wasn't kidding all those weeks ago when he said that being on tour meant you didn't get a minute to yourself. Just for a moment I relish the quiet, the stillness, the fact that I am completely alone. I feel myself settle. As my breathing slows down, my heartbeat slows too.

I move over to the rail where Nora has hung the dress we chose for me to wear. At first glance it is quite simple, a pale lavender charmeuse over an ivory satin slip, edged in soft blue velvet, but when the dress moves, the purple gleams and sparkles, like a piece of polished amethyst.

The dress itself looks like something from a hundred years ago. Sleeves that fall in tiers to the elbow, a bodice rather dashingly low cut over the bust, cinching in at the waist before falling in a full skirt to the floor. It has very fine silver embroidery in a vine-like pattern around the bodice, trailing down the sides and circling the bottom of the dress. Nora told me I would have to wear the proper underwear with it to make it fit, and so I agreed to a stiff petticoat and a corset, though I would not let her lace me up too tight.

"There's no point in wearing it if I can't eat in it," I said firmly.

I slip off my robe and step into the dress. The dress is heavy, and there is, I realize, a big difference between buttoning someone else into a costume and buttoning it yourself. There's a reason all those Victorian ladies had maids to help with their dressing and undressing.

I manage to get most of the buttons done up and I'm twisting myself into strange shapes in front of the mirror trying to do the rest when there's a knock at the door. I swing around to find Kit framed there, leaning with one shoulder against the door frame and an amused look on his face.

"Nora thought you might need a hand," he says. "But you look like you're managing just fine."

"Don't just stand there!" I huff, half-laughing in frustration. "Come and help me!"

He peels himself away from the door and steps into the room.

"Oh!" I exclaim. "You look so handsome!"

I don't think about the words before they come out of my mouth – it is as instinctive as telling Alma she looked beautiful – but I find that I am flushing a deep and unbecoming red. Thanks to the mirror in front of me I get to actually *see* my blush spread, which is an experience that I do not recommend. Far better to remain in ignorance.

Kit, to his credit, ignores me and moves forward to help me with my dress. I don't know why I am so flustered all of a sudden. It was just a shock, I suppose, to suddenly see Kit in evening wear. He's dressed in a close-fitting black tailcoat, with a matching waistcoat over a crisp white shirt with a white bow tie, and a pair of black trousers. His shoulders look broader in a jacket. His hair is lightly oiled and smoothed back away from his face, apart from a couple of unruly locks that fall over his brow. The oil has turned his hair a little darker, a touch more auburn. I've never noticed before that his face is such a nice shape, with such good cheekbones.

"Who taught you to tie your bow tie like that?" I ask, looking at him in the mirror.

"My sister," Kit says, coming to stand close behind me. "Now, what seems to be the problem?"

"It's just those last few buttons," I say, twisting slightly. "I think you would have had to be a contortionist to get yourselves in and out of these things alone. I suppose they had maids."

He does up the few remaining buttons on my dress. I have got my breathing back under control, but there is a moment when I feel his hands brush, ever so lightly, over the skin between my shoulder blades, and something peculiar happens to my knees.

"Are you all right?" he asks. His voice is low.

"I think I must be hungry," I frown. "It's been hours

since those jam sandwiches." My stomach growls, and I laugh. "You see?"

Kit does up the final button and steps back. "There you go," he says. "Let's go and find sustenance. Although ... take a look at yourself first." Our eyes meet in the mirror and his crease up at the edges in a faint smile. "You look very lovely."

I shake the lavender skirts out and tilt my head to the side. "I feel like I'm Cinderella, about to be swept off to the ball." I turn to admire the dress from the side. "I'll start making deep curtsies to everyone again, just like I did when I first started, and Mr Cantwell will sack me!"

Kit laughs. "I'm sure you can rein in the curtsies if you try."

"Perhaps, but I should at least have a fan that I can flutter coquettishly, and slap across people's wrist's while saying 'La!'"

"That is very specific."

"All right," I say, giving my reflection one more quick examination. "I'm ready, let's go."

Kit puts his hand to his chest, and executes a smart little bow, before holding out his elbow to me.

I slip my hand into the crook of his arm. The fine black material of his topcoat is smooth. "Don't bow, or I will start curtseying."

"Sorry," he says. "I think it's the dress."

We make our way down the corridor, and my beautiful dress rustles, whispering across the wooden floorboards like a secret.

"Are you ready?" Kit asks, a gleam in his eye, as we head towards the wings.

I glance at him. "Of course I am."

But I'm not at all. When we erupt on to the stage I come to a clattering halt, my gasp audible even above the record player that is sending slow, sweet music curling through the air.

As if we are in a play, the company stops what it was doing and swings around to welcome us, and there is a pause, a silence, that lasts only a moment in which I take in the incredible scene before me.

The stage is dressed like an enchanted forest in the snow. Beautiful silk screens, painted with slender, silver-trunked trees, stretch out around us. Impossibly, magically, there is snow on the ground coating the stage and building up into little piles at the side. A low, rosy glow is cast over the scene.

Running the length of the stage is a long banquet table, surrounded by seats with deep red velvet cushions. The table groans under the weight of pies and cakes and platters of fruit. There is cold roast chicken and a beautiful shell pink salmon. Nestled between the dishes are enormous, heavy candelabras, the lit candles in them shining like tiny stars. There are jars with candles in them dotted around the darkened auditorium, giving the feeling that we are standing amid the constellations.

"It's impossible," I whisper, and I feel the vibration of Kit's laugh under my hand. "How did you all do this? The *snow*?"

"Magic," he replies.

"No, but really," I ask. "How is this possible?"

"Tomorrow I will tell you the prosaic ways in which we create snow for the stage," he says. "Tonight, let's just agree ... magic."

"All right," I say. "Magic."

Sophie, in a gorgeous gold dress that matches Nora's waistcoat, fusses over the table, and Mr Pennington

– who really does make a very convincing vicar – is gazing adoringly at Eileen Turner, who is resplendent in a gown of midnight blue velvet, with a collar of sparkling diamonds at her neck. Ordinarily, I'd say the diamonds were simply glass costume jewellery, but tonight who knows? I wouldn't be at all surprised to find Eileen dripping with the Crown Jewels themselves.

Dan and Russ are both in full military regalia, and I'm reminded of the first time I met Russ. He looks just as dashing now. Next to them, Kit's outfit is stark in its simplicity, but somehow all the more elegant for it.

"Thank goodness you're here!" Nora calls over. "Now we can eat!"

There's a cheer at that, and we drop eagerly into our seats, talking all over each other and admiring one another's costumes, passing dishes around in an intricate dance as we fill our plates.

Mr Cantwell gets to his feet. He is wearing what looks like an Admiral Nelson costume, and it suits him extremely well. I particularly like the gold tassels on his shoulders, and his commitment to wearing the bicorne hat – it is the kind of whimsical touch that I would not have expected from him, and yet he looks in his element.

"A toast," he says, tugging at the cork on a bottle of elderflower wine. We all cheer when it pops. "To Runleigh and the warm hospitality we've enjoyed here. I have never found myself in a situation quite like this one, and yet I find that I would not change it for the world. Nor could I ask to be stranded with a more amenable group."

"To Runleigh!" we all chorus.

"To Hubert!" Eileen cries, causing the theatre manager to turn very pink.

"And to Sophie!" Nora joins in, turning to the woman beside her. "For keeping us poor souls fed."

"Hear, hear!" we cry as one.

CHAPTER TWENTY-FIVE

We eat and eat until we can eat no more. Or at least I do.

"Why did I ever agree to a corset?" I groan. "I should have worn something that fits me like a tent, then I could eat some more of that gooseberry tart."

"Perhaps just a little piece of the cheese?" Kit suggests. "On a cracker?"

I press my hand against my stomach, and wiggle experimentally. "I think the strings will hold up to another cracker and a sliver, just a *sliver* of cheese," I agree. "And maybe some of that quince paste too."

Kit prepares the cracker and hands it to me and I eye it appreciatively.

Russ shakes his head at me across the table. "I wish you'd look at me the way you look at that cracker," he says, looping his arm lightly around the top of his chair.

"I doubt I'll ever look at *anyone* that way," I reply. "I'm fairly sure no man can compare to a perfect sharp cheddar."

"How utterly depressing," Russ says.

"You're slipping, Russ," Viola says, grinning from further down the table. "Beaten out by a piece of cheese!"

Russ laughs but I think I see a flicker of irritation in his eyes. He reaches a hand across the table and takes mine in his own, running his thumb gently over my fingers. "Perhaps you'll give me another chance to change your mind," he murmurs.

I pull my hand away, feeling confused. It seems the more I put Russ off, the more interesting I become to him. I need to put a stop to it, but I'm not sure how.

I turn to Sophie.

"It was kind of you to supply this incredible dinner," I say. "My very wholehearted compliments to the chef."

Sophie chuckles. "This chef accepts them, and you're very welcome. I have to say it's not every day I get invited to a shindig like this." She glances at Nora from under her lashes, and Nora dimples in response. "And in such excellent company as well."

"But you must have theatre companies coming through all the time," I say. "It's a beautiful little theatre."

Sophie shakes her head. "Not really," she says. "The theatre *is* beautiful, but we're very out of the way. Hubert tries to keep it going – he loves the theatre, Hubert does – but earlier in the year he was talking about shutting it up. That's why it was such a relief when your Mr Cantwell added us to his tour."

"It's a shame we never got to put on the play. It's supposed to be our last night here tomorrow," I sigh.

Nora shakes her head. "Strange, isn't it? We'll just have to hope the snow thaws soon. I can only imagine how wild with anxiety Miss Meriden must be."

"Wild? Miss Meriden?" I ask disbelievingly.

"Underneath." Nora smiles into her glass.

"Underneath a very calm and capable surface, she'll be going wild with anxiety."

"Who fancies some dancing?" Russ's voice calls my attention back to him, and the others murmur in agreement. Someone puts on a different record. I stand to find Russ bowing over me. "Might I have this dance?" he asks, holding out his hand.

"Of course," I say lightly.

The left-hand side of the stage becomes our dance floor then, and it feels only right to be twirling around in the arms of a handsome man while wearing this beautiful dress. While Russ spins me around and around the stage, my skirts swirl around me, a vibrant Catherine wheel of purple and silver sparks.

We all dance: me with Russ, Kit with Alma, Viola with Dan who is saying something outrageous that makes her laugh. Eileen dances with Hubert who has the blissful expression of a man whose dream has become reality, and Nora holds Sophie close as the two of them sway gently around the dance floor. Only Rhys Cantwell sits at the long table, watching the rest of us with the look of an indulgent parent.

When the song finishes, I head over to Mr Cantwell and ask if he would like to dance.

"How very gallant of you," he says, "to take pity on a wallflower."

"Not at all," I admit. "Gallant would be volunteering to sit out the dance, but I'm selfish and I want to keep on twirling."

"Then I shall be happy to oblige," he says with a bow. He freezes. "That was not," he says sharply, "an invitation to curtsey."

"No, sir."

He dances carefully, politely, keeping a rigid distance between us. We don't talk very much, but I think he is enjoying himself.

I watch Kit who is now dancing with Viola. She reaches up and whispers something in his ear and I see his answering smile.

I dance with Dan, with Russ again – twice – and even with Hubert, who is surprisingly light in his feet, but it is a long time before I dance with Kit. I find that I am too shy to ask him. I look over at him often – I don't exactly know why. Perhaps it is still the shock of seeing him all dressed up. Kit usually wears scruffy trousers and a worn jumper, and seeing him turned out like this, all smooth and polished – it's as if it's turned him into someone else, someone I don't know.

By the time he does ask me to dance I am in a state of anxiety. I try to blame my breathlessness on the vigorous foxtrot I've just been executing with Hubert, but when Kit takes me into his arms I can feel myself trembling. We've danced together before, but this feels different.

I think he must feel it too, because his face is serious, the usual laughter gone from his eyes. I experience a brief instant of panic that somehow my friend has gone. I've never had a best friend before, but since that day on the train, Kit has stepped admirably into the role. He has become the person I want to share my good news with, the person I want to talk to all the time, the person who knows me best, and who makes me laugh. I feel greedy for his time and his attention. I force myself to relax. I'm just being silly. Everything feels unreal tonight, as though we've fallen right down the rabbit hole.

As we dance through the dusting of snow, his arm wrapped around my waist – none of the polite distance between us, just fine layers of purple silk and black wool – I rack my brain to think of something to say. I am finding it hard to concentrate on anything except the feel of his hand spread across the small of my back.

Finally, we come to a stop, having danced in total – and certainly uncharacteristic – silence. I step back from him, fanning my face with my hand.

"I'm so warm," I say, in a choked little voice that I am not proud of. "I think I need to stop and have a drink."

"Let me get one for you," Kit offers.

"No!" I exclaim, too sharply. "You should dance with someone else," I manage more calmly.

I hurry off the dance floor, just as Viola appears again to claim Kit's hand.

I make my way over to a seat, and press my hands against my cheeks, trying to cool them down.

"Let me pour you a glass of wine." Russ appears at my elbow. "This elderflower stuff is not bad at all."

"Thank you." I accept the glass from him. "I think I have danced my feet off."

"Perhaps we should move on to the next part of the evening?"

"And what is that?" I ask warily.

That Cheshire Cat grin appears. "The games, of course."

"What sort of games?"

Russ makes his way over to the record player, bringing the music to a clattering halt.

"What did you do that for?" Nora asks grumpily. She and Sophie were dancing again, and never mind the polite distances, you'd have been hard pressed to slip a sheet of paper between the two of them.

"It is time for the next portion of this evening's entertainment," Russ announces, like he's the ringmaster of this particular circus. "Games! And the first game will be ... sardines!" If he had a moustache, I think he'd be twirling it.

"Sardines?" Alma frowns. "What's that?"

"It's like hide-and-seek in reverse," I explain. "One person hides and the rest of us have to look for them. When you find the person hiding then you have to get in the hiding place with them."

"Like sardines in a tin," Nora adds. "The last person to find the hiding place loses."

"Plenty of secluded, darkened corners in an old place like this," Dan says, with a twinkle.

"Oh, yes, let's play," Alma says. "I've had enough dancing."

Even Viola agrees. Her cheeks are flushed and her eyes sparkling.

"I think it's time for the elderly folk to head home," Eileen demurs. There is a chorus of disagreement and she shakes her head. "It's been a wonderful evening, but it's well past midnight already, and the three of us are long overdue for turning back into pumpkins. You youngsters enjoy your game."

We bid Mr Cantwell, Eileen and an exuberant Hubert goodnight and it is decided that Kit will hide first. The rest of us count to a hundred before setting off in pursuit.

Once outside the halo of light surrounding the stage the rest of the theatre is shrouded in a thick, velvet darkness. It takes a moment for my eyes to adjust.

"I think that's the last we'll see of those two," Russ murmurs in my ear, as Nora and Sophie disappear down one of the corridors, the faint sound of laughter echoing behind them.

"Perhaps they're looking for Kit," I say. "He could be down that way."

"Perhaps," says Russ. "Why don't we look in here?" He leans past me and finds a door handle, twisting it open with a click.

CHAPTER TWENTY-SIX

"Which room is this?" I ask, disorientated, as we step inside.

"I think it might be Hubert's office," Russ says, swearing as he walks into the corner of the desk.

"Kit?" I whisper. "Are you in here?" There's no answer. I turn to Russ. "He's not here. Let's go."

"In a moment," Russ says, and then he pulls me into his arms, pressing his mouth against mine.

I make a muffled noise of protest which he ignores. I bring my hands up to push at his chest, but his arms only tighten, and so I bring my foot down on his, twisting the heel sharply.

He gives an exclamation of pain and stumbles backwards. "What did you do that for?"

I wipe the back of my hand across my mouth. "What do you think? You can't just go around jumping on girls in darkened rooms."

"I thought you wanted me to." His voice is sulky, like a child who has been denied a toy.

"I don't think I did anything to give you that impression," I say. "In fact, I *know* I didn't."

We stand there in the dark for a moment, and I can feel his animosity coming towards me in waves. "You seemed to want to be kissed well enough the last time," he says.

"Yes, well, I changed my mind," I snap. I feel curiously shaken and a bit sick. "You don't even like me, Russ, not really. This is just a silly game."

In the shadows I see his expression soften. He takes a step forward, "Darling, if that's what's worrying you..."

"It's not." The words stop him in his tracks. "I don't feel that way about you either."

"I see." His voice is cold now. "So you're just a tease, then?"

The queasy feeling in my stomach intensifies. "I don't know what you mean."

"Yes, you do." His voice is hard and scornful, and I don't recognize it at all. "I know you were just playing hard to get. You've been flirting with me for weeks, leading me on. You want to be careful about getting a reputation like that in this industry. People talk. Men don't like women who string them along. Just ask Viola."

"Russ." I struggle to keep my voice even. I take another step back to put more space between us. "I-I'm sorry if you got the wrong impression." I swallow, hating the fact that I'm apologizing to him. The man I thought was my friend has become something else entirely, here in this cold, dark room. I'm not at all sure what is going to happen next, and it's that uncertainty that scares me. "I didn't mean to upset you," I finish weakly.

There's a moment of silence, one that stretches out between us. Then, with a muffled expression of disgust, Russ turns on his heel and leaves the room. I sag against the desk, surprised to find myself trembling.

Nothing happened, I tell myself sternly. *Stop being so silly. Nothing happened, just a few mean words.*

Finally, I leave the room. The darkness has transformed the snug little theatre into something much more sinister, and I jump as the quiet is broken by the scattered sound of laughter in the distance. Russ and I had only been in the office for a couple of minutes. The game is still going on, and suddenly, I really do want to find Kit.

I stumble down the passageway, trying to get my bearings. I try a couple of the rooms off to one side, but neither of them open. Eventually I come to one that does, and I know exactly where I am. The costume cupboard is blessedly familiar, even in the dark, with only the pale silver light from the moon filtering through the high windows.

"Kit?" I whisper, moving through the clothes rails. "Are you in here?"

There's no answer, but suddenly a hand closes around my wrist, and I squeak in alarm.

"Shhhh!" Kit laughs. "You're the first one to find me. Come back here and hide."

I manage my own shaky laugh as I push the clothes aside and take Kit's hand as he helps me through to the gap between the rail and the wall. There's just enough space to sit down, and with the clothes pulled back in front of us, we're very nearly invisible.

"A good hiding place," I say quietly. "Very cosy."

"I thought so." Kit turns to look at me, his face half in shadow. "Is something wrong?" he asks sharply.

"Yes," I say, rubbing my arms. "Actually, no. Not really. I had a bit of a run-in with Russ. He doesn't take rejection very well."

There is a silence and I feel Kit stiffen. "Did he hurt you?

"No! I feel silly making a fuss about it. He just – said some things that weren't very nice." I take a deep breath. "I don't know why it bothered me so much. He'd been drinking, and—"

"I could wring his neck," Kit mutters. "There's no need for you to make excuses for him. If he made you feel uncomfortable or frightened then he was in the wrong."

"He – he said I should be careful about getting a

reputation, that it could hurt my chances," I manage, my voice small. "I suppose I am quite inexperienced."

"You're clever, and you're talented and beautiful," Kit says. "You don't need to listen to anything Russell Whitmore has to say on the matter. He's nothing but a pretty face, and deep down he knows it."

Kit thinks I'm clever and talented and beautiful. Or maybe he is just trying to cheer me up. Either way, I feel better. "All the same," I say firmly, "I think I might be done with romance."

Kit snorts. "That's because you've been romancing entirely the wrong person."

"Do you think so?"

"Yes, I do."

"You sound very sure."

"I am, in fact, absolutely certain."

We sit quietly then, side by side in the dark, surrounded by silk and tulle and taffeta.

"Do you think the others will ever find us?" I ask. "Perhaps I'm just too good at hiding."

"Well, *I* found you."

"That's true."

I drop my head on to his shoulder and he rests his cheek against the top of my head. I like it here, I think. I would like to stay in this dark little corner for ever. *Clever and talented and beautiful.* Those words settle around me like sparks of light – warm and comforting.

"I think you're clever and talented and beautiful too," I say dreamily. I feel him smile against my hair.

"That's nice," he says.

I pull away from him then and turn so that I can look him in the eye. Our faces are close together, almost nose to nose. In the smudged, silver moonlight Kit's eyes look almost pewter, the irises wide and dark. I've never been this close to him before. I could count the golden freckles scattered across his nose, sketch constellations in them. My heart is thumping, and when Kit lifts a gentle hand to push a strand of hair away from my face, I almost jump out of my skin.

"Freya," he murmurs, my name holding a question in it.

"Yes," I whisper, and I'm unsure if I'm asking a question myself, or answering one.

"Here you are." The acid voice of Viola makes us spring apart. The clothes are pushed unceremoniously to one side. "I do hope I'm not interrupting anything."

Part Four

Durham
December, 1931

CHAPTER TWENTY-SEVEN

Two days later we arrive in Durham.

We never did get to perform at the little theatre in Runleigh, and we miss our first night in Durham too, before the snow thaws enough to let us leave. There is still snow on the ground as we reach the city, our penultimate stop on the tour, but it is only a light, picturesque dusting.

Durham is a lovely place, dressed for Christmas, with lights strung up in the winding cobbled streets and shop windows full of plum cakes and piles of beautifully wrapped gifts.

Relations between the group have become strained. The morning after the party, Russ sought me out, and mumbled something about having had too much to drink, and worrying he'd not been "quite the thing". In the interests of the production and an easy life I told him that it was fine, that we were fine. But I have avoided him since.

Russ and Kit are also avoiding each other, and I get the sense that this is because Kit had some strong words to say about what happened. Then I too am avoiding Kit because I find the sight of him extremely confusing. Did we really almost kiss in the costume cupboard? Or did I imagine it? Viola seems to be avoiding me and spending as much time with Kit as possible. Dan appears bemused, while I think Alma has it all worked out, and Eileen and Mr Cantwell are either oblivious or hoping to ignore us all.

Needless to say, this made sharing the small, cramped dressing rooms rather testing. Nora was, at first, quietly amused, but her nerves – like everyone else's – have begun to fray, and at one point she asked quite forcefully if we could all "stop leaping in and out of rooms away from each other like bloody jack-in-the-boxes".

I wouldn't have thought it possible, but it is a relief to finally leave the tiny chocolate box of a theatre and head into new surroundings. When we pull into our accommodation in Durham and Miss Meriden steps out of the door, her neat little tweed suit completely smooth, every strand of her hair in place, a clipboard in her hand from which she starts issuing instructions, I feel that I could throw myself into her arms and weep.

It seems that Mr Cantwell feels the same, because he goes so far as to clap Miss Meriden's shoulders and press a loud kiss on each of her cheeks. "Thank god you're here, Meriden," he booms when she emerges from his embrace. "It's been one bloody disaster after another with you gone." As though Miss Meriden could have prevented the blizzard that kept us all stranded, or erected a five-star hotel with her bare hands.

"Well, you're here now," Miss Meriden says soothingly. "And I have rooms booked for you and Eileen down the road at the Grand."

"Bliss." Eileen briefly closes her eyes. "Not that

Hubert wasn't an absolute angel putting us up, but it was rather cramped for the three of us and I'm longing to spend several hours in a hot bath."

Our new digs on the other hand are a cold and draughty boarding house. A long corridor full of small, cell-like rooms containing two narrow beds each. After the peculiar magic of the theatre the rooms seem even meaner, but the relative privacy is a relief. Thank goodness for Alma, who at least is behaving normally. In this dingy room I look forward to the best night's sleep I've had in three days.

Once we've unpacked our meagre belongings it's straight over to the theatre for rehearsal. It feels good to sink back into the familiar routine, everyone playing the parts they are meant to play – both onstage and off. Nora and I are busy unpacking and steaming and mending and helping with the quick changes between scenes. I fly from place to place, my fingers always busy, demands ringing in my ears.

The performance that night is, I think, the best one yet. It's as if the energy has been building up in all of us for days, waiting for an outlet. The play runs thirty minutes longer because of the breaks we take for laughter and applause. The audience are readily swept up into the giddiness of the performance, hooting and cheering and falling about in their seats.

Out of everyone, Viola stands out as truly extraordinary. From the wings I watch with admiration as she blazes across the stage, holding the audience in the palm of her hand. She has never looked better, never performed better, and when she takes her bows, she glitters with the knowledge of it. Even Alma – good as she is – is a pale shadow in comparison.

I watch her carefully, but I can't put my finger on what it is that makes Viola so good. She works hard, true, harder than any other member of the company when it comes to rehearsals. I've never seen her shirk her responsibilities, whatever Russ has said in the past. I *have* seen her ask to do something over, and over until it was right. But it's more than that. It's as though no one else could play the part once she has made it hers.

It takes Nora and I ages to pack away the costumes and props, and we are the last ones to leave the theatre.

"I'm exhausted," I groan, when we finally leave the

building. "I'm going back to my room. I just want to curl up with my book and fall asleep."

"Oh, no, you're not." Nora takes my arm. "That was the best performance of the whole run, and you can't avoid everyone for ever."

"I'm not avoiding *everyone*," I mutter. "Just a few people."

I allow her to tug me towards the pub where the sounds of celebration are spilling out into the street every time someone opens the swing door. I am used to pubs like this now – the kind of bar with a late-night license that doesn't mind a group of noisy thespians and their various hangers-on. Hot and friendly, with worn leather bar stools, and floors slightly sticky with spilled beer. We make our way inside, and there are the calls of welcome, the jokes, the drinks thrust sloppily into our hands that I have missed these last few days.

It's nice to have the whole huge, noisy family back together again. Lindsey catches me by the arm and tugs me towards her group, begging for news of our snowbound escapades.

"I heard you had a masked ball!" she says. "Tell us everything!"

"Not quite," I laugh. "But we did manage a dinner party."

A voice I recognize, raised above the hubbub of voices, catches my attention. Lindsey rolls her eyes. "Oh Lord," she says under her breath. "Here we go again."

"Who is it?" I say.

"Viola," she says. "Whenever there's a scene, you can bet she's at the centre of it. I suppose we were due one – she's been surprisingly well-behaved this whole tour."

I crane my head to see, and sure enough, there is Viola. It is as though a spotlight is on her, even in this crowded pub. She stands, poised and elegant, and I realize with a sinking heart that she's facing Kit. A throng of people are not so subtly watching the drama unfold.

"What's going on?" I whisper to Nora.

Nora rolls her eyes. "Viola's about to enact a Cheltenham tragedy again. The way she was onstage, so keyed up – I knew she was spoiling for a fight tonight."

"Oh, no." Alma appears at my elbow, distress in her face. "I was afraid of this. Remember what she said? That she'd have Kit back by the end of the tour. Well, here we are."

"I love you, Kit." Viola's voice is carrying. The rest of the room falls quiet, but Viola doesn't seem to notice. She's blazing up at Kit. I half-expect to see electric sparks to flash across her skin. She laughs, a slightly giddy laugh. "I know you feel the same. I made a mistake, a bad one, but I can fix it. You know I'm sorry. We need to stop wasting all this time and be together."

"Vi…" I've never seen Kit look so pale. "Please don't do this here." He takes a step closer to her. "We've talked about this. I've said all I had to say."

She holds up an imperious hand. "You're saying that you don't love me, then?" Her tone is derisive, disbelief writ large in every word. It is, I realize, a tremendous performance, for all that the emotion in her voice is real. "But I know you do. I know it!"

Kit's face is bleak. He scrubs a hand across his eyes in a tired gesture. "Viola," he tries again in a quiet voice.

"Let's go and talk about this somewhere else. I don't want to…"

"Just a yes or a no, Kit." Viola looks at him with challenge in her eyes. The consummate performer, playing to the crowd. And it's working. You could hear a pin drop in the room. She's hypnotic.

Kit's shoulders rise and fall as he takes a deep breath. "No, Viola," he says gently. "I don't. I'm sorry."

For a second she stands there, stunned. "I know I hurt you," she says in a small voice. "But I apologized. And I need you. You know how much I need you."

Kit shakes his head. "You don't need me, Vi. But I'm your friend, you know I'll always be here for you—"

She turns away, cutting him short, and begins pushing her way through the crowd of people. She comes face to face with me for a moment and her face contorts with rage. "You!" she hisses. Her trembling finger points at me accusingly. "This is all your fault!"

And with that she leaves, slamming out of the door and into the night. The stunned silence holds for another second and then it shatters like a glass against a wall. Everyone is talking. Except for Kit. In the middle of the room, pale and alone, Kit stares towards the door, a look of such devastation on his face that I feel as if my own heart is breaking.

CHAPTER TWENTY-EIGHT

The next day, Viola and Kit are all anyone wants to talk about. It appears no one has seen either of them since their showdown at the pub. Kit left straight after Viola, and speculation was rife as to whether he'd gone to find her or not.

Of course, the peaceful night's sleep I had been looking forward to did not materialize. All night, whenever I closed my eyes, I saw Kit's face as it had looked when Viola left; so bleak, so helpless. I never thought to see easy-going Kit look that way, and it made something in my stomach clench.

I want to make sure he's all right, but I'm not even sure where to find him. His bed, apparently, has been slept in, but he was gone before anyone was up. Viola's door remains locked.

The day limps by, as we prepare for the evening's performance. We have only tonight in Durham and then two nights in Newcastle before the tour is over. It has gone so quickly, and yet when I think about my life before the tour it seems like the far-distant past – as though that life belonged to a completely different person.

When I set out with the company, six weeks had seemed an awfully long time. But now the questions are creeping in. What will I do afterwards? Will Nora keep me on for the next production? Will my family let me stay? My salary was so meagre that most of it has been spent, a handful of coins at a time, on our evenings out. I have no means to support myself in London – although I suppose Lou might put me up.

That thought is a bad taste in my mouth. When I first arrived in London, I thought nothing of staying with Lou. But things are different now. I have got used to my independence. Our digs may often be horrendous, but I work hard for them and I'm proud of that. I don't answer to anyone. It's intoxicating and difficult to think of going back.

And, more than any of that, I have found a place where – *finally* – I fit. It is even harder to imagine leaving that behind.

I am not the only one in an introspective mood today. Everyone is a little quiet, a bit snappish.

I catch Dan and Russ squabbling over a linen shirt.

"It's mine!" Dan says.

"No!" Russ exclaims, "Yours is over the chair, there."

"That's *yours*."

"Boys," I break in, "you're acting like children. Give me the shirt."

Sulkily, Russ hands it over, and I look closely at it, the telltale embroidery on the cuff. "It's Dan's," I say.

Dan makes a triumphant if slightly rude gesture at Russ, who glowers at me. "Of course you'd take his side."

"It's not a side, it's a shirt," I snap, flushing at this disjointed sentence.

"It always happens at the end of the tour," Nora says to me later. "Real life starts to impinge once more."

"That's just it." I frown down at the dress I'm mending. "I don't know what my real life is at all. What am I going back to?"

We're interrupted then by Miss Meriden, who comes flying into the room, as if the hounds of hell are on her heels, or – at least – at a most un-Miss Meriden like trot.

"Freya!" she exclaims. "There you are! Thank goodness. Viola is ill. She can't perform tonight."

I stare at her. "Viola is … ill?" I say slowly. My first thought is of her fight with Kit. Perhaps she can't face him. I get to my feet. "Has someone checked on her?"

Miss Meriden shakes her head. "She's refusing to open her bedroom door – says she is too ill to perform. So," she finishes, "we must get you ready."

"Get me ready?" I have the feeling that my brain is swimming very hard against an angry current. My knees start to shake.

"For god's sake, Freya," Nora says firmly. "Snap

out of it! You're the understudy. You'll have to perform tonight."

"Yes," I say, getting to my feet on such unsteady legs that I stagger slightly. "I need to get ready. To perform."

"Are you sure you can?" Miss Meriden looks at me uncertainly, no doubt worried about my ability to form complete sentences. "We could cancel the show, I suppose, although it would be an awful shame – it's going so well. And we had to cancel those performances because of the snow…"

Suddenly, I am calm. Uncannily calm. Ice-cold calm. I shake my head. "We don't need to cancel. I can do it," I say. I smile. "Everything is going to be fine."

"Well … good." If anything, Miss Meriden is looking at me with even greater concern than before.

"Let me do a quick costume fitting while she's here," Nora says. "I'll ask Lindsey if she or one of the girls can help out as a dresser tonight."

"All right, and then Mr Cantwell wants her in the theatre manager's office," Miss Meriden says, still eyeing me uneasily.

Nora makes a sound of agreement, and I continue to

smile serenely. I feel nothing. Absolutely nothing. I am a hollowed-out egg.

I am utterly composed as Nora dresses me and undresses me. She chatters away, a rattle of excitement. We'll have to alter Viola's dresses at speed, I am after all a lot rounder than her, and yet I don't feel worried. In fact, I feel nothing. I had thought I would have a lot of feelings about realizing my lifelong dream of acting on a real stage in front of a real audience, but apparently realizing your lifelong dream only makes you feel numb.

Kit appears at the door, his hair sticking out all over the place, catastrophically wild, worry in his eyes.

"Freya," he says. "Are you all right about going on? You will be wonderful, I'm sure."

Curious that this absence of feeling has stretched out to include Kit, I observe. I had been worried about seeing him, there was a lot I wanted to say to him, but, blissfully, none of that matters now.

"I'm fine," I say a little distantly. "I'm absolutely fine to go on, please don't worry."

Kit and Nora exchange a look. Normally that would

make me cross, but my reflection in the mirror does not flinch. It remains pale, stoic, unmoved.

The feeling of calm continues while people drop in and out of the dressing room, firing questions, whirring about in a desperate hive of activity.

"Bloody Viola," Russ grumbles when he comes in to wish me luck. "Typical of her to flake out on us at the last moment. She gets away with murder, that girl."

"She's unwell," Nora says.

"Sure she is," Russ snorts. "Sick of not getting her own way, and sick on her own drama. Still," he says, turning his winning smile on me, "it will be fun to be onstage together, won't it, Freya, my darling?"

I smile and nod. Russ and his behaviour mean nothing to me. I am the eye of the storm.

I suppose this is what it is to be a professional, I think. How nice that I have so instantly become one. This must be what happens when you train for something your whole life.

The feeling of complete serenity continues as I walk down the corridor, and it continues as I knock on the door of the manager's office. It continues right up until the point when Rhys Cantwell lifts his head and looks me in the eye.

"Oh god," I moan, promptly falling to my knees and vomiting into the litter bin at my feet.

And now, the numbness passes, and I find I am nothing but feelings. I am a raw nerve, exposed and vulnerable. My teeth are chattering. I crawl into the seat across from Rhys Cantwell and look at him in complete despair.

"I see you are ready for your big break," he says drily.

"I'm s-sorry," I manage. "I c-can't believe I just did that. I was so calm before." I want to be calm again, I want to feel nothing. Now my mind is full of clamouring, intrusive thoughts – thoughts of falling over onstage, falling off the stage, pushing someone *else* off the stage. I shudder.

"It's perfectly normal." Mr Cantwell presses his hands together on top of the desk. His calm voice dispels the mental image of me accidentally sending Eileen Turner flying into the front row. "Many of the actors I know suffer from stage fright, but they're all fine once they're out there."

"That's a relief, I suppose," I say. "And how many of them have actually been sick onstage during a performance?"

"None. Well, not yet anyway."

I manage a shaky laugh.

"Now, you've had plenty of rehearsals, you've seen the play a hundred times. You could do this in your sleep." He is matter-of-fact, not precisely kind, but more reassuring because of it. "Everyone is on your side. The cast and the crew. And the audience. The audience *want* to like you, so just give them what they want."

"But I can't remember my lines," I say. "I can't remember a single line." Panic rises up and I think I might be sick again.

"Dear me, you are smart!" Mr Cantwell says, and it takes me a moment to understand he is feeding me Algernon's line. The one before my first.

"I am always smart!" I say automatically, in a pathetic, reedy little voice. "Am I not, Mr Worthing?"

"You're quite perfect, Miss Fairfax."

"Oh! I hope I am not that. It would leave no room for developments, and I intend to develop in many

337

directions." My voice is firmer now. I take a deep breath.

"You see, it's all there," Mr Cantwell says. "It will come easily when you're onstage. This part is the worst."

"Did *you* ever act, sir?" I ask.

"In the beginning." He smiles. "A long time ago. But it was never really for me. Being onstage isn't what gets my blood pumping. Working with all the different departments, working with the actors, trying to create a single, beautiful whole out of so many moving parts – that's the thing I love." He peers at me over his glasses. "It can be profoundly satisfying, Freya."

"I'm sure it is," I say. I realize I have stopped shaking.

"You are looking much less green," he observes.

"I feel better, thank you."

"Good, then run along."

I get to my feet and make my way back to the door.

"And, Freya," he says. I turn back to face him, my hand resting on the door handle. "Break a leg."

But, please, god, I think desperately, *not literally.*

338

CHAPTER TWENTY-NINE

I'd love to say that it is a triumph. That I walk on to that stage a nobody from a village in Cornwall and walk off a star. I'd love for that to be true. But it isn't.

I was not terrible. I was not even bad. I got my lines right; I stood where I was supposed to stand. The audience laughed. They didn't laugh the way they laughed at Viola the night before, but they laughed nonetheless. Like Mr Cantwell said, they were eager to be pleased, and I could feel that. I could feel their eagerness and their anticipation. This was a treat for them, and one they were determined to enjoy.

Being onstage in a packed theatre was not like I imagined it. The lights were so bright that the audience became a single, shadowy entity. Before I walked on for my first scene I was shaking so much that Eileen, in her full, and very formidable Lady Bracknell costume, had to support me on her arm.

"*Courage, mon brave!*" she whispered in my ear. I don't speak French, but I got the gist.

And then we were there, onstage, and the audience was applauding for Eileen, and I glanced, stricken, at Dan, and he winked, the tiniest of winks, and I pulled my shoulders back and spoke. My voice was loud and steady, though to me it felt as though it was coming from somewhere far away.

I don't remember all of it. It's like a dream, shattered and fragmentary, just out of reach. I remember relaxing as the play wore on, I remember being relieved that things seemed to be going all right, that I hadn't made a horrible mistake, forgotten a line or fallen over. I had seen Viola play the scenes so many times I knew which lines to linger on and which to play for laughs. But I never, not for a single second, felt like Gwendolyn.

What I felt like was Freya, pretending to be Viola, playing Gwendolyn.

I was desperately aware of my self-consciousness. And being aware of one's self-consciousness is not terribly helpful.

By the time the play finishes I feel like a wrung-out dishcloth. I smile and step forward on Dan's arm, hearing the applause, and yet I know it is not really for me. I want to tell the audience it's all right, that I understand, that I did just enough, but I know I didn't give them what they deserved.

When the curtain finally comes down the others crowd around me, hooting and laughing.

"Well done, darling." Dan sweeps me into his arms and swings me around.

"You did it!" Alma's eyes shine. "That was so much fun!"

I think the benefit of low expectations is that by putting in a competent performance you convince people you've done well.

"My love, we must take you for drinks," Dan says. "To celebrate your triumph."

"Yes," I say. "Drinks."

In the dressing room I take off my costume with unsteady hands and a sense of detachment. I know this dress very well, I sewed these lace frills on myself. I trace the pattern with my finger, as I stand in my slip, shivering.

"There you are!" Nora exclaims, bursting in through the door. "You did brilliantly. Why are you standing about in your underwear? You'll catch your death."

She wraps me up in a dressing gown and pushes me down in a chair, wiping the make-up off my face. I watch her do it in the mirror, watch as she wipes the colour and life from my face, the mask I was hiding behind.

"I've seen this before," she says reassuringly. "It's just the adrenaline. You have to be so up when you're onstage that when you come off, you crash. Don't worry, you're just not used to it. You'll feel better in a bit."

"Will I?" I ask, my eyes filling with quick tears.

Nora misunderstands my emotion, smiling fondly.

"Of course you will. You're overwhelmed! It's a big night for you. I'm so pleased for you, darling."

With a bit more pulling and prodding, Nora helps me into my own dress. I've recovered some of my senses now, enough at least to put a brave face on. I can hardly consider all the thoughts running through my head, there are so many, and they are so overwhelming. I daren't start untangling them, pulling them out and examining them now, not while there are people waiting for me. It's too much.

"Come on, come on!" Dan sticks his head around the door. "We're all ready to go. Time to toast to your success!"

He puts his arm around my shoulder, and Nora sweeps along in our wake. We make our way through the corridor, and people keep stopping me to say well done.

"You did it!" Lindsey exclaims, squeezing my arm, as I walk past.

"I did," I say brightly. "I did it." Because that is completely true. I went onstage, I said the lines. I did it.

I just didn't do it well.

And I think if they'd had any expectations of me, then they'd realize that themselves.

We meet up with Alma and Russ and bustle out into the cold. They are merry and laughing and I am too, acting a thousand times better than I did on that stage.

We pour into the pub, and there's a crowd forming around me. It makes me feel hot and claustrophobic. I try to keep my breathing steady. I try to keep the broad smile pinned to my face.

And yet, even while I smile and thank them, there is something happening inside me that I can't articulate.

It feels like I am coming apart.

It was wrong. It was all wrong. It *felt* wrong.

And there's only one person I want to talk to about it.

It seems like an age passes before the crowd starts to disperse, before people drift off to chat in smaller groups. I sip my drink, wincing at the taste of gin. I don't know who ordered this, but it wasn't me.

At the first opportunity I slip unobtrusively out into the cool night air, drinking it in, feeling the cold snap against my heated cheeks. I head back to the boarding house, where I climb the stairs, quick and silent, then I knock on one of the doors.

A low voice answers. "Who is it?"

"It's Freya," I say. "Please, I have to speak to you."

There's a pause, a shuffling sound, and finally the lock clicks and the door swings open.

CHAPTER THIRTY

"You'd better come in," Viola says.

She is wearing a white nightgown and, shivering, she gets straight back into bed, pulling the blankets right up around her like a cocoon. Her hair is matted and her eyes have dark circles underneath them. Perhaps she really is ill.

"Are you ... feeling any better?" I ask hesitantly.

Viola tilts her head as though considering this. "A little," she says finally.

"That's good."

There's an awkward silence. I hover in the doorway, unsure of what to do or say.

"So you went on, did you?" she asks, and she gestures to the foot of the bed, where I perch myself gratefully.

"Yes." I hesitate, and then I look at her, really look at her. Straight in the eyes. "I wasn't very good."

Viola doesn't correct me. She doesn't rush to convince me otherwise. She simply nods, accepting the fact. "No," she says. "I don't suppose you were." The words sound like they should be cruel, but somehow they aren't. She's just being honest.

"You are the only person I can talk to about this." I twist my hands in my lap. "I know you'll understand. I need you to tell me the truth. Do you think I could be an actress?"

Viola doesn't answer. She reaches to her bedside table for a packet of cigarettes, tapping one loose and lighting it. I've never seen her smoke before.

She takes a drag and then slowly exhales. "If you're asking me if I think with work and training you could make a living as an actress on the stage, then the answer is possibly yes. But I don't think that's what you are asking me."

"What am I asking you?"

She looks at me steadily. "You're asking me if you can be great. And the answer to that is no."

I absorb this small hard truth into my body like a blow. "Perhaps I don't need to be great," I say weakly.

"Don't do that," Viola says sharply, pointing at me with her cigarette. "Don't turn away from your own ambition. You and I are the same in some ways and that's one of them. There's no point in doing it if you're not going to be the best. There's no sense in aiming for anything less than perfection. You could do a fine job. You could be..."

"*Competent*," I say, giving voice to an earlier thought.

"Competent, yes." She nods. "But you'd be miserable."

I am miserable now, I think. "It's all I've ever wanted," I say. My voice is small and sounds like it's coming from somewhere far away. There is a static buzzing in my ears, and a physical ache in my chest.

"I know," she says without sympathy. "But that's true for lots of girls. Not all of them can make it."

"But you can?"

She taps her cigarette into an empty water glass. Something flickers across her face. "Yes. I can. I will."

I believe her too. She has the talent, the determination and the strength to become a star, a household name.

"I knew it the second I was onstage," I say finally. "It wasn't like how it used to be, when it was just me and I could fall into it, lose myself in it. It hasn't been like that, even in rehearsals. I was trying so hard, too hard. I was trying to be you, thinking about what you would do. It just felt ... wrong. Up there, on the stage. It's not where I belong."

I think if I had tried to explain this to anyone else, even Kit, that they would misunderstand. They would tell me it was just one performance, that I would improve with time and work. They wouldn't understand the instinctive feeling of wrongness, the undeniable message my brain and my body were sending me, the one that I heard loud and clear. Viola does. I am grateful for her honesty, even if it costs me dearly. I know she understands, and though we are not exactly friends, in that moment I feel incredibly close to her.

Perhaps she is feeling the same, because she leans back against the pillows and closes her eyes for a moment. "I suppose they all think I didn't turn up today because of that stupid fight last night?"

I nod, because we are telling each other the truth. "Yes, I think most people do. *Was* it because of that?" She doesn't answer and I take a deep breath. "I know you think Kit and I..." I flounder here, because the truth is I'm not at all sure about Kit and I.

Viola rolls her eyes. "This is certainly not about Kit and *you*," she says, making me feel about two inches tall. "It's not even about Kit. I guess I thought he was so besotted he'd hang around for me. I couldn't imagine he'd turn me down." She pauses, bewilderment in her face. "But he's right, you know; there's nothing between us any more. Perhaps there was once, but I made the choice to end it. I went after someone more useful to my career." She pauses. "That didn't end well either, but I'd do the same again. I have to. There's nothing more important to me than the work. Nothing."

She leans forward, and her eyes are wide, willing me to understand. I nod. She slumps back on her pillows again, the spark gone, the weary look returning.

"Russ said I was naive about how things worked in this industry," I say. "He said I'd get a reputation, if I wasn't careful. With men, I mean."

She shoots me a thin smile. "Russ was presumably saying that after you turned him down." She takes my silence as assent. "God, he's predictable. Not that he's exactly wrong. Navigating this industry as a woman is an obstacle course. It's a very fine balance. Men can be useful, but they can also want more than you're prepared to give."

I think about this for a moment. Then I say, "So … this evening, were you really feeling ill?"

Viola hesitates and then she seems to make a decision. As if we've already spilled so much, let each other see so much, that there's no need to hold back now.

"Something happens to me," she says carefully. She closes her eyes. "I don't know how to explain it. It used to happen to my grandmother as well. She would say, 'I'm just having a funny spell.' It happened this morning.

I woke up and everything was just … grey. And heavy. And the thought of doing *anything*, I mean anything – brushing my teeth or walking downstairs or going outside – it seemed impossible. Completely exhausting. It's like a huge dark cloud descends on me and I feel … nothing. When it happens, I can't get out of bed. There's nothing I can do, except wait for it to pass."

"That sounds … hard," I finish lamely, kicking myself for coming out with something so paltry.

Viola nods. "It is hard. It's hard to have a reputation as a flake when all I care about is the work. When all I want to do is to be able to do my job." Her hands clench in fists at her sides.

"Have you told anyone?" I ask.

She laughs mirthlessly. "Oh, they'd all love that, wouldn't they? Can you imagine how Dan would react? Or Russ? Your little friend Alma, who would kill for my parts – they'd be spreading it round that I was mad. No one would work with me. Better to be considered a temperamental starlet, that's what they expect me to be – though if I was a man, no doubt it would be a sign of genius." Her voice is hard, bitter. I can understand why.

"Kit knows," she says at last. "You and Kit. The only ones."

"Did the fight with Kit," I hesitate, unsure how to phrase my question, "cause the … um … spell?"

Viola makes a noise of impatience. "Nothing *causes* it," she says. "I wish it did. I wish there was some rhyme or reason to it, but there isn't. If anything the fight with Kit was part of it. Sometimes I know the crash is coming because I feel the high beforehand."

I remember how Viola looked last night, glittering with energy. I think I see. At least some of it.

We sit silently for a moment, just looking at each other. It's strange. We don't like each other very much, but I know what it has cost her to be honest with me, in exchange for my own vulnerability. For once, between us, there is no acting, nothing but our real selves, stripped bare.

"I hope you feel better," I say at last. "I'll leave you to rest."

I get to my feet and move towards the door.

"Goodnight," Viola says.

"Goodnight," I reply. "And thank you."

"For what?"

"For telling me the truth."

I slip back into my own room. Alma is still out and I slump on to my bed in relief. Relief at being alone. I press my hand to my chest, almost too afraid to think about what has happened, to sift through it, because I know how much it will hurt.

Whenever I have imagined my first night onstage – and I have imagined it many, many, many times – it never ended this way. It never ended with this feeling of hopelessness, of being lost and alone. It never ended with me, curled up under the sheets, crying as though I was never going to be able to stop.

Part Five

London, again
December, 1931

CHAPTER THIRTY-ONE

I move through the final days of the tour like a sleepwalker, going through the motions. I sew buttons, fix hems, tidy up. I go to the pub and stand quietly at the bar while people chatter around me.

Viola is back at work the next day as though nothing has happened. A couple of people make some cutting comments about her diva-like behaviour, but she ignores them with her chin held high. It is her armour, I know now, this icy hauteur – it keeps them all at a distance while she focuses on what matters.

She and I do not allude to our conversation. It was a temporary truce, that spilling of our secrets, and now we are back to business as usual.

Only nothing is usual for me. My dream has died, and that is what it feels like: a death. I feel bereft. The thing that I have been chasing all my life, the thing I have always been the most certain about, has gone. And in its place, there is nothing – just emptiness, and a sense of failure that gnaws at me, eating me up inside.

I watch the play being performed three more times. There is a line which Dan delivers that always gets a big laugh.

He says, "Lady Bracknell, I hate to seem inquisitive, but would you kindly inform me who I am?"

And every time Dan says the line, I think, *That's what I want. I want someone to tell me who I am.* I have to pretend to laugh to hide the tears that sting in my eyes.

I feel as though the rug has been swept from under my feet. And where the rug had been is nothing but a gaping hole that I am falling into deeper and deeper. I am Alice in Wonderland all over again, only this time the dream feels like a nightmare.

Kit tries to talk to me, more than once.

"Are you all right, Freya?" he asks outright on one occasion. "I'm worried about you."

"I'm fine," I say, in a tone that is bright and brittle as the ice in the streets.

"Well, I'm here," he says. "If you want to talk. If there's anything…" He trails off. "I'm here." The words are like a promise.

I can tell he is hurt and confused that I have withdrawn from him, though – to be fair – I have withdrawn from everyone. But he is here. He keeps his word. In the evenings he sits beside me in the crowd, not talking, simply being there, occasionally putting food in front of me, or a glass in my hand. I don't even thank him. I say nothing.

And then, just like that, after six busy, beautiful, heartbreaking weeks, it is all over.

When Nora drops me off at Lou's house, we say goodbye, her wool coat pressing against my cheek as she gathers me in for a hug.

"Here," she says, handing me a parcel wrapped in

brown paper. "This is for you."

"Thank you," I say. "For everything."

Nora hugs me again, until I gently pull away. I notice her eyes are suspiciously shiny.

Then I let myself in with the key Lou gave me and I go up to my little yellow bedroom and sleep for eighteen hours.

When I wake, Lou is sitting on the end of the bed.

"Hello, stranger," she says.

I fling myself into her arms and cry like I am a small child and she is my wise, capable big sister. Which, I suppose, is completely accurate.

"I take it something has happened," Lou says, when my tears have reduced themselves to very undignified snuffling sounds.

"My dream is dead!" I intone, flinging myself back against my pillows.

"Oh dear," says Lou mildly. "I'm sure it's not as bad as all that. Why don't you wash your face and get dressed and come downstairs?" Lou's unruffled demeanour reminds me for a second of Midge, and I feel a wave of homesickness that threatens to crush me.

"There's tea and toast and jam tarts, and I've found that dreams have a way of reviving on a full stomach."

"If only it were that simple," I sniff, disconsolate. "Jam tarts, did you say?"

Lou nods.

"Did you make them?" I ask suspiciously.

"Robert did."

"Maybe I'll come down, then."

Soon I'm sitting on the sofa in Lou's living room, wrapped in an enormous striped woolly cardigan that Midge sent for Lou with one sleeve longer than the other. ("Stripes now," Lou says despairingly. "She's extending her repertoire.") A mug of steaming tea is cradled in my hands and I am three jam tarts and two pieces of toast deep into my breakfast.

"Now," Lou says encouragingly. "Tell me everything."

So I do. I leave parts out, of course. I don't tell her about Viola's revelations. I don't mention Russ's unwelcome advance. I don't mention the fact that Kit and I almost kissed or how mixed up I feel about that. But I tell her about the theatre, about my experience of going onstage, and how it all went wrong.

"I know how it feels to be lost," Lou says gently. "I felt like that after Alice got married. I didn't know what I was going to do with myself or who I was. I was so scared I would never find my place or what I wanted to do. But I did."

"That was different," I object. "You didn't know what you wanted to do. I *knew* what I wanted to do. I *knew* who I was. There wasn't a single doubt in my mind, not one, not for as long as I can remember, and now it's all gone. Just like that. It feels like my idea of what I wanted to do was so tangled up with me, that without it I don't know who I am. The entire career I imagined for myself is over."

"Are you sure?" Lou asks. "You can do the work and improve, can't you?"

"It's not that I'm scared of the work," I say, leaning forward earnestly. "If I thought work would fix it then nothing would stop me, I'd work myself down to nothing."

"That would rather defeat the object."

"You know what I mean. I would do anything to get better. But up there onstage – I knew, then, that it was

362

all wrong. It wasn't like when I would put on things at home. It wasn't like when I did that silly audition for Mr Cantwell. I couldn't lose myself in it. There was no ... *joy*."

Lou sips her tea, thinking that over. "And you think an actress needs to feel joy in performing?"

"Of course she does. If there's no joy in it, it's not real – for you, for the audience."

"You seem to have a good understanding of it," Lou says. "You clearly learned a lot on this tour."

"Yes. I suppose I did. About a lot of things." I lean back and bite into another jam tart. "There's a lot of world out there, it turns out. Outside of Penlyn."

"Yes, I know." Lou smiles. "And somewhere in that big, wide world, is a future for you. One that fits, one that *does* bring you joy."

I shake my head gloomily. "I find that hard to imagine. Acting was all I wanted to do. There is nothing else for me."

"And I find *that* hard to imagine. Imagination has always been your greatest gift. Don't give up on it now. You are bigger than this dream, Freya. You are still you,

with or without the acting. And you are wonderful –
clever, strong and brave. You made the last six weeks
happen. You did. No one else. You took your destiny in
your own hands and you built something. You can do
that again."

I try to take in what Lou is saying, I try to share
some small part of her confidence. And yet, where she
describes a future wide and open, all I see is a blank
space.

CHAPTER THIRTY-TWO

Days pass and I do very little except mope around Lou's house and play sad songs on the record player. I sit in the yellow bedroom and watch the street through my window. The tree that was full of vibrant autumn leaves is a skeleton now, tapping its bony branches against the glass like it wants to be let inside.

We're only a few days out from Christmas, and there are lights up and down the road, twinkling like sequins. Robert arrives home from work one night, pink-cheeked and pleased with himself, dragging an enormous great tree that takes three people to carry it in, and which they then have to cut down by about a foot so that it will fit in the house.

"I thought the ceiling was higher," he mutters, bewildered.

"This is exactly what you did last year," Lou laughs, reaching up to kiss his cheek.

He and Lou string the now battered tree with lights and ornaments and put a gaudy gold star on the top. They play Christmas carols on the record player and sing along. They hang stockings, including one with my name on.

It makes me sick.

"Come on, Freya," Robert calls. "Help us with the tree."

"Bah, humbug," I reply, shuffling off to my room with a tray full of their hot mulled cider and mince pies.

There's something *so* awful about being miserable when the world around you is turning into a joyful, festive, carol-filled wonderland, that being miserable almost becomes its own twisted version of pleasure.

I understand Scrooge now, I think, pleased, and then I remember I never need to understand a character again because I will never play a part again, and I sink into an exquisite spell of melancholy that lasts the rest of the afternoon.

When a group of carollers turn up at the door that evening I tug the pillow over my head and tell myself it would be very wrong to hurl projectiles out the window. As I listen to their cheerful voices harmonizing on "Deck the Halls", I can't help but feel they are placing an unnecessary emphasis on the fact that I am supposed to be jolly. I turn my mind again to my plans for the empty future gaping before me.

It is during this period of reflection that I come to a decision. After Christmas, I will go home. It is the sensible thing to do now that my artistic dreams have gone up in flames. I will go back to a quiet life on the farm. Pa will always be glad of an extra pair of hands and perhaps while I am there I will come up with a plan for what to do next. Maybe a typing course, so that I can move to a bigger town or city and find work. That could be nice. Safe and sensible, and unlikely to leave me with a heart smashed to smithereens. I pen a quick missive to Midge, letting her know.

I feel a certain sense of relief at this decision. At least it is done now and I can begin to put my childish fantasies behind me. Perhaps I will become a serious person, one who alphabetizes things. The sort of girl that even Aunt Irene will approve of. Yes, I think; now my life is devoid of all joy, who better to model myself upon? I wonder if she might like a companion? I too could dress in black and disapprove of everything. I wonder – for a startling moment – if Aunt Irene is the product of a broken dream.

I practise in the mirror, looking at my pale, unhappy reflection. "Foolish girl," I say in Aunt Irene's voice. "Causing nothing but trouble and strife for everyone, running off with your head stuffed full of ridiculous nonsense. Well, look where all that dreaming has got you!"

"Oh, shut up, Aunt Irene," I mutter. "What do you know?"

I flop back on to my bed.

Now that the matter of my immediate future is

sorted, I am able to unpick a previously unexamined thread from the general tapestry of my misery. I glance over at the parcel Nora gave me, still unopened in the corner of the room.

I miss my friends.

I miss all of the people I spent the last six weeks with. Well, maybe not *all* of them – I don't mind if I never see Russ again. But I miss Nora and her keen intelligence and glamour, the flash of her red nails as she wields a needle. I miss sharing a room with Alma, whispering late into the night, laughing over silly stories, her quick understanding. I miss Dan and his sharp tongue and ability to gossip anywhere, with anyone. I miss watching Viola on the stage, her charm and vanity, her brilliance and her steel.

I miss Kit.

I think about him – I would estimate – perhaps a hundred times a day. I want to talk to him about every thought that passes through my brain. I want to lay my troubles at his feet. But I can't. He is a talent, like Viola. Not a failure like me. And I spent the last few days of the tour, and all the time since then, completely ignoring him. He must feel like I don't care about him at all.

Maybe he's given up on me altogether by now, realized that I don't belong in his world any more.

Finally, fed up with doing nothing, I decide to write him a postcard. It has a picture of a flaming Christmas pudding on the front, and when Robert is next going into town I ask him to leave it at the theatre. I assume Kit will be dropping in for his final meetings with Mr Cantwell and Miss Meriden. No doubt they're already talking about the next production.

On the back of the postcard I write:

"I hate people who are not serious about meals.
It is so shallow of them."
   Merry Christmas,
   Love
   Freya

It is nothing really. A line from *The Importance of Being Earnest*, a smoke signal, a way of reminding him that I am here. In case he is thinking of me too.

Two days pass and my moping only gets worse. Perhaps I shouldn't have sent the postcard after all. Would he think it was odd? I think about that night in the theatre when we were playing sardines. I think he would have kissed me if Viola hadn't arrived. I think I would have liked him to.

I am checking the hall table for post for the hundredth time when I run into Lou, who is just back from visiting a friend. Her cheeks are pink from the cold.

"For goodness' sake, Freya," she says, tugging her hat off her curly head. "It's like having the ghost of Christmas Yet to Come in the house. I know you've had a setback, but can't you *try* for a little merriment?"

"It's not that. I've decided to turn my back on my career and that's the end of it." I sigh. "If you must know, I am having a dilemma of the heart."

"Well, that's a different thing altogether." She strips her gloves from her hands. "Come and tell me all about it."

We sit together on the sofa, the tea tray at the ready. "The thing is," I say, after I pour everything out over several cups of tea and three mince pies, *including* the almost-kiss during a game of sardines this time, "I don't really understand how I feel or what I want."

"It sounds like you're very fond of him," Lou points out.

"Oh, I am!" I say. "I feel comfortable with him. Sometimes we can have whole conversations without saying a word. And now, I miss him so much, it's like an *ache*."

"It sounds," Lou pauses delicately, "as though you might be in love with him."

"In love with him!" I clutch at my skirts. "No! It's not that. It can't be. He's never made me want to miss a single meal. He's never made me cry or feel sick and faint with longing."

Lou laughs. "But being in love isn't all weeping and wailing."

"Isn't it?" I ask doubtfully.

"Maybe on the stage it is," Lou says, "or in novels, though I'd never put that sort of nonsense in mine. And I don't act like that around Robert, I never did. I eat very well when he's around, and you can't tell me you don't think we're in love." Her cheeks go pink. "Because we are, quite desperately, actually."

I think about this. It's true that Lou and Robert have seemed always very comfortable together. I remember this when we first met Robert and he came to visit the farm. They seemed relaxed around each other.

"And Alice and Jack are the same," Lou goes on. "They've always just … fit. Love doesn't have to be a great thunderclap and choirs of angels. Love can start as friendship. You don't want to be with someone who breaks your heart or treats you badly or tries to control you – you want someone kind, steady, thoughtful. Someone who really *sees* you. It might not sound glamorous, but it feels wonderful when you find someone like that. It's bigger than just passion, that kind of love – it's a gift. Passion alone burns out when it becomes miserable."

"I suppose," I say.

"Imagine living inside *Wuthering Heights*." Lou shudders. "What a nightmare Heathcliff would be. Only think how miserable."

"I was thinking more *Romeo and Juliet*."

"Well, either way, everyone dies. I don't call that romantic."

"I guess not." I think this over. For a novelist, my sister can be very practical. "Do you really think I'm in love with Kit?"

Lou laughs. "It's not for me to say, Freya. I think you know yourself, one way or the other. Don't you?"

I'm left to mull that question over for a while. In search of a distraction I settle on Nora's parcel. After she gave it to me I left it languishing in the corner of my room, too heartsore to look at it. I didn't want to be reminded of Nora; I didn't want to think about any of it.

Taking a deep breath, I pull the brown paper open. Inside is a dress. It's a simple day dress in a warm, mossy green fabric. There's a note on top of it in Nora's hand.

You deserve a dress made just for you

N x

I unfold the dress, shaking out the creases. It's lovely. I try it on immediately, and it fits like a glove. It wraps around at the top across my bust, and the neckline is

wide, sitting on my shoulders, cut into a V shape that
is deep enough to be just the right side of scandalous.
The skirt hugs my hips and flares out around my calves.
I look in the mirror and smile, because I understand
what Nora has done. She's made a dress for me. The
colour, the fit, the style, they're all mine. It's not one
of my sisters' hand-me-downs, it's not Lou's London
wardrobe, or a golden dress for a romantic heroine,
it's not an amethyst gown or a Victorian street urchin
costume. It's me. Freya.

Just then, the front doorbell rings.

"Freya," Lou's voice calls through from the hallway.
"It's for you."

"For me?" I clatter down the stairs and make my
way through to the front door. Lou steps back, past me
and away, a smile playing around her lips, and there,
standing at the bottom of the front steps, with my
postcard in his hand, is Kit.

I look at him wordlessly for a moment. His face is
impassive, his grey eyes serious, searching.

"Oh!" I say. "You're here."

"I'm here."

And then he smiles.

The smile is slow, it lights his eyes, his dimples deepen, and suddenly I know, with my whole heart, that every word Lou said was right.

I walk out of the door and straight into his arms.

It's as easy as that.

I lift my chin, his lips come down on mine, and the whole world disappears. Kit cradles my face in his hands, and his mouth is soft and warm. His thumb strokes my cheek. My knees tremble, and I lean against him, his arm moving to wrap around my waist and pull me closer. My fingers slip inside the dark wool coat he wears, and I feel his heart hammering madly in his chest.

Finally, we break apart, and he rests his forehead against my own while we both catch our breath. Slowly, I open my eyes, and see that his are still closed, long golden lashes against his cheek.

I smile. His eyes open, pupils wildly dilated.

"Thank you for the postcard," he says huskily.

"I missed you."

"The feeling was mutual."

And then he kisses me again, slower, sweeter, taking

his time, and I am dimly aware how funny it was that I ever thought he was just a friend, that I thought Russ with all his polish, and the girl in the golden dress could ever be the real deal. And then I'm not thinking of anything at all, except the feeling of his lips on my skin and his hand in mine.

CHAPTER THIRTY-THREE

After we have thoroughly scandalized Lou's neighbours for several minutes, Kit notices that I am not wearing a coat.

"You're shivering!" he says.

He takes off his blue scarf and wraps it around my neck. It is warm and it smells like him.

"You should go back inside," he says, though his arm remains wrapped quite tightly around me.

"Not yet," I reply. "I'll get my coat. Perhaps we could go for a walk?"

He pushes my hair back. "I'd like that."

"I'm going for a walk!" I call in to Lou as I snatch her coat off the hook.

"Don't take my—"

"Byyyyye," I call, closing the door.

Kit laughs, and he pushes my frozen, fumbling fingers aside, buttoning the front of my coat. There are soft woollen gloves in the pockets and I pull them on. He takes my hand in his, and we set out.

"It's been snowing," I say, finally noticing that a thin sheer of soft white has settled over the road.

"All day. Didn't you see it earlier?"

"I've been avoiding the outside," I say. "Much easier to mourn your broken dreams indoors."

He squeezes my hand. "Do you want to tell me what happened?" he asks. "Not that you have to," he adds hurriedly. "It's just... I've been worried about you. And so have the others."

"Have they?"

He nods. "You weren't yourself at all the last few days of the tour. I wondered if it was because you'd been onstage and then you had to go back to being the wardrobe assistant..." He trails off uncertainly. "But you seemed so unhappy, and so far away, I didn't know how to help. Even Mr Cantwell was worried about you, said you'd seemed in a strange mood. I believe his exact words were, 'disturbingly quiet and much less irritatingly buoyant than usual'." He flashes a lopsided smile and lets out a long breath. "I thought you might not want to see me. You were so distant at the end. We didn't even properly say goodbye." My heart twists at the flash of unhappiness in his eyes. "And then Robert left your postcard at the stage door, and I thought, maybe you wouldn't mind seeing me after all."

"Thank goodness for Robert."

"You can say that again. Apparently, he caused quite the stir at the theatre, by the way."

"I can imagine."

It's early evening and it's starting to get dark now. The lights strung above us in a looping zigzag shine white against a royal blue sky. We're walking further into a residential bit of the city, and the windows in the tall houses glow, warm and welcoming. Some contain glimpses of decorated trees, of brightly coloured paper chains, and jewel-like glass ornaments.

"It wasn't that I wanted to be back onstage," I say finally. "It was that I didn't."

Kit frowns. "I don't understand."

I take a deep breath. "All my life I've wanted to be an actress. It's been my North Star, the thing I've thought about, worked towards for as long as I can remember. But when I was onstage that night I knew it wasn't right. I wasn't right."

"You were good," Kit says. He sees me shake my head. "You were," he insists. "You had hardly any rehearsal, you had no warning, and I don't think anyone would have noticed."

"Maybe I was passable," I say, "but that's not enough. Not for me."

Eventually, he nods. "I can understand that."

I reach for his hand once more, tangling my fingers with his.

"I feel all … untethered, as if I've lost a huge part of myself."

We walk on further, our bodies pressed close

together, leaving matching pairs of footprints in the snow.

"What are you going to do?" he asks.

I shrug. "Go back home with my tail between my legs, I suppose."

"You can't go back home!" he exclaims, horrified.

"I don't think there's much choice," I rub my nose. "I can't just hang around Lou's house for ever. I'm already feeling like the world's biggest third wheel, one of those Penny Farthing type ones. You wouldn't believe how many times I've walked in on Lou and Robert in a clinch. The two of them can't keep their hands off each other, and all the mistletoe they've hung is the perfect excuse," I finish with a grimace.

Kit wraps an arm around my waist and pulls me close. "Mistletoe sounds like an excellent idea," he murmurs into my hair.

And then, we're kissing again and it's bliss and I begin to see the appeal of strewing the house with mistletoe after all.

"It's snowing again," I murmur, dazed, when we come up for air. Fat flakes drift in drowsy curlicues to settle in Kit's hair, on his dark wool coat, to melt against my warm cheeks. In the early evening light, the world around us is fairy-touched, shining silver.

"I hope you're not feeling so averse to romance any more?" Kit asks.

I laugh. "Now that I know what it really feels like, I've decided I'm very much in favour."

"Good. We had better go back, before we're caught out in another blizzard."

I don't want to let him go. "You can come in for a hot chocolate. Meet my sister."

"I'd love to. For one thing, I hear the place is covered in mistletoe."

I shove him gently and we turn back towards Lou's. "Actually, it's a good job we're going back," I say. "I'm starving. I haven't eaten for days. Well, I've *eaten*, of course – but not at my normal capacity."

"I came prepared." Kit reaches into his pocket and pulls out a bar of chocolate.

"This is why you're the best person in the world," I say, taking it.

"I'm only surprised you left the house without a

satchel full of sandwiches."

"*That* was a good day," I say, thinking about that magical afternoon at the abbey. Staging Kit's play, the set coming to life in my mind from the skeleton of a ruined abbey.

"It was a lot of fun," Kit agrees, and the words ring in my ears.

A thought strikes me then, a thought so wonderful it's as if lightning parts the sky and shoots right through me. I freeze, glued to the spot, my eyes wide, my breathing suddenly rapid.

"Freya?" Kit turns to me, concern writ large across his face.

"It was fun," I say. "It was the *most* fun I ever had. It brought me joy. It felt *right*."

"Ye-es." Kit's confusion is clear. "That's good."

His confusion is not dispelled in the slightest when I begin to laugh manically. I whirl towards him, reaching up on my tiptoes to plant a swift kiss on his lips. "I have to go!" I exclaim. "I'll explain later, I'm sorry, but ... there's something I need to do."

"Wha—" Kit starts, but I reach up and kiss him

again, because I can, because I want to.

And then, I swirl away and begin to run, leaving him standing in the falling snow.

When I reach the theatre, I head directly to the stage door. They will be preparing for their evening's performance. The touring company may be finished, but the theatre's own production of *The Nutcracker* runs right up to Christmas Day. And I know Mr Cantwell and Miss Meriden have meeting after meeting lined up in the building.

"Hello, Joe!" I call, as I bustle through the door, shaking snow from my boots. "I need to see Mr Cantwell. It's urgent."

"Mr Cantwell's not here, miss," Joe says, his crumpled face appearing at the window.

My face falls.

"Miss Meriden is in her office, mind," Joe adds, and I'm already moving, calling my thanks over my shoulder.

I knock on Miss Meriden's door, my knuckles beating a jittery tattoo.

"Come in," I hear her voice call and I push the door

open. "Freya!" she exclaims, startled, taking in my flushed cheeks, my dishevelled, just-run-through-the-snow appearance.

"Miss Meriden, it's so good to see you!" I say. And then, "I need to see Mr Cantwell," I blurt out with no finesse at all. "Do you know where he is?"

She turns the gold watch at her wrist to look at its face. "We're going to meet a producer for dinner. He's due any minute."

I sigh gustily with relief. "May I wait with you?" I ask. "There's something I simply *must* talk to him about."

"Of course," she says, gesturing to the seat across from her. "Why don't you sit? I must say, I'm glad to see you, we didn't get a chance to talk after we got back and I wondered…"

The door swings open.

"Blast it, Meriden, it's bloody snowing again and that ass Thurlow is going to want us to traipse halfway across town…" Rhys Cantwell notices me and stops, his bushy white brows shooting up.

"Miss Trevelyan. About time you showed your face

around here."

"S-sir?" I say, momentarily thrown.

"I understand no one's seen hide nor hair of you since we got back to London. Shouldn't you have turned up asking me for a job by now?"

"Well, actually, that's why I'm here." I twist my hands anxiously in front of me.

"Good. I understand Nora has been very pleased with your work, and I'm sure…"

"I'm not here about my old job." I glance at Miss Meriden whose face is a smooth mask of polite interest. "I'm here about a different job."

Mr Cantwell sighs. He looks for a moment as though he has a toothache. "If it's acting work you want, Freya, there's nothing right now," he says heavily. "You do need training. I can perhaps introduce you to…"

"No, it's not acting work I want either. But training is precisely what I'm here about," I break in eagerly. "I realized I don't want my old job, not as a wardrobe assistant or as an understudy." I pause. "The job I really want … is yours!"

"Mine?" His brow crumples. "I'm afraid I don't

understand."

"I want to direct," I say, and I know as I say it that I do want it, more than anything in the world, and it feels real this time, not like a dream I can't remember being without. "I'm not made to be an actress, I know that now, and I thought it was the end of everything, but then it hit me – what I loved, all along, was making something. It's the creative vision, the idea of bringing all the pieces together into something better than the sum of its parts. Just like you said."

"I said that, did I?" he mutters weakly, casting a hopeless glance at Miss Meriden, who is pressing her lips together as though to try and hide a smile.

"Something very like it," I reply. "When we were in the abbey working on Kit's play, I don't think I've ever felt more alive or full of joy than I did then. And as soon as I understood, I just had to come and ask you, Mr Cantwell, whether you might consider taking me on, as as an assistant."

He frowns. "I don't have the time to train someone."

"I wouldn't be a burden," I insist. "I want to learn, and I want to learn from you. I can do this. Give me this opportunity and let me prove it to you."

"You *did* say she showed excellent instincts," Miss Meriden breaks in.

Mr Cantwell glowers.

"Oh, *did* you?" I ask, delighted.

"Harrumph," says Rhys Cantwell.

"And you know you could use another pair of hands," Miss Meriden continues ruthlessly. "I'm stretched desperately thin, and things are falling through the cracks – why, look what happened at Runleigh. I'm sure I could squeeze a little out of the budget."

I hold my breath as Mr Cantwell glares at me. "It would be a *very* little out of the budget," he says finally.

"Oh, Mr Cantwell!" I exclaim, flinging myself at him and kissing him on the cheek before whirling round to do the same to Miss Meriden. Miss Meriden laughs then, a startlingly loud and unruly arpeggio, quite at odds with the rest of her.

"You won't regret it!" I turn back to the director. "I promise you won't."

"I already told you, Miss Trevelyan: don't make

promises you can't keep."

I beam beatifically. "But this time, sir, I know I can keep it."

Epilogue

Eight months later

It is my second ever opening night. And this time, I don't watch from the wings, but from a seat in the audience, and we're not in Oxford, but in London. As soon as the tour reviews started rolling in, Miss Meriden found herself inundated with invitations to stage Mr Cantwell's next project, trying to tempt him away from the Queen Anne, but they decided to stay. It's home – at least for now.

At my side Mr Cantwell, smart in his tuxedo, sits very still. I riffle through the programme, my fingers tapping nervous patterns on the arm of my seat as we wait, the heavy red curtain like an impenetrable wall before us. I turn anxiously to look around and watch the seats as they slowly fill up.

"Freya, if you don't stop wriggling I will have you ejected from this theatre," Mr Cantwell grinds out.

I still instantly. "Do you think Viola took the note about her entrance? In the dress rehearsal it didn't come off exactly right..."

"It's done," Mr Cantwell says. "There's no more you can do now. This is the moment of truth, where you let it all go and see if it can walk on its own." He turns to me, his expression grave. "This is an important lesson for you. What you're about to experience is simultaneously the best and the worst moment of directing – the part where you find out if your job is done."

I take a deep breath, letting his words wash over me. Striving for some kind of calm. This production of *A Midsummer Night's Dream* has been all that has occupied my mind for months. My new job has proved even harder work than my last one, and I've loved every moment of it. I have learned so much, and I'm still learning, watching, taking it all in. Most of what I've been doing has been grunt work, real bottom-of-the-ladder stuff. Let's just say I've been making a lot of cups of tea, and that Mr Cantwell takes his with milk and one and a half sugars.

But, *but* there are a couple of my notes that made it into the play we're all about to watch, and that feels incredible. And, after I lobbied for it doggedly, with detailed notes as to how it would not only work but offer a fresh perspective on the role, Mr Cantwell agreed to cast Viola as Puck, and that has proven to be a wonderful decision. Big things are going to happen for her, I know they are. Finally, she is on a London stage, where she has long deserved to be.

It all feels good.

It feels right.

I twist around in my seat.

Somewhere behind us in the dark auditorium are my family. Midge and Pa came all the way from Cornwall, with Alice and Jack ... and Aunt Irene. No one was more surprised than I when the old bat herself arrived, but apparently she insisted. While she's made her opinions of my life choices very clear, she hasn't quite been able to conceal the tiny hint of pride.

"You should have heard her all over the village," Alice told me, wide-eyed. "It was all, *my niece, yes, the one working with Rhys Cantwell, she's a close personal friend of Eileen Turner, of course*." Alice's Aunt Irene impression is always spot on, and I could imagine the scene exactly.

Lou and Robert are here as well. Lou finally put Robert out of his misery and she proposed to him under an apple tree in Cornwall. They're waiting for Caitlin and Lucky to come over before they get married. Apparently Caitlin has a lot of *plans* for the wedding and there have been several entertaining long-distance phone calls taking place.

I'm so glad they're here to see this. Robert and Lou sent an enormous bunch of roses to the theatre and I put them into a vase in the office, next to the daisies from Kit.

My other family is here too.

Right now, I know that they're running about

backstage, a perfect swirl of organized chaos. Nora will be there, buttoning people into their costumes and adjusting hems with the help of her new assistant, Martin. (Russ would have been devastated, I'm sure, but he got another job with a different company, and we don't see much of him these days.) Alma, with whom I now share a very mean flat that rarely has hot water, but where we are both blissfully happy, will be muttering lines under her breath. And Kit, with whom I share my whole life, will be busy shouting instructions at people hauling scenery around, and thinking, perhaps, of me out here and of the play we're working on together.

Maybe he's thinking of a small jewel of a theatre, and the little manager there who is only too happy to stage the work of an up and coming playwright, and a young female director this Christmas. Particularly as they seem to be the only people other than Rhys Cantwell who can tempt Eileen Turner out of retirement.

Maybe he's thinking about the party we'll be having tonight with all the people we love. Where we'll laugh and dance and he'll whirl me about in his arms like he'll never let me go.

When I think about it, about all of these people, coming together in one place, in this golden, perfect moment, I feel as though my heart may burst.

I know that I am exactly where I am meant to be.

Ambition. Opportunity. Want.

The curtain rises.

ACKNOWLEDGEMENTS

This book was written during an extremely strange and difficult time for all of us, and it certainly wouldn't exist without the very vocal and enthusiastic encouragement of many people.

Chief of these is my agent, Louise Lamont, who loved this book when I couldn't, and who saw what it was going to be even when I was in the depths of despair. Thank you so much for being Freya's biggest fan and for long, gossipy phone calls and for *Babylon Berlin*. I'm so grateful for you.

Thank you to Gen Herr, who made my job so much easier, and who worked like an absolute demon to get this done. I'm so thankful for your encouragement and your insight. You make everything better. I love writing books with you.

Thanks to Jenny Glencross for copyediting – I'm so happy that you were involved in a bit more of Lou's story, which is only right. Thanks to Pete Matthews, Lauren Fortune, Harriet Dunlea, and the rest of the team at Scholastic – truly the best of people. Thank you AGAIN to Jamie Gregory and Yehrin Tong for their beautiful work, and for making my books the best looking on any bookcase.

Thank you as always to my family and friends. You have all made sure I kept my sanity while writing a book during a global pandemic, which is a real miracle. I love you all so much. Special thanks to my lovely friend Ben Fowler, who acted as my theatre consultant and answered all my daft questions.

Finally, I have to say an enormous thank you to you readers who loved *A Sky Painted Gold*. I can't tell you what it has meant to me to hear from so many of you.

Thank you for loving Lou and her family as much as I do. Thank you for cheering me on, for sharing the book, for your beautiful pictures and words. I hope that this book makes you happy – I wrote it for you.

Laura Wood is the winner of the Montegrappa Scholastic Prize for New Children's Writing. She has a PhD from the University of Warwick studying the figure of the reader in nineteenth century literature. She is also the author of *A Sky Painted Gold*, *Under a Dancing Star*, *Vote for Effie* and the *Poppy Pym* series.

lauraclarewood.com
Follow Laura on Twitter – @lauraclarewood
Instagram – @lauracwood

Also available from Laura Wood

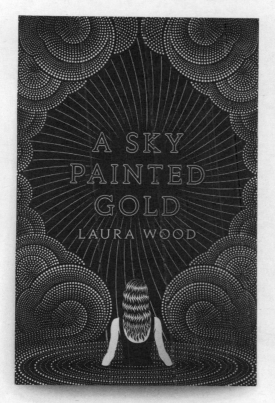

When the Cardews arrive in her sleepy Cornish village for the summer, Lou is quite swept off her feet into a world of moonlit cocktail parties and glamour beyond her wildest dreams. But is there something darker lurking at the heart of the Cardew family?

"A brilliant, beautiful book. I loved it"
Louise O'Neill

Also available from Laura Wood

In grey, 1930s England, Bea has always known she will one day have to marry someone of her parents' choosing. When she gets the chance to spend the summer in Italy, she meets Ben, a cocky young artist who happens to be infuriatingly handsome. Can Bea and Ben put aside their teasing to have the perfect summer romance?

"Heady, sun-drenched and achingly romantic"
Observer